THE BLUE FOLIO

MATT MCMAHON

BLACK OSTRICH PRESS

NEW YORK, NEW YORK
2014

ISBN: 978-0-9907103-0-1

Follow Matt McMahon at
MattMcMahonBooks.com

Dedicated to
Mary
&
Christine
my
sine qua non
(without which nothing)

ACKNOWLEDGMENTS

My special thanks to a team of gifted editors and designers who helped make this book a reality.

Editorial

Diane O'Connell, Developmental Editor
Daniel Sheridan, Line Editor
Michael Trudeau, Copyeditor, Belle Étoile Studios
Katie Sherman, Proofreader
Angela Amman & Mandy Dawson, Beta Readers, Bannerwing Books

Design

Gabi Anderson, Cover Design, Gabi Anderson Studio
Sandra K. Williams, Interior Design, Williams Writing, Editing & Design

PROLOGUE

The White House, May 6, 2059

Bill Waverly didn't hesitate for a millisecond as he slipped into the Roosevelt Room of the White House amid mouths opening into ovals. Usually loud, the media — pasted against the wall to his right — quieted to a suspicious hum at the sight of the president's attorney. He expected as much. There would never be a need for the president to have her attorney at one of these ceremonies. They were routine. Just photo ops. But Bill knew he would be needed.

He positioned himself just to the side of the door that led from the Oval Office into the Roosevelt Room, judging that it gave him the best vantage point to control the frenzy once it started. His presence could provide a headline, but it was a risk he had to take. And there was no way he could hide.

The top of his bare head gleaming under spotlights, the thin swatch of lightly salted, pepper-colored hair around the back and sides of his head, and his bulging midsection from too many hours of sitting in front of screens and books made him conspicuous. But his looks didn't advance his career, so he just stood there, looking like Friar Tuck in an expensive black suit draped awkwardly around his rotund body. In comparison to the others crowding into the Roosevelt Room, he appeared sickly.

While carefully observing Senator Delois Nath and Congressman Kelvin Lynn extol the benefits of the South American Free Trade Act (SAFTA) to the media, he tried to blend into the background. It was their baby. They proposed it, a power given to Congress in 2037. The more they bragged about their multiparty support for the legislation, the less attention on him.

Everyone wanted a piece of it. The senator was Patriot Party, the congressman a Democrat. But additional support from the Republican Party, the People's Party, the Independent Party, and the Conservative Party is what made it newsworthy. He could use that to put some distance between the president and the legislation.

In one form or another, he had started preparing the president for this meeting more than three years ago. When Congress sent the act to her eight days ago, those preparations became daily. They practiced careful scripts of what to say and how to answer questions. She complained about the hours and the repetition. Mostly she complained that he was treating her like an idiot, like she didn't know what she was doing.

He didn't fear her intelligence. She was smart. He feared that she could be hotheaded, aggressive. That she could blurt out thoughts as quickly as they popped into her head, rather than sticking to the scripts. She didn't understand the danger. He did. It was the reason the president needed him, and it made him feel clever.

The White House never listed this as either a signing ceremony or a veto ceremony. How that got past everyone, Bill couldn't figure. Maybe it was just a sign of the skyrocketing trust in politicians over the two decades since the Second Constitution became final. From the jovial mood, he gauged that everyone assumed it to be a signing ceremony. Logical, he thought, since it passed with sixty percent support in both houses and President Beth Roche-Suarez never spoke out against it. But he knew better.

Seconds before 9:00 a.m. and the reporters along the wall seemed to be getting used to his presence. They included the usual White House correspondents and a few younger ones from smaller outlets. Blogs with a few hundred thousand followers and small city newspapers. Correspondents who would be eager to assert themselves. Less disciplined than the hardened veterans.

The dignitaries took their seats around the longer sections of the rectangular, dark American walnut conference table, facing the empty chair at the head of the table where the president would sit, closest to the door Bill was guarding. Quick entrance, quick exit, he thought.

As President Suarez strode into the room, everyone stood to attention and applauded. She waved to the media as if they were the reason she was attending. Cameras and microphones were hidden in the decor, but Bill knew that she always played to the cameras. He saw her do this hundreds of times and he knew the effect. On-screen and in person, people liked her. Nocturnal eyes, big and round, with pupils spread so wide that they hid the color of her irises. Her tiny frame, only 157 or 160 centimeters tall he calculated, still not completely comfortable with the metric system fully adopted fifteen years ago. In any event, she didn't quite reach the top of his shoulders, and she was only a wet napkin's weight over forty-five kilograms. All this made her approachable, lovable, he thought. With his help, she never showed her other side to the people.

Before settling into her chair, the president gave quick handshakes to the senator and congressman without any conversation. The trade act lay on the table in front of her, next to her official stamp, a pen, and the official blue folio she brought with her — a dark royal-blue leather folio with the presidential seal emblazoned in the center of the cover. Fifty-one white stars encircling a spread eagle, its head facing left toward the olive branch in its dexter talon, away from the thirteen arrows in its sinister talon. The folio would usually hold her signing statement, giving the president's understanding of the new law and how it should be enforced by her administration. A copy of the signing statement along with one of the many pens used to sign the legislation were customarily gifted to the proponents.

As the initial commotion hushed, the president slowly opened the folder. Bill made eye contact with the press secretary standing in the center of the media and then turned to catch the eye of the president's Secret Service agent standing at the other side of the door frame. He felt confident that everything would go as planned.

"Good morning, ladies and gentlemen," the president began, looking toward the hidden cameras mounted just above the gaggle of reporters huddled against the wall and ignoring the people at the table in front of her. Bill's eyes focused on the faces of the senator and congressman, both holding relaxed smiles of anticipation. Their bodies sitting erect, preening for the cameras, for their photo ops.

She continued, "After a great deal of research and deliberation, I have come to the determination that I must veto the South American Free Trade Act—"

"I beg your *pahdon*," gasped Senator Nath in her Boston accent.

Congressman Lynn jumped to his feet. "When did this happen? When did you change your position?" he demanded. The Secret Service agent took a quick step forward, placing himself in the line of view between the congressman and the president. Just as Bill had instructed before the ceremony.

Along the wall, the reporters swarmed like fiddler crabs at low tide, thrusting claws in the air, grabbing for recognition, for the chance to shoot a question. They couldn't ask questions without first being recognized by the press secretary. Bill could taste their frustration, especially the young ones. He counted on it.

"Why didn't you tell us you were doing this?" Congressman Lynn shouted above the rustle of the reporters.

Turning first to the senator and then to the congressman, the president started to answer. "It was—really I just—" she stumbled.

Bill's pupils narrowed as he focused on the president. Her eyes darted from the media to the senator before fixating on Congressman Lynn. Her hands drew together tightly in front of her, as if she could hold something in. Bill knew what she wanted to say, that they should all just be grateful for the good things she'd done and accept her judgment. Her hesitation, her stumbling, wasn't uncertainty. She was fighting the urge to speak her mind without his filter. He needed to get her back on script.

He shuffled to his right, which placed him along the wall directly behind her seat. With a slight lift of his leg, his knee pressed into the back of her chair. Confident that no one saw the gesture, he could see that it startled the president out of her inner dialogue.

"I can assure you both, and the American people, that this was not a light decision. I gave it a great deal of consideration. I simply do not think it is in the best interests of the country at this time," she concluded, back on script.

"*Naught* in the best interests?" Senator Nath mimicked, cocking her head back in disbelief. "You told us you supported SAFTA. You campaigned on this," she continued, her voice rising.

"That's right, I did initially campaign on this," the president responded, drawing out the word *initially* for emphasis. "There was a time I believed it was right for the United States. Recently"—she stopped herself—"I mean, after long deliberation, I came to the conclusion that while it would provide cheaper goods for Americans for a while, any benefit would be short-lived and it would eventually cost American jobs. It is not in the best interests of the country," she repeated.

Bill cringed when he heard her utter *recently*. It's exactly what he told her to avoid, any hint of when she made her decision. He tried to talk her out of the veto, to make her see what could happen to her, but she was stubborn. Either way, he damn well meant to protect her, to protect his golden goose. At least she didn't complete the sentence. Minimal damage, he thought, but he sensed that she might slip again.

"Did you change your mind before the election?" shouted a young reporter from the far end of the media pack lined along the wall.

Bill nodded to the press secretary, swallowing the sense of self-satisfaction rising to his lips. He knew they couldn't resist.

"Ladies and gentlemen, we will not tolerate outbursts. You know it's against protocol. You know better," the press secretary scolded, following Bill's instructions. "This meeting is over," he declared as he personally ushered the frustrated reporters through the far door amid their protests and apologies.

With the media gone and the ceremony concluded, the senator and congressman dropped the formality. "What the hell did you do? What are you doing to us, Beth?" Senator Nath demanded.

"Who got to you?" Congressman Lynn carped, taking a decisive step toward the president to make certain that it was clearly an accusation and not a question.

Bill nodded to the Secret Service agent, who put himself directly in front of the angry congressman, as if he was going to restrain him.

"This meeting is over," Bill ordered.

On cue, the president responded, "I am sorry for your disappointment.

As I have said, I believe it is in the best interests of the people that I veto this act." She stood and left through the door toward the Oval Office, followed by her Secret Service agent and Bill.

The president continued into the Oval Office while Bill hovered in the hallway, listening through the closed doors as the two members of Congress vented. He heard confusion and outrage. But he didn't hear the word he feared. Just as he thought, coyotes howling at the moon, complaining that they can't be men and powerless to change what they are. It was an image that brought him comfort, and just a little sense of approval, if only from himself.

Media attention would be intense for the next few days, but he could handle that until the public lost interest. As long as the one skeleton stayed buried, she would get away with it. He was confident that it would stay buried. At least he hoped it would.

CHAPTER 1

New York City, September 29, 2059

In the short walk from the elevator, Bill was gripped by a feeling he couldn't identify. Frustration, anger, dread, hate, disappointment were all part of his climb to the top of the shark-infested waters of law and politics. But this was different, unfamiliar, counter to the instincts that helped him crush anything that stood in his way. Admitting to fear was like cracking a vial of cyanide between his teeth. The poison would surely paralyze him within seconds, making him useless.

He had calculated that showing up without an appointment gave him the best shot of meeting with his old professor, George Comstock. In person Bill could argue his way into anything. He was the master of not taking no for an answer and the stakes were just too high for polite niceties. Shoving the alien emotion into that place where he quarantined things that didn't suit him, Bill opened the green-frosted glass doors to the offices of Comstock, Krause, Bitterman, and Tao on the 37th floor of New York's iconic Freedom Tower.

The reception area invited rather than intimidated, an accurate reflection of his old professor's personality. He felt instantly at home, as if walking on a beach. Overstuffed neo-deco cream cloth chairs dotted the muted sea-green carpet, like white caps on a tropical sea. Princeton grad or pauper would feel equally at home, Bill thought. But the surroundings didn't have the same effect on him.

He consciously relaxed each facial muscle, as if he were preparing to be hypnotized, while he walked toward the semicircular reception desk in the vast reception area. By the time he reached the beanpole male receptionist, every muscle down through his legs was relaxed. A long-practiced ritual to hide any hint of anxiety or doubt.

"Good morning. Could you please tell Mr. Comstock that Bill Waverly would like to speak with him?" he asked, distracted by the swatch of blond hair, razor-cut and angled from the crown of the young man's head toward his left eye.

"Do you have an appointment?" the receptionist politely asked in a slight drawl, his hairless eyebrows, a recent trend that Bill couldn't understand, rising as he checked the display in front of him.

"No, but I'm sure he'll see me," answered Bill in a deep, calm voice. The receptionist examined Bill's face as if he knew him but just couldn't remember his name, even though he had just heard it twice. Bill was used to the reaction — people who knew they knew him but didn't know how. A background celebrity.

"There's a Bill Waverly here. He would like to see Mr. Comstock but he doesn't have an appointment," the receptionist announced, seemingly into open air, as Bill rambled over to peruse documents hanging on the wall of the reception area. It gave him a few more moments to continue his relaxation ritual. After a few hurried words that Bill couldn't make out, the receptionist ended his conversation and joined him at the other end of the room.

"Of course Mr. Comstock will see you. He always has time for the president's counsel," the young man said, the tips of his ears turning bright red and his eyes unable to connect with Bill's. "His assistant will be out in a moment to take you back. Can I get you anything? Tea? Water?"

"Thank you, no. I'm fine," Bill answered, not deflecting his attention from the original documents gracing the walls. Letters penned in the hands of Thomas Jefferson and George Washington; Martin Luther King and Mahatma Gandhi; Supreme Court Justices Thurgood Marshall and Chloe Adee, whom Mr. Comstock clerked for after law school; President Barack Obama and President Souta Dozono, the first Asian American president. But the prized possession, the one that sent chills up the spines of even such hardened political players as Bill, was the original copy of the Second Constitution, signed by all of the reframers, including George Comstock.

Bill could hardly believe that it had been ten years since he last came to the 37th floor to call on his favorite professor. Only weeks before, he attended the fifty-eighth anniversary service of the 9/11 terrorist attack with President Suarez. But the president's schedule didn't permit a visit. Anyway, he didn't want to speak to George with Beth nearby. It would be hard enough to get them both to agree to what he had in mind without them clashing heads, and he knew they would clash. Opposites who could never attract each other.

Standing back from the historic documents, Bill struggled to keep the alien emotion segregated. Anyone would be nervous meeting a man of George's stature, he thought. But the extra moisture filling the pores of his hands wasn't awe — he knew it was fear. Fear that the one person who could save the president might not.

"Good morning, Mr. Waverly," George's assistant announced, startling Bill, who hadn't heard her come up behind him. "Mr. Comstock is happy to see you," she explained. "Currently he is in a meeting, but he would like you to wait in his office. I'm certain that he won't be long."

"Thank you, Ms. Tinsley," Bill gently responded, catching the slight blush of her cheeks, revealing her surprise that he remembered her name. They had met only briefly a few times, but he made it a habit of memorizing the names of staff members, just for this purpose. Powerful men and women could get him what he wanted. Their staff could grant him access to them.

It was a short walk to George's office. The firm was small in relation to its importance. The other named partners had all worked for George as associates. Most likely the three current associates would someday become partners as well. Working for George was a lifetime commitment that Bill understood. They advised clients on constitutional issues. From the largest corporations to dirt-poor inmates. Fees assessed on ability to pay, not on the time spent on a case. Rare for attorneys, even in enlightened 2059.

Bill took it as an intentional sign of respect that he was allowed to wait in George's private office by himself. On the other hand, he knew that George probably insisted on that courtesy for everyone, even thieves.

He looked around as if he were in a museum. Awards of every kind; pictures with heads of state, the greatest minds in science, politics, law, and the arts; George's own books and hand-inscribed first editions of equally famous authors; and small tokens whose meanings were known only to George. A metal Roman centurion proudly facing forward on his desk; a brass horseshoe holding three old pennies; an inexpensive pocket watch, its face open and its hands still; a wax seal; and a plaque with the inscription *We've blown past the ethical standards; we now play on the edge of the legal standards. — Sen. Chuck Hagel.* Anyone questioning their meaning got the standard "Oh, it's nothing" response or the more restraining "It's a private little joke" from an uncharacteristically reticent George.

Within a few minutes George burst into the office, hand outstretched to greet his former student. The physical differences between the two men could not be starker. In his mid eighties, George was tall and lean. Pure white hair framed penetrating sky-blue eyes. The outlines of his well-defined arms pressed against the sleeves of his crisp dress shirt with a sleeveless cardigan sweater on top.

More than thirty years his junior, Bill looked older than George. At least closer to death. Fashion had no meaning for him. His complexion bore the scars of his drive to the top, never letting exercise, nutrition, leisure, or even family stand in his path. Something his ex-wife and estranged sons would readily certify, Bill figured. He believed that his dowdy carriage made him less threatening to those who assessed danger by outward appearance.

"Always a pleasure to see you! I hope you haven't been waiting long," George offered, his grasp cutting into the circulation of Bill's fleshy hand. At George's gesture, Bill settled into a silk-covered armchair in front of George's handmade wooden desk. He looked at George and still saw his favorite teacher at William & Mary Law School. Remembering his passion and enthusiasm for the Constitutions, he revered the man who could accomplish so much and yet think that his accomplishments were so common.

It was no secret that George had twice refused appointments to the Supreme Court of the United States, despite there being no doubt that he would be confirmed. He was the true omni-partisan candidate to fill every vacancy on the court. It was such a natural position for him, yet he avoided it, refusing to interpret what he had written. Years before, he had confided to Bill that he feared he would too easily succumb to vanity, like an artist who paints himself into a picture, perverting its beauty and its art.

"I'm certain that you didn't come here just to pass the time of day," began George, cutting short the usual pleasantries as he lowered himself into the chair next to Bill. "Is this about your employer?" he asked, leaning toward Bill like a priest ready to take confession. Bill took a moment to compose his response before speaking.

"Yes," he replied, quickly adding, "but before we go further, I need to know—I have to make sure you don't have a conflict of interest. Have you spoken with anyone regarding her? Regarding her present difficulties?"

Thinking for a moment, George replied, "The best I can tell you is that I haven't agreed to be involved in the case. I haven't given any advice regarding the case." Reaching over and placing his left hand gently on Bill's right forearm, he added, "By the same token, I assume you know I would have said *no* to the president as well."

"We knew you wouldn't represent her—that's the only reason we didn't ask," Bill responded, adding the white lie. While George was the absolute best at constitutional law, he was never a trial lawyer.

"Paul Gordon is one of the best. I'm certain that the president is well represented," George opined as the two men nodded in silent agreement. "I'm not sure how I could be of any help to you?" George asked, his pitch rising at the tail of the question.

"I understand," Bill answered. "It has nothing to do with the trial or the appeal, of the case itself."

"Then what?" asked George.

"Your life has been a monument to your greatest work," Bill began slowly. "It is also a monument to your integrity. Your willingness to make yourself available for those ideals that you personally helped to bring back to our great nation." Bill saw George's eyes floating away, breaking contact—the sign of impatient tolerance that he saw whenever a student was making an irrelevant point. "As a result, your presence is your conviction," he added, forcing the final words through a gripping throat that surprised him.

"I appreciate the sentiment," George interrupted. "What do you want?"

Bill knew he had exhausted George's endurance for flattery, no matter how sincere.

"Your presence in a matter shows your belief in the righteousness of its position. That belief can carry more weight than any precedent or evidence. It can even quell an angry *lynch mob,*" he concluded.

"Ah yes — sentencing," George whispered as he stood from his chair. He picked up the pocket watch lying on his desk and walked over to the tall window framed by fine blue drapes. Rhythmically winding the watch, he looked out of the window toward the Hudson River without saying a word. It made Bill fidget.

"We must be prepared for anything," Bill interjected, his voice cracking slightly. "High treason still carries the death penalty. . . ."

George spun around like a lion ready to lunge, locking his laser gaze on Bill. It rekindled feelings of intimidation that Bill remembered when arguing in his class more than twenty-five years earlier.

"Not a single person has been executed for treason since 1942 — and you know that," George expounded, his conviction and his strength flaring. Bill knew the history from his work on the death penalty. Herbert Hans Haupt, a German-born citizen, came to the United States as a child and became a US citizen at the age of ten. During World War II he was found guilty of plotting with the Nazis and died in the electric chair on August 8, 1942. It was an important case used by George W. Bush in 2001 to try US citizens involved in the 9/11 attacks in a military tribunal. Ironic, Bill thought, as he stood in the phoenix of what used to be the World Trade Towers.

"Yes — but no president has been tried for high treason until now," Bill shot back. "If she's convicted, and mind you I'm not saying that we think she will be, there are already cries for the death penalty. We must prepare; we must be prepared so that will never happen."

George's stand on the death penalty was well known, especially to Bill. His eloquent appeals to ban it in the Second Constitution were thwarted by a few states that protected their power over life and death like Roman emperors. He never gave up that fight. Only two states still had death penalty statutes on their books, California and Florida. Neither had used it in more than two decades, and the only crime that still carried the death penalty under federal law was high treason.

Bill became intimately familiar with George's abhorrence of the death penalty while attending William & Mary several years before the 2037 Constitutional Convention. The top of his class and a member of the Law Review, he earned a coveted place as one of a dozen research assistants assigned to help George prepare for the convention. His research on the proposed constitutional clause banning the death penalty gained him a chance to work intimately with a reframer. It also landed him a job with the American Civil Liberties Union, the ACLU, after graduation, the last position he held based on moral conviction.

The conversation grew more deliberate. Bill remained silent, carefully considering each question and comment before speaking. After several minutes George cut the discussion short.

"Honestly, Bill, I don't think I can help you. If the jury finds her guilty of treason, I wouldn't want her to get away with a token sentence. The protections from the constitutional changes are too important."

"I perfectly understand," Bill responded, growing formal, as if he had just stepped into a courtroom. "Our purpose — my purpose is to see if you would argue solely against the death penalty. Just in case. That would square with your ethics and give you an excellent pulpit to continue campaigning against the death penalty. . . ."

George paced around the large office as he periodically glanced at the old pocket watch still cradled in his hand, avoiding eye contact with Bill. "Do you really think the prosecution would seek the death penalty?" George asked, quickly pivoting to look directly at Bill. With some degree of internal swagger, Bill noted that the trademark move didn't affect him this time.

"Yes. If she's convicted, I'm convinced they'll seek death! They're willing to kill her — just to send a message." Bill huffed, gritting his teeth. "The danger of giving power to the people is that they will eventually become a lynch mob — and I am afraid that I can already see them building the gallows." His head dropped, his voice lowered. "It cannot happen! We cannot let it happen!"

George walked back to the seat next to Bill and sat silent for a few moments, shifting his gaze between the family picture on the credenza behind his desk and the tall window. "I must discuss this with my partners — and my wife," he explained. Bill doubted that he needed to ask his partners' permission for anything, but he equally knew that such a monumental commitment required Mrs. Comstock's consent. George always spoke of the cost his part in the Second Constitution had on his wife and kids. "They will of course keep this confidential, but I cannot give you my answer until I discuss it with them," he concluded.

Bill wondered if maybe his apathy to the effects his relentless climb had on his wife and children is what led to his own divorce. How could trying to get ahead ever be bad for a wife and children? He would rhetorically ask himself this to soothe any remorse over relationships lost.

"Of course! Discuss it with them, but please make certain that they know not to tell anyone that we've talked. The media frenzy alone could convict her," Bill pointed out. Not wanting to chance George changing his mind, he immediately stood and handed George a card containing a private number for him to leave a message of simply *I'll do it, I can't help,* or *let's meet again.*

As the elevator descended from the 37th floor, Bill assessed the outcome of the meeting. He was encouraged by George's decision to discuss it with his wife. He didn't say no. Fear was gone, but another alien feeling grew. An unclean sense in his gut — an oily, unholy feeling that he was spoiling something sacred. By the time the elevator stopped he had banished that feeling to quarantine, freeing him up for his next meeting.

He needed his wits at their sharpest. With all of the media attention, it was getting harder to schedule private meetings. Meetings he didn't want Beth to know about, he wouldn't want George to know about. Celltops were out of the question and he knew he was being watched anytime he left his apartment or the White House.

He arranged to meet his handler in a bathroom in Penn Station. Anytime he used a public bathroom, his Secret Service agent would clear it out and post himself outside to keep anyone from entering. It would keep the meeting private, but still he worried. He didn't want his handler to know that he met with George, or why. There was no way to know how his handler would react.

CHAPTER 2

Philadelphia, May 25, 2037

The stillness hit George Comstock like a thunderbolt as he stepped from the eighteenth-century redbrick row house in Philadelphia's Society Hill. His home for the next four months. An eerie silence hung over the Old City section of Philadelphia, as if even the hushed roads understood the significance of the day. Surrounded by silence, George let his eyes follow the slivers of golden light as they crawled up red, white, and blue banners draping the sides of buildings facing Independence National Historical Park. The crystal spring sunrise felt like a good beginning, a good omen for the Second Constitutional Convention, he thought.

Each building was required to block any view of the park from prying eyes by covering the park side of the building with a full length banner. They could choose what would be printed on their banner. Advertisers dangled fortunes to place messages or logos on the banners. But none of the endless special interests, each vying for every conceivable syllable of the Second Constitution, would be allowed to place any message where the fifty delegates to the conventions, one from every state, could see.

Glad to be free of dogged solicitations, George welcomed the silence. No hum of electric cars, no groans from hybrid buses, no sound of a million footsteps, no planes or helicopters above. Nature triumphed over the mechanical noises created by humans, he gloated as he listened to the soulful *oo-wah-hooo, hoo-hoo* of the mourning doves. It was as if all humanity had been vacuumed out of the city and the delegates had been sent back 250 years to the world of the First Constitutional Convention in 1787.

But his thoughts, his feelings, didn't match the sereneness of his surroundings. Eagerness, bordering on childishness, swirled with terror like yin and yang. *Those who can't, teach,* repeated in his head, echoing his doubts with each step toward Independence Hall. As a professor, even a leading expert on constitutional law, he never had to achieve a result. It blessed him with the luxury of only having to look at the best of all possible worlds. What should be, not what can be.

Unlike judges and practicing lawyers, he didn't have to worry about stare decisis, the doctrine of *let the decision stand.* Old case interpretations were hard to change in a courtroom, even when change was logical. In a classroom, however, it took nothing to criticize old decisions. But it felt dishonest to George. Like a boxing critic who never stepped into a ring, even for something he believed in.

The snowy white tower above Independence Hall glared down at him as he walked north on 6th Street. In contrast to its pristine history, he felt impossibly inadequate, an imposter. He never stepped into the ring, even for his passionate opposition of the death penalty. Every few years he convinced a student to take up the fight by joining the ACLU, knowing the daily torture of having their clients' lives hanging on the threads of their abilities, knowing the guilt they would feel as they watched a client slip into death at the end of an IV needle because they couldn't sway jurors to acknowledge doubt or show mercy, because they couldn't overcome outdated cases. But he could never take on that responsibility himself. He couldn't take the pressure of having someone die because he wasn't good enough. How could he now hold the fate, the freedoms, of the country in such timid hands?

His gaze drifted down, away from the spire, focusing on each sidewalk flag in front of him. The bright concrete flags, lit by a strong morning sun, turned dark. A shadow caressed the tip of his shoe, forcing him to stop and look up. He had reached the far edge of the shadow projecting from the tower, several times longer than the tower was tall.

A block away and he could hear the hum of low voices. His footsteps quickened along with the rhythm of his heartbeat. Arriving at

Independence Square, the small park just south of the entrance to Independence Hall, the difference between *what should be* and *what can be* welled in the pit of his stomach like a rancid piece of meat. The expectation of having to achieve a result scared him to the bone.

The delegates outside the entrance stood silent, barely speaking, content to be part of history by approximation. As lifeless as the pillars lucky enough to be witnesses to history, along with the churchlike iconic spire of Tower Stair Hall towering above them. George rationalized that maybe they felt as small as he did. It was comforting.

He mingled with the others, instinctively shaking a few hands, bowing to others. He uttered his first greeting to Anaihyia Alman, the delegate from Illinois. They had become friends during the fifteen-year struggle to make the convention a reality, first meeting at the rally of five million in 2023.

As a physician from the South Side of Chicago, her adamant defense of abortion conflicted with his. But disagreements didn't mean they couldn't work together. What was freedom of speech, if not disagreement? He admired her willingness to protect the increasingly large portion of the population edged out of a meaningful voice in their own destinies. It was their shared value, their shared goal. Her tiny frame being dragged by handcuffed arms had become a mighty symbol of women's rights. A modern-day Rosa Parks for a woman's right to control her own body.

The two talked as he followed her through the white double doors into Tower Stair Hall. She was a friend, a fellow *scholar* delegate, one of twenty-four. Some questioned her informal designation as a scholar because of her passion for her proposed clause on abortion. George knew she would never hold the right of the people to control their government hostage to that agenda. She was dedicated to the single principle of taking the government out of the hands of special interests and returning it to the people. The defining principle of the scholars.

"Sorry," he cried as he nearly ran over her. She had come to a sudden stop with an audible gasp, just inside the twenty-eight-foot-square hall. Rays of sunlight from the large window above illuminated fine particles hanging in the air before landing along the light blue walls. Rays like those beaming through the great dome in St. Peter's Basilica and the high Gothic windows in the Cathedral at Reims, the coronation site of the French monarchs, George reminisced with awe. But what he saw at the end of the rays was more sacred to him than any tabernacle.

The beams lit up wooden display cases containing documents along the northwest and western walls of the small square hall to his left. Original signed copies of the Declaration of Independence, the First United States Constitution, and the Bill of Rights, where the delegates would pass every day into session. A powerful reminder that they were in America's maternity ward for such radical ideas as *freedom, a government of the people,* and the *pursuit of happiness,* George thought, feeling the weight of their message.

"There's my guy," Anaihyia whispered as she casually glided over to Jack Connors standing in front of the document cases. It didn't sound so duplicitous when she said it, George thought with a sigh, but it still went against his grain as he looked for *his guy*—as he looked for Sebastian Irving, the *political* delegate from New York.

The tight coalition of scholar delegates had assigned one scholar delegate to each of the political and patronage delegates to act as a liaison, an ambassador for the reform that the people so desperately wanted. For the life of him, George couldn't figure out why they assigned him to shadow Sebastian, especially if the rumors were true.

Never serving a day in public office, Sebastian was virtually unknown to citizens even in his native New York. His backroom political brokering earned him the reputation as the great-grandson of St. Tammany, the sixteenth-century Native American Chief whose name was adopted by Tammany Hall politicians for nearly 170 years. He rose like a modern-day Boss Tweed for the growing conservative sentiment in New York City. Originally a Democrat, he switched to the Republican Party, where he single-handedly converted wealthy Manhattan Democrats to the Republican faith, commanding the upper class with the assumed modesty of a Uriah Heep, the humble clerk of Dickens' *David Copperfield.*

It made sense that Sebastian would want to keep the government as it was. His buddies benefited from the status quo, George thought, remembering how they fought the Constitutional Convention right up to the doors of Independence Hall. But this was worse. Hints that a shadow government was growing in the background, in the underground, in the event that the convention succeeded. One that could still control the economy and mount a sustained battle to undo any meaningful protections in a Second Constitution.

George kept one eye on the entrance while he examined the sacred documents. They spoke to him in whispers of condemnation. Like a parent expressing disappointment. As if Washington and Franklin and Hamilton and Madison disapproved of his agreement to shadow Sebastian, to try to influence him. As if they knew he had no chance of stopping or even slowing Sebastian's plans, or so it seemed to him.

A flash of Sebastian rushing through Tower Stair Hall, without a glance at the display cases, interrupted the voices in George's head. Sebastian's wide torso barely fit through the doorway between Tower Stair Hall and the vestibule. George's stomach twisted at the sight. Not from Sebastian's size, but from the uncertainty he harbored at his assigned task. A clandestine task. George believed it to be right. But plotters always believed themselves to be in the right. Even the bad ones.

He scurried through the doorway into the vestibule, looking for Sebastian, then passed through the small doorway to the Assembly Room, to the east of the vestibule. Sebastian stood by a table greeting political delegates with a slap on their shoulders, as if he were a prince at a receiving line.

Not wanting to interrupt, George shuffled around the forty-foot-square Assembly Room — the room where the First Constitution was signed. He studied the changes made to the room to accommodate delegates instead of tourists, patiently waiting for an opportunity to approach Sebastian. Railings, carpets, and antique furniture had been removed. Only one original table and chair remained, perched on a small platform at the east end of the room, between two large fireplaces. George recognized the "rising sun" carving at the top of the chair, which was used by George Washington during the First Convention. A hopeful symbol of a rising nation. Another good omen, he prayed, hoping the knot in his stomach would untangle. Portraits of the most well-known founding fathers hung on the walls, standing sentry. He felt their eyes glaring down on him as he walked about the room.

When Sebastian was finally alone, George rushed over to where he was half seated on the edge of the long rectangular table. George didn't know what to say. They had met maybe twice at preconvention meetings but had never spoken. Other than occupying this moment in history, he couldn't think of anything they had in common, any topic to spark a natural conversation.

"Nice to see you again. George Comstock," George began, introducing himself just in case.

Sebastian grasped George's hand and pulled him a half step closer. Sebastian's pat on his right shoulder felt like a hammer hitting an anvil, jarring him out of his awkwardness. It seemed so out of the moment that George stifled a laugh.

"Mr. Naïve Intentions," Sebastian declared in a tone that George could not immediately interpret. Mocking? Admiring? Telegraphing a strategy?

"I'm honored that you read my book."

"Oh — no, I'm sorry," Sebastian shot back, still shaking his hand. "I didn't actually read it. Too *scholarly* for me. I'm just a public-school kid." His Bronx accent seemed exaggerated for effect. George felt suckered as he tried to find a way to steer the conversation.

"I wonder if Ben Franklin was this nervous?" George bumbled, retracting his hand from Sebastian's grasp and unconsciously rubbing his palms together, as if washing them.

"Oh. Ah, yeah," Sebastian responded, his eyes squinted, his head skewed slightly. George realized how silly the question seemed.

"Have you seen the Supreme Court room yet?" George asked, pointing across to the chamber on the west side of the vestibule. He grasped Sebastian's elbow and led him away from the table.

"No, not yet?" Sebastian replied, seeming surprised by George's insistence.

Entering the Supreme Court chamber, George began to lecture on the changes made for the convention. The original tiered wooden jury and spectator boxes had been carefully modified to fit forty-seven delegates in three boxes, each with five rows. Each row had bench seating, like church pews, with small wooden shelves for tablets, netbooks, or notepads. High-density foam cushions lay on the seats and hung on the backs of each bench.

"An accommodation to more tender bottoms than existed at the founding of this country," George quipped, showing a little of the humor that made him popular with his students. Sebastian did not respond.

The *rap-rap-rap!* of a gavel against solid wood sounded in the Assembly Room. It pierced George's concentration and brought first silence, then a sigh of hushed laughter from the delegates. Without a word, Sebastian headed to the small doorway leading to the Assembly Room and disappeared inside. This isn't going to be easy, George thought, lagging behind.

"Hear ye, hear ye, hear ye. All those having business before this, the Second Constitutional Convention of the United States of America, draw near and be counted," Henri Ormond, the sergeant at arms, announced in a loud, formal voice from the head of the Assembly Room.

George tried to paste himself next to Sebastian, who was walking in and out of the five rows of tables, looking for a seat. They were assigned seats in the Supreme Court room, where all arguments would take place, but not in the Assembly Room, where final votes would be taken and the Constitution would be signed. Sebastian plopped down between two delegates in the second row. George could swear that Sebastian threw him a triumphant smile as he sat, like a commuter evading a pesky subway prophet.

As the roll was called, George's mind slipped from his clandestine task. His thoughts returned to the historic journey that brought him here, brought all of them here. A chance to make things right. Each step of the journey continued in his mind with the call of the delegates by state. He mentally prepared to give his own response as the alphabet wound up to his birth state.

"Minnesota — George Comstock."

He held a tear from breaching the edge of his eyelid as he stood and responded, "Present."

It all still seemed like a dream. Making history instead of just teaching it. He knew that his adopted state of Virginia would choose a political tiger, not a monkish professor. He had become the unofficial spokesperson for the Second Constitution ever since the *Newsweek* article quoted his rambling observation that it was absurd and dangerous not to have periodic Constitutional Conventions. But politics was never part of his résumé.

Before Virginia had named their delegate, Minnesota announced him as their choice. No interview, no vetting process that he was aware of. Just the announcement that came shortly after Congress passed the bill authorizing the convention and it was signed into law by the president. Perhaps the only one stunned by the announcement, George had the initial reaction to turn it down. He fought so hard to make this a reality but never thought of himself occupying one of these seats. These seats were for brave men and women, not him, he worried as the roll call continued in the background.

"Rhode Island — Chloe Adee."

George could hardly hear her cheerful "Present" above the spontaneous applause at the mention of the former Supreme Court justice's name. Rising from his chair, he led the chamber to a standing ovation.

By the time the concept of the Second Convention became accepted as a possibility in the early 2020s, Justice Adee increasingly lent her support through her decisions. Writing dissenting opinions more often, she explained in detail why portions of the Constitution should be changed. George proudly followed over the years as she reviewed the road map of how interpretations were moved from people-centric to business-centric, from citizen-defined to business-defined, money-defined.

Clerking for Justice Adee out of law school, George understood both her incredible powers of logic and her unwavering commitment to the most basic founding principle of a government empowered by its citizens. Her later decisions didn't surprise him. Only the thirst ordinary citizens had to read her opinions surprised and encouraged him. Scholar delegates celebrated her appointment and resolved to have her elected president of the convention. It would be their first test of solidarity. George was so excited by her upcoming election that he barely heard the remaining roll call.

When the roll call ended, Henri Ormond called for nominations for president of the convention. Dr. Alman immediately shouted, "Justice Adee!" The response was so overwhelming that Dr. Alman suggested a vote by acclamation. At Henri Ormond's call for a vote by acclamation, a single "Yea!" blared from the mouths of the delegates with the force of the shot heard around the world. Justice Adee was now President Adee.

Looking around, George couldn't be sure if Sebastian had cast an answer, yea or nay. Sebastian's puffy face, creases streaking down his cheeks to the line between his first set of chins, took on a darker shade of red. His lower lip pushed past his upper, like a child opening a wrapped package of coal on Christmas morning. Sebastian certainly didn't expect to be nominated, let alone elected president of the convention, George assumed. But clearly he had someone else in mind. Some other plan now being foiled by a unanimous vote, by a single voice not in tune with his own.

The oath was given and a short recess ordered before President Adee's opening speech in the Supreme Court chamber.

■ ■ ■

The narrow wooden aisle in the third row of the center jury box creaked as Sebastian straggled to his seat, echoing throughout the Supreme Court chamber. With the maneuverability of a bear in a small cage, Sebastian struggled past George and dropped onto the last seat on the closed end of the box.

Once all of the delegates were seated and the creaking silenced, President Adee entered the chamber from the vestibule. George followed her small, weathered frame as she sprang across the floor and hurdled the stairs to the three chairs atop the judicial bench at the front of the chamber. As she stood in front of the middle Windsor chair, only the top third of her body was visible.

As she spoke, George listened with an intensity he wished he could command from his students. The road to the Constitutional Convention had too many potholes, too many dead ends, too many blind curves to trust the leadership to the wrong person. Justice Adee was the right person, he envisioned. Maybe the only person who could realign the polarized ends of politics that threatened to break the social contract.

Her words were calm, familiar, like a shared family story told at a reunion. "In the debates to come, do not become like Dante's Satan," she advised, "a winged beast trapped in a lake frozen by the frigid blasts of air from wings viciously flapped in anger. Look for what is right in each position. Try each proposal on like a new suit. Live with it for a while. Look to see how your ideas can help it grow, not how you can destroy it. How *you* can put us back on the right path."

The delegates watched with quiet admiration, many holding a hand over their hearts. Buoyant, George was certain that her instructions, her logic, would convert even the most cynical, the most opportunistic. His eyes floated around the room, trying to capture mental snapshots of what history looked like. Descriptions he could gift to his grandchildren. As his eyes rolled to his left, he saw Sebastian slumped forward and scribbling in a notepad, which was perched on the small wooden shelf in front of him. He looked annoyed. Still pouting over the vote by acclamation? Or upset that President Adee's descriptions hit too close to home? It disturbed George, distracted him. No other delegates were writing. All were listening, except Sebastian.

As President Adee's last words vibrated against the yellow-painted wood-paneled walls, George, still distracted by the note taking, aimlessly stood with the house. He observed Sebastian scratch his final marks, close the notepad against prying eyes (against his eyes), push himself to a standing position, and offer fugazi applause—hollow, silent claps.

A pale of despair gripped George. The way a drowning man must feel when he realizes he will never take another breath, he thought. Powerless to inhale anything but an endless ocean of destruction, and aware that it was of his own doing, the product of his own weakness. He didn't make Sebastian what he was; he didn't bring him to this hall. But he realized how powerless he was to stop such a dedicated political terrorist, an antichrist of the Second Constitution, a leader of a different America.

CHAPTER 3

New York City, September 29, 2059

As he sank into the plush seat in the rear of the train car, Bill looked forward to forty minutes of quiet time. The meeting with George Comstock gave him hope, although he knew President Suarez wouldn't share his enthusiasm. Forty uninterrupted minutes was a vacation. Since the indictment for high treason, he had abandoned all wireless communications and video conferencing. Aware that wireless communications could be intercepted, he limited important conversations to in-person meetings in bug-free locations such as his office, the White House residence, or his home. He only picked up a land line or participated in an on-screen conference if it didn't involve the president or her treason trial. Almost nothing these days had to do with anything other than the treason trial.

The Secret Service agent seated two rows in front of him placed a yellow ribbon across the aisle to keep other passengers away. Bill unfolded all four paper thin panels of his celltop and laid the laptop sized tablet on the tray in front of him as the 2:36 Acela MagLev Express left the station with barely a whisper. Moving at speeds up to seven hundred kilometers per hour, its powerful electric magnets suspended the train away from any physical contact, away from any friction or bumps. The combination of quiet and motion perfectly suited his task.

Pulling up yesterday's transcript, he started to analyze each question and answer in the same way he had done for twenty-five years. Other attorneys teased him about the practice, calling him old-fashioned. He was trained this way as a young lawyer, before the on-screen system became standard. But it wasn't just habit. He could review a written transcript of six full hours of testimony in about an hour. Reading, instead of seeing and hearing the testimony, took out inflection. It left only the logic of what a witness said. Later he would review select portions of the on-screen videos for inflection, in the same way that the jurors saw it in the privacy of their homes or offices. If other attorneys didn't understand the advantage to this method, he had no plan to educate them.

One quarter of the way through its case, the prosecution had already put forth damning evidence. But was it enough to convince a grand jury, twenty-three citizens, to convict the highest official in the country of the highest offense? The president needed only one vote against conviction to hang the jury. He spent all of his time trying to find a hole in the prosecution's case big enough to give them at least that one juror. Huddled over his celltop, he feverishly grabbed portions of testimony with his right index finger and glided them into his notes on the left side of the display.

His notes formed a virtual outline of the prosecution's strategy. They began by detailing Beth's rise to power. How on the surface she complied with each of the safeguards in the Second Constitution, but in reality she paid them no more than lip service. Never holding any office for more than two terms or staying in political office for more than twelve years without removing herself for the required four-year period, her compliance seemed insincere.

In contrast to most public servants who just returned to their pre-publiclives after the maximum two terms or twelve years, the prosecution painted Beth's precise four-year hiatuses as proof of a desire to acquire power. The four-year absence from public service requirement was a cherished protection against politicians who sought power instead of service. Bill could see that it resonated with the jury. As did the job she landed when she first stepped away from politics.

When it came time to leave politics for the first time, she didn't go back to being a social worker. Instead she became the highly paid vice president in charge of international relations at Global Mundo Corporation. A worldwide conglomerate with heavy emphasis in Central and South

America, Global Mundo used political connections in foreign countries to stockpile favorable trade agreements—the type of political access that became almost impossible in the United States after the Second Constitution. During Beth's four years at Global Mundo, she learned to speak Spanish fluently. She also met Bill, who immediately spotted his opportunity.

After five years of long hours, low pay, and little recognition as a second-string ACLU lawyer, Bill had made a promise to himself: he would never be on the bottom of the food chain. He wanted money, he wanted respect, and he wanted power. A sevenfold salary increase made leaving the ACLU painless. As an associate and later a partner at the top law firm in Chicago, he infiltrated the inner circle of mega-businesses, especially Global Mundo, and developed resources not available even to government officials. After several years, he left the firm to become general counsel at Global Mundo and a close adviser to its charismatic CEO, Manuel Suarez.

He placed Beth Roche on, Mr. Suarez' radar, certain that he could control her and provide Global Mundo with direct access to the United States government, if he could push her into national politics. Support for her social agenda from his covert resources blinded her to the favorable agreements and bits of legislation they wanted in exchange. Either the prosecution didn't understand the importance of this relationship, or it chose not to include it as part of its case. Either way, Bill happily worked behind the scenes without having his history with the president infused into the case.

Bill's eyes were diverted from the transcript when his Secret Service agent intercepted a passenger heading to the ribbon barrier. From their exchange, Bill quickly figured that the woman posed neither risk nor benefit. He studied her briefly to see if it was someone of renown, someone he would want to meet. Just someone who thought they knew him from the past, he thought, as he pushed her from his consciousness and returned to the transcript.

The prosecution hit close to home when it portrayed her time at Global Mundo as a move to gain the financial backing of a large corporation looking for friendly government officials while building her Hispanic support. To win any statewide or national office, she needed the endorsement of the Hispanic community. Global Mundo and Manuel Suarez could give her that endorsement. This became an overriding basis of Beth's early relationship with Bill.

The one area where the prosecution's investigation fell short, Bill thought, was how Beth ended up marrying Manuel Suarez. Their only evidence on this point was circumstantial, witnesses who testified that the relationship seemed to be nothing more than business. That they only met once or twice a year at large executive meetings. That they never dated during the four-year hiatus.

The last week's testimony focused on how Mr. Suarez lent his name, his reputation, and his company's resources to her first statewide campaign. With his support, she easily captured a seat in the United States House of Representatives for two four-year terms. It propelled her into the national politics of Washington, just where Bill wanted her. Would someone with no relationship do that and expect nothing in return? That was the question the prosecution wanted the jury repeating in their minds. It was an effective attack on the president's ethos, her character, Bill worried. It paved the way for the jury to believe that her veto of the South American Free Trade Act was a premeditated act of treason.

He finished his review just as the train pulled into Union Station, confident that the testimony would not be enough, not yet. The Second Constitution kept the requirement that treason requires *the testimony of two witnesses to the same overt act.* Circumstantial evidence would never be enough. The prosecution had to show the act of treason by at least two eye witnesses, and all they had so far was a theory.

After leaving the train, Bill's Secret Service agent led him to the shuttle level well below the train levels. Even the president used the small electric shuttles that ran from Union Station to the Supreme Court building, congressional offices, Capitol Hill, the attorney general's office, and the White House. Only members of Congress, the Supreme Court, the attorney general, the FBI chief, cabinet members, and the president and her closest advisers had access to the shuttles. No one, including the president, could bring an unofficial guest. His agent commandeered a shuttle.

Arriving at the White House just past 5:00 p.m., Bill went directly to the presidential residence and notified Beth's private secretary that he would wait for the president there. On days of testimony, usually three days per week, White House business began after 5:00 p.m. Although President Suarez was only going to appear in court on the day she testified, if she testified, she and Bill watched the proceedings on-screen fanatically.

He found it hard to watch with her. She would shout at the screen and type endless notes onto her celltop to her trial attorney, Paul Gordon, during the trial. So many furious, almost incomprehensible notes that it was more distracting than helpful. At crucial times, he saw Paul throw a piece of paper over his celltop while standing in the courtroom. When Beth found out about this practice, she scolded Paul like a schoolboy. But he kept to the practice, making sure that her rights were protected, even against herself.

Alone on the sheet-covered couch in the living room of the presidential residence, Bill watched the day's news on-screen as he waited for Beth. The room hadn't been cleaned in a few days, but there wouldn't be time to call in a cleaning crew now.

"Did you get *His Majesty*?" Beth asked, referring to George, as she strode into the living room and closed the double French doors behind her. Her green and yellow tweed pantsuit seemed more appropriate to riding a horse on a country estate than running a country. Deep blue cloth buttons, pocket piping, and rear collar stand lent an air of wealth and sophistication. It was how she projected herself outside of the public eye, both in dress and manners. Elite, aristocratic, above those around her.

"It doesn't work that way," Bill answered, ignoring her sarcasm. "It's a decision that will take some time for him to make."

"I don't see what all the fuss is about. Why do I even need this guy? This is all a bunch of crap," she responded in her typically belligerent fashion toward the charges. It frustrated Bill. She refused to understand the gravity of the charges. She refused to believe that anything she could do was wrong.

"Madame President . . . we've been over this time and time again —"

"Don't patronize me! This is all bullshit and you know it," she shouted, unleashing the sailor's tongue behind her lofty facade. Bill stood and took a few steps along the red Persian carpet to the fireplace, staring at it as if there were a blazing fire. He just didn't want to look at her face. He didn't want to see the pouting, spoiled child in her, even though he was the one who spoiled her, by feeding her ego to get her to do what he wanted.

"They're just mad because I knew what I wanted and I went and got it," she continued, pouring a short glass of scotch and taking a long gulp. "I'm a politician; what do they expect? Is it a crime now to be a politician?"

"Public servant! Public servant — Paul has repeatedly told you to always refer to yourself as a public servant, not as a politician," Bill chided her, turning from the fireplace to look at her as she stood by the mobile server stocked with bottles and glasses.

"Yeah, yeah, yeah," she chanted. "How do they expect people to get elected — by divine right? It's all crap," she concluded emphatically.

"You have to stop this, Madame President — you have to face this," Bill admonished. She rolled her eyes in disgust. "These are the most serious charges ever brought against a sitting president in the history of the United States. You may disagree with the charges, but you can't disagree with the law. To beat this, you must accept the law as it is, not as you think it should be."

There was a soft knock on the white double doors leading to the living room. One door opened and Paul Gordon slipped in, silently closing the door behind him. His appearance hardly matched his status as one of the top trial lawyers in the country. Standing only 165 centimeters, he had short curly black hair that thinned at the top of his head. His face was round and childlike, but his deeply set dark eyes revealed the intensity that made him so effective in a courtroom, which made Bill insist on having him represent the president. Paul was a partner at the two-thousand-plus attorney firm of Morehouse & White when Bill started as an associate.

Even when Bill started there, Paul refused to take part in running the firm. His sole job, his sole passion, was the courtroom. Bill respected that. He envied that. Paul's early trial experience came from representing petty criminals in federal court, pro bono. It wasn't that he cared for their causes or believed that they were treated unjustly; it was a great way to get the courtroom experience he craved.

Bill worked with him mostly on commercial trials. Lawsuits against government regulating agencies, corporations battling each other over contracts and antitrust claims. Boring cases in anyone else's hands. The criminal cases he worked on with Paul were white-collar crimes — bribery, insider trading, fraud, and embezzlement. His most relevant experience was, of course, his successful defense of Lorimar Petite, the only automobile executive to escape conviction for treason at the hands of Keri Eversley Marshall, the special prosecutor now prosecuting the president for high treason. Many thought Petite got off because Keri Marshall had stepped down as the attorney general before the case came to trial. Bill stayed convinced that Keri could never stand up to Paul.

Beth planted her empty glass next to the other empty glasses on an end table and sat across from the fireplace in one of the two gray leather tufted chairs resurrected from the Ford administration. Bill took the other seat and Paul stood before them. Paul preferred not to sit. He could look down on the client and it sent a clear message that he wasn't staying for dinner. He could also use the marker boards and exhibits lined up on easels to explain the trial to Beth. All upholstered furniture was covered in acknowledgment that the room would not be used by the family. It was off-limits to everyone except the president and her attorneys. Not even cleaning staff was allowed in the room without Bill present. It was their war room.

"Any highlights from today that I should be aware of?" asked Bill.

"Pretty much the same thing she's been doing for the last couple of weeks — mostly background," Paul relayed. "She tried to use your former friend, Mildred Renne, to suggest that you married your husband for ambition and not for love. But it backfired," he added casually. "I looked at the videos of the jurors' expressions when I cross-examined her, and they seemed to understand that it was ridiculous for a woman like Renne, who has been married and divorced five times, to give an opinion as to the genuineness of love." The three snickered.

"I wondered why Keri Marshall listed her as a witness. It didn't make sense. But it sounds like it went well for us," Bill concluded.

"Yup," responded Paul. "But she had better success with her next witness — Kym Massie, the manager of your congressional race," he said, looking directly at Beth. "He testified that you were obsessed with finding every loophole in the restrictions on public service."

"Why didn't you object?" demanded the president. "I don't understand why you're not objecting to these things. Essentially he testified that I was trying to obey the law as a way to suggest that I'm a traitor? You should be objecting all over the place!" she barked.

"Madame President, that's not how it's done. If I object — if I just keep making objections — the jury will simply think we're trying to hide something. It's better to point out the ridiculousness of his assumptions. I did that on cross-examination. I showed that your obsession could be, as you suggest, an obsession at keeping the law — not breaking it. But that's not done through objections," he instructed, somewhat impatiently.

The fact that Beth was not a lawyer made it more difficult for her to understand the subtleties of the court. Lawyers shied away from politics after the Second Constitution. They didn't like the transparency it infused into high politics. It took away the type of deal making that historically made them flock to politics as a profession. No president since 2045 held a law degree. Where more than eighty percent of congressional members were lawyers in 2037, by 2059 only thirty-two percent of Congress had law degrees.

"The next day of testimony?" asked Bill.

"Not till next week — next Tuesday. Tomorrow is an off day and Friday we'll argue our motions over the prosecutions' witnesses for next week, so the jury won't hear anything until Tuesday."

"Good! That gives me time to catch up on some of the videos. And Beth can attend to her presidential duties," said Bill as he walked Paul into the hallway.

Once they were alone in the hallway, Bill whispered to Paul, "How's it looking?"

"A lot depends on those motions. This Carroll witness is a problem."

"How much of a problem?" Bill asked, knowing the answer. It was the skeleton lurking in the closet.

"Could be enough to give her the death penalty if we don't stop him," Paul replied.

Bill knew that Paul would do everything to stop her former senatorial and presidential campaign manager, Aiden Carroll, from testifying. If he couldn't stop him altogether, he would limit what he could say and discredit him in any event. What Bill didn't know was whether that would be enough.

After Paul left, Bill lingered in the hall for a few minutes. Images of Beth coming to him in tears the day Aiden quit flushed into his head. She knew she fucked up that day, but he knew she wouldn't remember it that way. He paced the wide hallway outside the living room, debating with himself, which drew looks from the Secret Service agents. Should he reach out for help? Help that might silence Aiden more quickly than Paul could. He didn't want to talk to his handler about it. All help came with a price, and he wasn't sure he could pay it. He wasn't sure he could get Beth to pay it.

Aurelius, his handler, had left him with a dossier of dirt on Aiden. One of their blue leather folios bursting with newspaper articles and photos. He could make the Carroll problem disappear, if Bill wished. Perhaps a feigned heart attack or car accident.

In the old government, before the Second Constitution, this was common. Businesses probably still did that sort of thing, he realized. But he couldn't. The idea of having someone killed for political reasons — which had been off the table for the last twenty years — seemed honest-to-God horrible.

Then what? he asked himself, walking back into the living room.

CHAPTER 4

Washington, DC, August 5, 2023

Keri Eversley's home for the rally sat two miles southeast of the Capitol. With upward of five million people expected to come, she praised God for such a wonderful gift. Hotels booked up a year ahead. Her fellow law students from Arizona State couldn't get closer than fifteen miles. They would have to watch on outdoor screens or their tablets. But thanks to the generosity of Chad and Ashley Calise, she would be close enough to see the main speakers and meet one of her best friends for the first time.

She found Ashley and Chad through the social media site Vouch-4, which matched hosts and guests through a trust rating algorithm based on a six-degrees-of-separation schema. Keri used up only three degrees to connect with Chad. It didn't hurt that they wanted their daughter to learn the PawTab and that Keri was an expert with the one-handed typing tablet.

"I'll never get it, Ms. Eversley," said Tia. Keri and Ashley sat with her in the front room of the early-twentieth-century Henry Wardman row house.

"Sure you will, Tia. You're a *millennia,* just like me," Keri answered, patting the six-year-old's hand on her PawTab.

"You mean she's a *vampire,*" joked Ashley as she grabbed her daughter's sides and tickled her into a frothing laughter. The reference made Keri laugh.

Millennia, those born starting in 2000, devoured vampire books and movies like they were sucking blood to sustain life. Vampires were the symbol of their generation. A culture that banded together, neither beholden to their ancestors nor fettered by convention. Born in 2000, Keri was a true millennia, the dawn of the millennia, and nothing epitomized the difference between the millennia and their predecessors more than the PawTab.

Released as a tablet game in 2015, it quickly caught on with tweens and teens. She was fifteen when it came out. Anyone older than that found it almost impossible to remember the one-handed chord patterns, like adults who tried to learn a second language after their brain's language circuits calcified.

With one hand, Keri could type over ninety words per minute. Countless hours zapping letters, numbers, and symbols by tapping the correct chords to score points had fused the patterns into her brain. She thought of a word and her hand flew into the correct chord combinations, each of the five fingers pressed in a forward or back position or lifted off of the tablet. The most frequent characters had the easiest chords. *E* required only a tap of the middle finger in the forward position. A tilde (~) required the awkward placement of the pinky in the forward position and the ring finger in the back position. She hated that combination when playing PawTab games, but she loved the challenge.

She learned to use it with either hand. It was an icebreaker, like juggling, except that she typed like a piano virtuoso and everyone wanted to type just like her.

"I can't thank you enough," Ashley offered. "Chad and I have tried to learn it, but" — she hesitated — "I guess we're just too old."

"You can't be more than ten years older than me," Keri responded. But she understood the difference those ten years meant. Ashley was a millennial, those born in the decade before 2000.

Keri's generation was different, defined by instant access to a world of kids their own age. They didn't rely on traditional media, and they never trusted politicians. They were coming to the political age of reasoning just as the nullification wars erupted. The millennia watched as small groups of radical politicians representing people so frustrated with the money politics that blocked them from access to their government that they held the country's economy ransom. Refusing to fund the government, refusing to allow the country to borrow to meet its obligations, to try and break the special interests' hold on government access, to try and give the people equal access. A gallant attempt, but naïve, Keri reasoned. No wonder her millennia only trusted each other.

Each other meant millennia from anywhere in the world. They viewed mainstream news like reality shows, entertaining but not very real. All other forms of communication seemed to be pushing a point of view. Millennia liked to make up their own minds.

Whyers, the moniker for Generation Y, born between 1980 and 1999, invented this instant worldwide connection. Facebook, Tagged, YouTube, Twitter, Myspace, LinkedIn, Instagram, and a bunch of others. But the millennia used it as their primary source of information. To inspect the horse's mouth, not just hear someone tell them what it looked like. Like water finding its way through every crack in an old barrel, the millennia found their own sources of truth. The Washington rally was the logical consequence of such a large population with access to unbiased news.

"So I guess you understand this *eminent domain* sh — stuff, being a law student and all?" Ashley asked, stifling the more colorful description of what she didn't understand to protect her young daughter's ears.

"I'm just picking it up as I go. I don't take constitutional law until next semester," Keri responded, hiding her obsession with the issue. She followed the ups and downs of the eminent domain situation in Hamelin, Oregon, for four years. Chatting with former residents, she felt their anger like they were her next-door neighbors. Millions of Americans shared that anger, shocked that this was the law in the United States. It seemed so un-American.

"How could this have happened? Why weren't we aware of it before?"

"It's just one of those things businesses manipulated over the years. It was supposed to be a shield — a protection — to limit the taking of private property, but instead it became a sword, a weapon to take property."

"I didn't even know that was part of the Constitution," Ashley confessed.

"It's at the end of the Fifth Amendment. Just a few words that say private property can't be taken without just compensation, and only for *public use,*" said Keri.

"The problem came from how Supreme Court decisions changed the meaning of *public use* to include public benefit through improving blighted areas, then *increased tax revenues* from a century-long barrage by real estate developers." Subtle semantics formed on the twin tips of high-priced lawyers' tongues, Keri thought. But its impact was neither subtle nor limited to semantics. "A town's tax roll now has greater protection under the Constitution than a citizen's right to enjoy her own home," she continued, not realizing what parts she was thinking and what parts she was speaking.

"So who's this friend you're meeting?"

"Marlen? I met her on Tagged about four years ago. She posted about losing her home and having to fit in at a new school. It grabbed me right away. Her mom passed away the year before."

"That's horrible."

"Yeah. Within six months over two million people were following her posts. I showed her how to put ads on her blog so that she could help her dad financially. We started chatting directly after that."

With each detail, Keri saw Ashley step closer to Tia, as if to protect her, while Tia proudly formed chords on her PawTab. It was the stuff they never showed in mainstream news, Keri realized. How Marlen was drawn to the IKEA built on top of her home. How she would stand in the part of the store where her bedroom used to be, picturing her mom singing her to sleep, kissing her good night. Her last memories of feeling that the world was right. Her last memories of her mom.

Not in America, Keri thought at the time. Not in America, she thought now as she got ready to go to the rally.

"The people of Hamelin lost," Keri explained, her tone turning fierce, her eyes fixed and intense. "*Hild versus Town of Hamelin,* decided by the Supreme Court in 2021, provided the final bulldozer to uproot people from their couches who were weary of what seemed like a corrupt government." She explained how Justice Chloe Adee's historic dissent went instantly viral. The justice's use of the catchphrase *inbred reasoning* epitomized the canyon that existed between the people and the small, wealthy, powerful few that controlled their lives. "*Like the offspring of too many close relatives, business, government, and even this honorable court have been stacked with the descendants of a handful of universities, their thinking far removed from the vast majority of American citizens, allowing access to the government only to their own members,*" Keri quoted from memory.

Few remembered what she said or even what it all meant. But Justice Adee's use of the image of a factory worker's curses making more sense than ivory-towered judges spinning ordinary folks' hay into corporate gold hit home. It stuck.

"How's Marlen doing now?" Ashley asked.

"Still not a lot of friends, but she's really looking forward to college. The money from the blog will help. Plus her blog got her a great scholarship to Berkeley." She had to push the last words through choking pride. "She starts in three weeks. I can't wait to meet her."

"I can't wait to hear all about it. You'll post everything for me?" Ashley begged, walking Keri outside onto the front porch.

"Of course. And I'll tell you everything when I get back tonight. Assuming I can make it through the crowds," she laughed, pointing to the carnival-sized crowd lined up on the street. The three-block walk to the Potomac Avenue Metro Station would take longer than she thought, but it was the fastest way to get to the Grant Memorial, directly in front of the Capitol Building, where Marlen was scheduled to speak.

▪ ▪ ▪

The rectangular swatch of beaming white sky visible at the top of the stairs grew bigger as Keri sprinted out of the Eastern Market Station, feeling lighter than air. The hum of the monstrous crowd filled the stairwell between her and daylight. Just before emerging, she caught her first glimpse of what five million people looked like compressed into a fifteen-mile radius.

Thousands and thousands of legs, barely moving, looked like tree trunks in a dense and impenetrable forest. She was still a mile from the epicenter, the single outer bull's-eye of a dartboard, but it was as far as the pass Marlen provided would get her. She had to walk the rest of the way. When she climbed fully out onto Pennsylvania Avenue, her eyes fixated on the Capitol dome, barely visible above the buildings in the mile that separated her from Marlen. She thought of it as the star that guided the wise men to Jesus, a beacon.

She stopped the first person with a red, white, and blue T-shirt and matching baseball cap with "REFRAME 2037" emblazoned on the crown.

It was too loud for speech, and the young volunteer looked at the pass and walked her toward the tree-lined median, between four traffic lanes on either side of Pennsylvania Avenue. The crowd parted like the Red Sea to let her through. Anyone with a pass must be important to this shared cause. In the middle of the grassy area, the volunteer clapped her on the shoulder and pointed down a narrow corridor, barely big enough for one person to walk, in the direction of the Capitol. The crowd kept to either side of the lines painted on the grassy path, happy to help anyone willing to help them. Her hopes soared as she walked on legs weakened with awe over the reality that this was happening. Without warning, a middle-aged woman on Keri's right gently grabbed her arm. Above the roar she barely heard the woman yell "Thank you!"

Thank you? she wondered. Why is she thanking me? A man on her left yelled "Bless you!" pointing to the small, unadorned silver crucifix pinned to the pocket above her heart. "Bless you," "Bless you," others repeated. For the life of her, she couldn't figure out why they wanted to shake her hand. Pride coursed through her veins, muddling her head with the same sense of salvation she felt the day of her rebirth in Christ. This is what it feels like to be an American, she thought, tears streaming down her face.

"Thank you, bless you!" she shouted back as she pushed on along the path to the dome. Like most people, when Keri first heard of the concept of the Second Constitutional Convention, she thought it had taken place in the early 1800s. It didn't concern her very much until her church advocated it as a way to bring back Bible values, especially the sanctity of life, to the government. Sacredly pro-life, she followed the movement with diminishing hope when it didn't travel very far. The town of Hamelin changed that.

Now she found herself walking through a sea of neighbors. Millions united in a single belief, committed to a mutual love of their fellow citizens, a community of 350 million citizens caring about each other. The same feelings of love she experienced at evangelical meetings. The jelly in her legs stiffened, her steps quickened. She grew closer to the center, effortlessly, as if she were walking on a moving floor in an airport.

At the intersection of Pennsylvania and Independence Avenues, the buildings changed from stores and residences to huge, cold marble government icons. The Library of Congress, Cannon House, Longworth

House, and the Rayburn House Office Building. It felt foreign, impersonal, powerful, oppressive.

Only her pass got her into the area walled off by National Guard troops. Narrower, but just as packed as Pennsylvania Avenue, it was also just as loud. Some had passes because they were speakers or, like her, invited by speakers. Others won passes in lotteries designed to ensure a representative crowd of two million Americans packed along the National Mall from the Capitol Building to the Lincoln Memorial, the inner bull's-eye. The largest crowd on the mall in the history of America. The largest rally in the history of the world.

On Independence Avenue, she could only move with the crowd. Not walking, but being conveyed as part of a single organism, a chubby caterpillar crawling through a long tubular cocoon. Branches of the organism broke off at intersections. She folded into the right-sided caterpillar, circling the park below the long cascading Capitol steps.

The organism came to a stop a football field's length from the Grant Memorial, where Marlen waited. She raised her pass to show its large blue star and the words *Grant Memorial* boldly printed. Gold stars granted access to the Capitol steps, green stars to the Summer House past the Grant Memorial. The crowd did whatever it could to create tiny crevices. A lifetime's worth of squirming in and out of the maze brought her to the paved pedestrian path. She began to panic, picturing Marlen waiting for her, worrying about her impending speech. She was the fourth scheduled speaker.

A volunteer by the paved path shoehorned Keri into the heel-to-toe single line moving in the right direction. Only a crawl, but it was moving. Movement gave her hope.

Just before she reached President Garfield Circle, she felt her tablet vibrate. The millions present hushed. Conversations ended and the crowd came to a motionless attention. The first speech was about to begin. The pause provided the gap she needed to scamper around Garfield Circle. The path widened and flowed smoothly.

You could hear an eggshell crack as the speaker at Arlington Cemetery took the podium, displayed on large screens around the Capitol and through CNow on every tablet.

A few steps past Garfield Circle, she spotted Marlen jumping up and down and waving like a NASCAR flagman warning drivers of a danger ahead. She didn't shout to Marlen out of respect for the Arlington speaker and the audience. Something about the cost of freedom, the price paid by American heroes. Keri wanted to hear every word, but right now she was too excited. She wanted to get to Marlen, to meet her in person, to be there for her.

Keri hit the sculpture of a mounted Ulysses S. Grant running, vaulting up the white marble stairs to Marlen. They embraced, silently crying tears of joy. After the Arlington speaker stopped there was thunderous applause and shouts. It was impossible to speak, so they held each other. She was content to finally be with Marlen. They had a few minutes before the next speaker from the Lincoln Memorial, on the other side of the mall. At last they could talk.

"Isn't this wild?" Marlen asked, walking Keri to the edge of the huge block of marble at the base of the sculpture of Grant sitting on his horse. It dawned on Keri that Grant faced the National Mall, toward the Lincoln Memorial. His horse's butt faced Congress. Did they know then how unpopular Congress would become now, she mused, laughing to herself at the irony.

When they turned the corner of the marble base, Keri's breath leapt from her lungs, propelled into the ocean of people occupying the National Mall. If the air could somehow return to her lungs, if she could speak, no words could describe what her heart felt. Unthinkable fear, like watching a tsunami crest above her head, an avalanche tumbling toward her, picking up speed, volume, sound, everything in its path. Rapture, like the first step through the pearly gates, knowing that it was something she would have for eternity. A feeling of absolute love, as if the entire human race stopped thinking about themselves for one brief moment and cared for their neighbors, if only for the first time.

There was no scale she could understand. The Washington Monument obelisk pierced the sky in the middle of her view, surrounded by a shifting sea of people as far as she could see. Surely every citizen of the United States must be here? Shiny white clouds hung in the upper atmosphere. It must be the same around the entire globe, she fancied. No birds, no planes, nothing flew above the crowd. How could they? There couldn't be any spare oxygen above the mass of people.

They stayed on the mall side of the monument as the next speaker began. They could talk on the mall side without disturbing anyone.

"Are you nervous?" Keri asked.

"Hell yeah," Marlen exhaled, and they laughed. It was the closest that either would ever get to a curse. They had chatted about this moment since Marlen was selected three months ago.

"With you here, I'm sure I'll be fine," Marlen whispered.

Keri tried to follow the speaker's words, but it was too exciting and too nerve-racking to focus.

Keri's tablet vibrated again as the speaker finished, hardly distinguishable above the vibrations from the crowd's acclamation. The next speaker was George Comstock, the first speaker at the Capitol Building. He would introduce Marlen at the end of his speech. Keri turned to say something to Marlen, when one of the volunteers interrupted them to escort Marlen to the Capitol steps. Keri watched with fear and love as Marlen walked along the cleared path to the long steps leading up to the Capitol in preparation for her speech.

Keri climbed onto one of the bronze lions guarding the corners of Grant's likeness. The podium on the top of the Capitol steps appeared as high as Mount Olympus. She alternated between looking at the podium and looking at the close-up on her tablet.

She was surprised by George Comstock's appearance as he walked to the podium. In his late forties, tall and athletic, he wore a corduroy sports jacket and dress pants. Not the type of jacket with private-school emblems or professor patches on the elbows. A simple jacket with a plain shirt and an ordinary tie. He was handsome, she thought. Younger and taller than he appeared in pictures and videos.

She had read everything he wrote about the proposed convention. From his book *Naïve Intentions* to articles on eminent domain and his proposed treason clause. She looked forward to his speech like he was a rock star, and she gleamed with a mother's pride at the thought of him introducing Marlen.

The crowd grew perfectly quiet as he came to the podium.

"I am happy to inform you," he began in a sober voice, "that there *will not* be a test on today's lecture." Laughter burst from the masses like steam from a broken pressure pipe. The type of relief that cleared the mind, prepared it to understand new ideas.

"There is truly only one lesson to be learned from history," Professor Comstock continued. "That is, that human nature never changes. Amass a mountain of gold and the most aggressive among us will look to steal it. Ordinary thieves are easy to spot. But benevolent thieves, those wrapped in the suits of politicians and cloaks of judges, claiming that everything they do is for our benefit while they loot and plunder our tax dollars through institutionalized corruption, are harder to spot and have proven almost impossible to stop."

Keri knew his arguments, the great study and writings that he and other professors made to expose the hidden changes to the United States' system of government. A government that granted access only to huge corporations that could contribute more money in one donation than millions of ordinary people could in their lifetimes. Political Action Committees with no limits on spending for campaigns and lobbyists. But hearing it from Professor Comstock's lips, put so simply, was as powerful as her rebirth.

"Two hundred and thirty-six years ago, a group of brilliant patriots knew this," he went on to a hushed mall. "They built fences to protect the rest of us. They created a Constitution that embraced this reality." Keri listened, searching off to the side of the podium to pinpoint Marlen. She heard the professor explain how "the most aggressive among us" spent those 236 years tearing down those fences, but her mind was shifting to Marlen.

At the end of his speech there was a standing ovation and more than five minutes of applause. Keri imagined Marlen standing in the wings, scared beyond anything a seventeen-year-old should have to face, and Keri felt every twinge as if she were the one about to face the millions. Her vicarious fear multiplied with each minute of applause. Finally, the crowd quieted and Professor Comstock began his introduction.

"Heroes come in all shapes and sizes — and all ages," he began, his voice soft and sincere. "I would like you to welcome one of *my* heroes. A girl who at the age of twelve faced the horror of a government more bent on tax revenues than on her need to grieve. A girl who by the age of twelve decided that she had to do something about that. A girl who at the age of twelve could bring a nation together in a way *grown-ups* never could." He paused. "A girl who at the age of twelve knew the exact cost of the Supreme Court's decision in *Hild versus Hamelin.*" He paused, turning to Marlen. "Please welcome Marlen Hild."

Millions of hands clapped in chaotic beats and pounding booms. Cries of admiration, sympathy, and frustration blared across a shrinking sky— earsplitting screeches of support and hope. Keri could not think. She worried that the reaction would mute Marlen. Would anyone be able to hear a word after the applause stopped? she wondered.

Her eyes followed as Marlen walked to the podium and stood on a box so that she could be seen above it. The crowd hushed. Marlen stood silent. From her vantage point, Keri couldn't see her eyes, couldn't see where she was looking. She hoped Marlen was looking at her, that she could see her and speak as if only talking to her. Thirty seconds passed, and Marlen still stood silent. The crowd rustled.

In the distance, someone yelled out, "Take your time, honey; we're here for ya." The knots in Keri's stomach tightened, like a watch wound to the breaking point. Just read it, Keri thought, trying to mentally transmit the thought to Marlen. Another twenty seconds and she saw Marlen shuffle the pages just a little, take a deep breath — as if she heard Keri's message — and then start.

"Hi." She paused to the utter quiet. "My name is Marlen, and I'm a Hamelin survivor."

"Hi, Marlen," echoed millions of voices as if an unseen conductor had cued them with the point of a wand. A single voice that made the earth and air rumble. They planned the introduction as an icebreaker, a play on the Alcoholics Anonymous introduction. But it hit a different chord. It released from the sea of people every frustration, every sense of helplessness that they had swallowed for generations.

The applause finally receded and Marlen began, slowly, awkwardly, reading from her notes. It was a short speech. More of a thank-you for their support. Keri realized that it didn't matter what she said. Everyone knew her story. They just needed to see Marlen, to know that she was real. To know that the "Hild" in *Hild versus Town of Hamelin* was a person, just like them. Her youth and innocence made her the sweetheart of the movement to limit eminent domain, the poster child of the call for the Second Constitutional Convention.

"Re-frame; re-frame; re-frame . . .," the crowd chanted the second Marlen issued her final thanks. The din grew louder and louder, causing the bronze lion under Keri to quake so violently that her teeth chattered. There was no control. This could never be controlled. It could never be hidden from the people again, she thought, knowing that somehow she would be part of this. She offered up her will to the crowd. "Re-frame; re-frame; re-frame; re-frame . . .," she prayed, feeling that she could ascend into Heaven.

CHAPTER 5

Philadelphia, June 20, 2037

"Treason!" shouted the tall burly representative from Oklahoma as he jumped to his feet, spewing pellets of spit as if to make certain that his anger was not ignored. Delegates in the pews in front of him reeled from the falling globs, trying to avoid the rabid saliva.

From his seat in the middle jury box, George turned to his right just in time to watch the falling spray land on the repulsed delegates. The words were venomous darts that struck George like arrows through his heart, bleeding pangs of guilt from his exposed nerves. The barb caught more meat than Arthur Hanley's reputation should command.

"Order! Order! I'll have order!" cried President Adee, feverishly banging the gavel.

"You are guilty of treason," Arthur Hanley continued, ignoring the calls for order. His eyes fixed on George, his finger, shaking with anger, pointed at him for all to see. George gasped, feeling his face swell with rushing blood. "All of you are guilty of treason," Arthur continued, jabbing his finger over and over, pointing at everyone who disagreed with him. "Anyone who would weaken our country is guilty of treason."

Oklahoma's delegate was living up to his reputation as a WMD patriot, George reasoned, trying to release the blood trapped in his facial capillaries. One who could be wound up with fury just by framing the argument as either patriotic or anti-American. Like those who cried "treason," "unpatriotic," or "anti-American" to any opposition to the second Iraq War. Blinders that suspended reasoning, which made facts irrelevant.

Most Americans ignored WMD patriots. They were puppets, wound up and set loose by power brokers hiding in the shadows. Swords wielded by undisclosed foes. You couldn't defeat the sword, George surmised, you could only defeat the holder. If you could find him. The holder of the sword, the wielder of such an offensive weapon as Arthur Hanley, had to be uncovered to be defeated. But for now, George struggled between the urge to fight the accusation of treason and his fear that he was doing something wrong, something corrupt.

A deep, resonant *twang* of vibrating wood snapped George's gaze to the front pew of the left-hand box. Arthur's counterparts were rising to the fight. Melissa Gould, herself an atheist intellectual, one who automatically opposed any argument containing the words *God, Jesus, Bible,* or *church,* sprang to her feet like a Jack Russell at the scent of a fox. Before she could speak, President Adee grabbed the growing tension by the throat.

"Mr. Hanley!" she shouted in a voice devoid of the subtle niceties that made her an effective consensus maker. Her voice—stern, cold—commanded immediate attention and obedience. George watched Mr. Hanley plumb to attention; his pointing finger dropped to his side and his eyes diverted toward President Adee's diminutive presence looming large behind the judicial bench. Melissa Gould and the other intellectuals regained their seats without a word.

"Mr. Hanley," she repeated, even louder. "This is not a barroom. You will get your chance, *when—I—recognize—you.* Until then, sit down and *listen* to what the other delegates have to say. You might learn something," she concluded with a subtle sarcasm. He slowly returned to his seat, puffing short bursts of moist breath as he meekly raised his hand in the proper gesture to request recognition to speak.

"If I may, Madame President," George quietly uttered, also raising his hand to be recognized. Even though he had just finished presenting his proposed treason clause, he wanted to respond to Arthur's accusation of treason.

"You may not," President Adee directed at him sharply, but not bitterly, making him feel transparent.

The idea for the treason clause grew out of years of discussion in George's constitutional law class at the Marshall-Wythe School of Law in the College of William & Mary. He began the fifth class of every first-year constitutional law course by starting a free-for-all. "Under our current Constitution, do we have a government by the people, of the people, and for the people, or do we have a government of the special interests, by the politicians, and for the corporate interests?" he would begin.

No one sat on the sidelines. The entire class erupted, purging their inner frustration at the question — the same frustrations and suspicions that had grabbed a majority of the population tired of being blocked out of their government by special interests, and sick of politicians who only cared about themselves.

George asked the question without having formed an answer for himself. A tool to incite passion, to test his students' understanding of the founding principles of the Constitution. Over the years, the answers seemed pretty similar. But one student's response, an answer that he initially dismissed with little thought, took seed in his mind and germinated through successive semesters . . . until the professor finally understood how much that student had taught him.

"As long as politicians can get away with pursuing their own interests or the interests of special-interest groups, it will never be a government by the people and for the people," the student, whose face and name he long forgot, had argued.

"How would you stop them?" George remembered asking in a short, lordly snap.

"Try them for treason," the student answered, with that degree of absolute certainty that only a law student, untested and untried in real-world battles, could possess. "Isn't that what they'd be guilty of? Selling out the interests of the people of the United States for their own gain." But of course it was treason, George eventually accepted. What else could it be when politicians use the trust and power of their high office to defraud the people of the country?

It was only an academic idea at the time; George knew it would take some unexpected event, something that hit the hearts and souls of the entire people as so unforgettable, unforgivable, that they couldn't turn their attention as they had done with short-lived scandals over the centuries. That would take generations, he reckoned, if ever. But he continued to use it as the discussion point for the fifth class of every first-year constitutional law course he taught.

George followed President Adee's eyes as she scanned the faces attached to each raised hand, including his. She took her time picking the next speaker. He felt uneasy, wondering what she was looking for. Was she a friend or foe of the treason clause? he worried. Her gaze glided back to his pew and stopped on him. Their eyes locked for the space of a breath, and then her eyes shifted to his left and fixed on Sebastian sitting next to him.

"Mr. Irving," she called.

Sebastian's political skills represented the height of his profession, at least to those who considered politics a profession, George mused. The product of the City University of New York education system, he was not as finely educated as the majority of delegates. In the world of politics, he was a street fighter who adroitly moved up the ranks from a Democratic Party office worker to the behind-the-scenes Republican power broker for most political seats in New York, including governor. Backroom power instead of front-office titles. Political power built strong by judiciously supporting winning candidates while brokering all manner of deals across party lines.

When the Patriot Party, the ultraconservative spin-off of the Republican Party, as well as the political child of the Tea Party movement, made a play for a foot in the door of New York politics, Sebastian named his price. He switched to the Patriot Party and became their broker, procuring the election of a Patriot Party governor, about one-third of the New York seats in Congress, and one seat in the Senate. In exchange, all he wanted was to be appointed as the New York delegate to the Second Constitutional Convention.

The day he was appointed as New York's delegate, he opened an additional office in Washington, DC. Heads of the largest industries — energy, pharmaceutical, defense, insurance, auto, airline — paid large sums to consult with him, but he never seemed to do anything for them. No press conferences, no lobbying in Congress or in New York. Rumors flooded the media and conversations of the other delegates before the convention.

Were they hiring him to sabotage the Second Convention? To insist on industry-friendly wording? Or something else? Something worse?

Rising — slowly, deliberately — Sebastian paused five seconds beyond a comfortable silence before he began to speak. It was an effective technique for quieting an audience and focusing their attention completely on him, George estimated. By the time Sebastian's lips parted and his words broke the silence, every eye in the small chamber was fixed on him, every ear cocked ready to hear what he had to say.

"This clause is either the worst idea or the best idea of this convention," he began. Unexpected words to George. The unexpected held his interest, and the ears of the chamber, he could see.

"I don't doubt that Mr. Comstock intends this clause to be the best for our country, that his intentions are undoubtedly patriotic — even noble." The added word seemed deliberate to George. A faint attack. An allusion to the conspiracy to influence Sebastian? Or was he just being paranoid? Feeling guilty?

Sebastian paused and shuffled before turning to his right, exiting the row to plod down to the platform in front of the judicial bench. George's eyes followed in anticipation of the inevitable *but*.

Wooden planks sagged when Sebastian stepped onto the platform, his right hand rising in acknowledgment to President Adee. He turned to the caucus, his eyes seemingly fixed on every delegate. "I cannot help asking myself, as I think we must each ask ourselves, whether Mr. Comstock's proposal is just a trifle too naïve — and I mean that in a complimentary way," he added, looking at George with atoning eyes, his head tilting slightly to the side like a puppy trying to understand its master's words.

Mr. Naïve Intentions — Sebastian's greeting from the opening day streaked through George's mind. A long-plotted strategy revealed. Knowing his game would make it easier to counter, George thought, if President Adee would only give him the chance.

"Were it to work perfectly, it could eradicate all measure of nepotism, narcissism, and picked-pocketism from politics and even from the corporate world. But" — Sebastian continued slowly, deliberately — "we don't live in a perfect world. We're not perfect creatures. Politics, I believe, is the practical expression of our perfect ideals." A strange position for a political horse trader, George thought. But he feared that the audience seemed to be following the argument.

George knew that every vote was critical for the treason clause, which he had thought out, modified, and refined for more than fifteen years. He would have to argue for every vote, fight for every vote against seasoned political manipulators. Something he dreaded but was determined to do.

In its final form, the clause possessed the type of simple elegance found in the words of the original framers. It added a definition of *treason* as "Committing a fraud upon the people of the United States of America, and when committed by a Public Servant it shall be High Treason." Twenty-four plain words that could guarantee freedom from the abuses carved into the original Constitution over 250 years.

Sebastian's opening comments made it difficult at first to tell if the logic of George's presentation was making him reconsider the clause or whether he was leading the logic down a primrose path to the edge of a cliff. He suspected the cliff. Either way, George kept keenly tuned to Sebastian's every word.

"Certainly," Sebastian continued in a louder-than-life voice, like a ring master, a Monsieur Loyal, announcing the acts to follow, "we can all think of situations where politicians *must* misrepresent to keep our enemies from gaining an advantage. Misrepresenting troop strength, diplomatic negotiations, trade agreements, or any number of things in progress. Under this clause, such strategic communications could be the basis of not only treason, but *high treason.* And that would certainly give our enemies aid and comfort." George sat up straight, his chest expanding with deeper breaths at the sight of more and more heads bobbing in agreement. Heads that had bobbed in agreement when he presented the clause, now bobbing in tune with Sebastian.

"I fear it would weaken our country and our economy. It would make us vulnerable, in favor of the wonderful concept of *simple truth.* I'm not certain that our nation can survive such a naïve concept. I am certain that it will not thrive under such a naïve concept as simple truth. Simple truth is simply not practical," he concluded, his closing mantra echoing in George's mind.

A full one-third of the delegates burst into applause, George estimated with increasing dread. Sebastian's words seemed so reasonable after Arthur Hanley's tirade. Like a salesman closing a deal by offering the affordable car after pitching the top-of-the-line sports car. Would those heads have been nodding along if they hadn't followed Hanley's outburst? Or were they the product of relief, the desire to maintain a sense of sanity, a sense of order? The status quo, the opiate that the Sebastians of the world relied on to corral the masses. His hopes revived a bit as the applause quickly waned when it did not increase after several seconds.

With his hand raised high and waving, George watched President Adee continue to scan the pews for the next speaker. Over and over she passed his waiting gaze in favor of someone else. He would have suspected that the order was planned, had it not been President Adee who made the choice. After granting a succession of delegates opposed to the clause ten minutes of discussion each, she eventually returned to Mr. Hanley.

Considerably calmer now than during his initial outburst, Mr. Hanley was struggling to constrain his emotions as he walked to the platform. The first three precious minutes of his ten-minute allotment were spent apologizing profusely to the president and to the delegates for the tone of his outburst, before turning to George to continue his argument.

He launched into well-worn comparisons between Americans of the 1780s and modern Americans, keeping his eyes focused solely on George. His words were slow and articulate, stopping for elongated breaths between sentences. The extra moments keeping a tight grip on his composure before continuing each portion of his argument, George thought.

"The average American, as you well know—as anyone who has ever held office well knows—is more concerned about adding inches to their television set than protecting someone's constitutional rights." The immediate laughter seemed to startle Mr. Hanley, who hesitated, as if he had to check his fly to see if it was open. "This is the reality of it. It's not lofty, it's not honorable, but you all know it's a fact," he emphasized, pointing to several delegates in each of the boxes.

"One minute!" Henri Ormond announced, rapping his small wooden cylinder.

"We must keep our government strong at all costs, to protect against terrorism, and keep growing our economy, providing jobs, providing a lifestyle which defines Americans as the happiest people in the world." Pleased that Mr. Hanley gave up his personal attack on him, George saw that the more reasoned appeal after his initial outburst was having an effect.

President Adee turned to the sergeant at arms and signaled for the dinner break. George saw lines of disappointment and frustration on the faces of many of the scholar delegates as they left their pews and exited Independence Hall for dinner and their informal debates. They had not had their say. It seemed unfair.

■ ■ ■

For dinner, most delegates chose the nineteenth-century Beaux-Arts-style Bourse Building, a short walk from Independence Hall. Its majestic marble atrium, encased by wrought-iron balconies, lined with rows of white incandescent light bulbs strung like pearls, provided a cozy yet grand backdrop for their informal debates. Seated around long rectangular tables butted together to form a square in the center of the atrium, they could debate face to face over the informality of breaking bread together.

President Adee never attended the table square debates, but George wished she came this evening. More often than not, the debates were presided over by Reverend Jack Connors and Dr. Alman, sitting together in the middle of one of the sides of the square. Reverend Connors represented the conservative faction, Dr. Alman the liberal. Despite their opposing views, they could argue without getting personal. George went directly to his usual seat toward the end of one of the perpendicular sides, hoping for a chance to respond to Arthur Hanley's attack.

Dr. Alman began the evening's debate while most of the delegates were still foraging at the large self-service buffet tables at opposing sides of the seating square. "I'm sure it's no surprise to anyone that I find Mr. Hanley's comments offensive," she began. A delegate started to laugh, until Dr. Alman looked at him with eyes that imparted the seriousness of her comment. The fierceness of her passion commanded respect, if not outright fear.

Her passionate defense of the treason clause echoed throughout the atrium. A momentary silence, which seemed to test whether she was going to continue, was broken by Jack Connors, the prominent evangelist preacher and delegate from Arkansas.

"Please!" he said mockingly in his slow Southern drawl, all eyes turning to him. "The people get to choose who will govern. That is democracy. To allow them to choose *how* to govern is insanity. It invites anarchy." His voice grew louder, quivering with the slight vibrato that made popular preachers effective.

George started to stand and answer, when Anaihyia Alman bellowed, "Amen, brothers and sisters," returning Reverend Connors' sarcasm as she raised her hands, fingers spread, shaking like flickering butterflies. This time, there were no burning glances in response to the overt laughter from around the square. Even Reverend Connors' mouth spread into a genuine, warm smile.

The debate continued for two hours. Heated, but kept within bounds by Dr. Alman and Reverend Connors. George was satisfied that his clause was being taken seriously, although he recognized that it might not overcome the opposition.

"We should get back," Dr. Alman reminded the group, standing from her seat.

"George," Sebastian interrupted in a strong but casual voice as the delegates just began to stand. "There's something I don't understand. Maybe you can clarify it for me." The atrium was silent, anticipation thick as oatmeal as they sat.

"Why does this have to be in the Constitution? Don't we have laws that cover the same thing? If not, couldn't Congress make laws to cover this?"

George sensed that Sebastian's timing was not accidental. The delegates would vote whether to send the treason clause to committee, where it would get a final vote at the end of the convention, at the end of the debate. If it didn't get the vote of half the delegates, his fifteen years of work would be thrown in the trash. He welcomed his chance to explain the clause, but sitting across from Sebastian, he worried that he was being led into a trap.

"That's a great question," George started confidently. As he spoke, his demeanor morphed from the academic — intimidated by the stature and power of the other delegates — to something more than a professor, more than an advocate. A parent protecting a child, a pastor disseminating belief. His identity, his ego disappeared, replaced by the vision of a government staunchly responsible to the people.

"It has to be in the Constitution to keep it out of the reach of politicians, to restore faith in our system," he extolled, his face red with fervor. "People are sick to death of seeing politicians resign over money scandals and getting pardons by a friend in the White House. Enough," he demanded. Delegates who had started to leave returned to the square and listened in silence as he continued.

Institutionalized corruption, unspoken pacts between special interests and politicians, fueled by unrestricted political contributions from corporations, was what suppressed the voice of ordinary citizens, George realized. But it was not the straw that made this moment possible. The people needed something more human than money, power, or corruption. They needed a face, a face they could not wipe from their minds or their hearts. They needed Marlen Hild crying in an IKEA to ignite them, to keep the flame hot through the years leading up to the Constitution. Her image gave him courage.

"No law written by politicians will ever be able to get back the trust of the people. That is why it must be in the Second Constitution," he concluded, gazing at Sebastian with eyes bulging intensely, nostrils flaring with the commitment of a general ready for a long, bloody battle.

All eyes turned to hear Sebastian's response. "Thanks," Sebastian meekly responded, adding, "we better get back before President Adee gives us all detention." No one laughed. They stood silently and headed back to Independence Hall.

Before entering the hall, George realized that Sebastian wasn't with them. Looking around, he saw Sebastian on 5th Street, heading to the side of Independence Hall. Odd, George thought. Sebastian always returned after the table square debates. But, if he wasn't present for the vote, it improved the chances of the clause being pushed to committee.

Two more hours of debate in Independence Hall, with an hour remaining in the evening session, and all discussion abruptly stopped. No more hands raised for recognition. Delegates talked among themselves, as if there were an intermission. What conversations George could hear seemed to be about other things, not the treason clause. It was time, he realized. The vote would soon be called. Before he had time to worry, Henri Ormond banged his wooden plug.

"The debate on the Comstock treason clause is now closed," he announced. "Forty-nine delegates being present—" He paused. The delegates hushed and turned their heads simultaneously to the sound of footsteps bending the wooden planks as Sebastian labored up the stairs to his pew without explanation or apology.

"Correction," Henri Ormond continued, "all *fifty* delegates being present, it will require a vote of twenty-five delegates to move this clause to committee." George readied himself, less hopeful now that Sebastian had returned, and seeing the puzzled expressions on many faces looking toward Sebastian as he planted himself onto his seat.

"All those in favor of moving the treason clause to committee, please raise your hand." Some hands quickly raised, some more slowly, more tenuous. Mr. Ormond waited a full thirty seconds of agonizing silence before beginning to point to each raised hand as he deliberately, silently, counted, moving his lips along with his finger.

George tried to count the hands. An impossible task, he realized. As monumental at the moment as proving Hawking's M-theory. But it seemed close. Many of the scholar delegates and several political delegates had their hands raised. He lost all count, along with his breath, as he turned to his left and saw Sebastian's hand, half raised.

"There being twenty-eight in favor, the Comstock treason clause is hereby approved for review by the committee," Henri Ormond announced with a final rap of the wood cylinder.

George exhaled fifteen years of tension as Sebastian stood and started to push past him to leave their pew. He put his hand on Sebastian's shoulder and whispered, "Thanks."

"No problem," Sebastian answered. "Politics makes strange bedfellows."

This isn't politics, George thought, holding the comment to himself out of shock or gratitude. But it bothered him as the chamber emptied.

The summer solstice approaching, there was a hint of sunlight reflected in the sky as George headed home just before 10:00 p.m. He floated aimlessly, unaware of anyone or anything around him, wrapped in a blanket of hope from the vote for his contribution, his *naïve* suggestion.

Mulling over the presentations of the day, trying to give unbiased consideration to the opposition's arguments, he found himself at the threshold of the Georgian-style row house loaned to him by a history professor from the University of Pennsylvania. He stepped into the narrow darkened entranceway, onto the black and white marble tile without looking down. His foot briefly slipped forward, aided by a square ivory envelope. It bore his name in handwritten script, and now a faint imprint of the sole of his shoe.

He flipped the hallway light switch and placed his keys onto the antique mahogany server placed along the narrow hallway. Uncertain of what to do, he stared at the envelope for a long pause, until the sound of the door falling shut behind him jarred him to action. Reaching down, he picked up the envelope and quickly opened it, still standing only inches inside the front door.

June 20, 2037

Dear George:

There are several matters where I believe you and I can provide a great service to the convention. To that end, I would like the opportunity to meet with you in private to discuss how we can together best serve our common cause.

Please join me for a light breakfast tomorrow, June 21, 2037, at the City Tavern at 7:30 a.m. I am,

Sincerely yours,

Sebastian Irving

Private meetings weren't forbidden, but George wasn't aware of any. The thought scared him. Sebastian's two-hour absence from Independence Hall scared him more. Had he left Independence Park? Had he spoken with anyone? Were others involved that no one knew about? The one thing he did know was that it would be a long, sleepless night.

CHAPTER 6

Elkhart, Indiana, October 8, 2059

The sun cut into Aiden Carroll's eyes like razor blades, forcing tears to trickle down his cheeks. The white dishes, water glasses, and silverware on the table in front of him beamed as bright as stadium lights, as if he wasn't uncomfortable enough with this meeting. It was just one of those unfortunate seats where the bright sunrise pierced the window at such an angle as to make it impossible for him to keep his eyes open beyond bare slits. The sun rose late in Elkhart, almost an hour later than in D.C. and New York City. Another couple of weeks, he couldn't remember precisely, and the end of daylight saving time would have raised the angle of the sun high enough to be deflected by the window awnings.

A quick look at his watch, as if it could tell him why his host was late for their breakfast meeting, while he shifted from one side of the bench seat to the other to cut off the ray of sunlight viciously attacking him. Out of frustration, he stood and switched to the other side of the table, placing his back to the warming sun. It took several minutes for the burning in his eyes to cool enough to allow him a leisurely sip of coffee. His nerves settled a little, but the question that nagged him all night put fuel back on the fire of his anxiety. Why had Bill Waverly called this meeting?

What did he want? Was this leading him into some ethical trap? Did he have something on him? The thoughts ran through his mind faster than birthday money through a seven-year-old's pocket. He spent enough time with Bill on the campaign trail to know to be afraid.

Strange, he thought, looking around and realizing that there were no other diners in the room. The restaurant, a quaint inn twenty-five miles to the Ohio side of Notre Dame University, was popular with the bed-and-breakfast crowd, parents visiting the university, and locals. He never saw any one of the three dining rooms completely empty. It felt like he was trapped in some horror movie where everyone knew what was about to happen but him. Lively conversation and the clacking of dishes from the other two dining rooms made it worse as he sat alone in the silence of the empty dining room. He nearly spit out his last sip of coffee when Bill suddenly appeared, motionless in front of him, as if transported to the spot.

"My apologies!" Bill shouted, cupping Aiden on the back. Before he could stand or speak, Bill grabbed his hand. "I hate to use the presidential privilege," he joked. "But you know that when you work for the president of the United States, everyone else has to come second."

Aiden knew from personal experience that working for Beth meant that everything else came second, whether she was president of the United States or the village dog catcher. "No problem, I could use the quiet time," Aiden replied, pushing the words through a dry larynx.

As Bill slid into the seat facing the window, Aiden saw him place a letter-sized leather folio on the table. At first it looked like the folios he had seen in the White House, but something was different. A lighter shade of blue than he remembered, a metallic blue, lighter than the presidential blue. And the seal was different. Set on the bottom right corner of the cover, instead of the center. No fifty-one white stars encircling the eagle, and a distinctly different eagle. A swopping eagle, a clutching eagle about to capture its prey, instead of the spread eagle he was used to.

Bill's words blurred into the background as Aiden continued to focus on the seal. In an instant, Bill turned the folder over, hiding the seal as if it was something he didn't want Aiden to see. A puzzling maneuver, Aiden deduced. Bill wouldn't have put the seal side up if he didn't want Aiden to see it.

"How you holding up?" Bill asked, drawing Aiden's eyes up from the folder.

"I'm fine. Why do you ask? Why wouldn't I be fine?" Aiden shot back.

"You know we didn't want to bring you into this? Beth never would have dragged you into this mess."

Aiden saw Bill carefully assaying every twitch and gesture on his face. It creeped him out.

"She wants you to know that Paul Gordon will not use your personal life — you know, your family history — as fodder for cross-examination," Bill said, opening the blue folio. Aiden felt his large boyish physique contract into a slump. It hid the full breadth of his 193 centimeters, tall enough to be a shooting guard on a professional basketball team, covered in muscles, padded with thick skin — endomorphic skin, which he knew made him look larger, younger, physically immature. His eyes shot to the papers within the folio.

Some kind of official report on top of loose pages. News articles that had followed his family for generations, which made them move from Utah to Indiana when he was a kid. Which made them consider changing their last name.

His paternal grandfather, an elder in a small fundamentalist Mormon sect that practiced polygamy in New Mexico, when polygamy was still illegal, made national news before Aiden was even born. One of his grandfather's wives, his grandmother, was only thirteen when they married. It was a stain that could destroy him and his family. His grandmother was only fourteen when Aiden's father was born. His grandfather was forty-one. She left the sect and moved to Provo, Utah, rejoining the main Church of Latter Day Saints, when her husband was imprisoned for statutory rape.

Wherever they lived, everyone seemed to know about it, and comment on it. Aiden's intense feelings of shame required lengthy therapy. By the time he was a wide-eyed political science major at Harvard, he had made peace with his family's past, at least he thought so.

He looked up from the folio, studying Bill's face for signs of what he was up to. Bill's eyelids closed to slits, obliterating the whites of his eyes, as if they could betray his motives. The little black beads, Bill's pupils, shifted back and forth, looking to pierce his defenses, Aiden thought. Bill made no threat, not even a mention of his grandfather. But Aiden knew that his reaction betrayed his fear.

"Should we be talking about this?" Aiden asked, squeezing his quivering words through clenched teeth. "I didn't ask the prosecutor if this is okay—as you asked—but I'm not a lawyer. Are you sure it's okay for me to be talking to you?" He fought to steady his voice and keep it below a scream.

"Yes, yes, of course. I'm not asking you to do anything illegal," Bill assured him, reaching across the table to pat his arm like a puppy he was trying to train. "My job is to make sure that nobody in the White House does anything illegal, and that begins with yours truly." That would make sense, Aiden thought, but he didn't trust Bill.

"Besides, I'm not asking you to lie or to make anything up. I'm here to make sure that the prosecutor isn't asking you to lie." Aiden reeled from the suggestion that the prosecutor would ask him to lie. Keri's reputation for honesty when she was the US attorney general was unquestionable. She entered the political arena solely to serve a civic duty and then pass the torch on as she returned to the business of living life. She set the example of what a public servant should be, Aiden thought. He got to know Keri and her associates pretty well over the last two months. Nothing ever made him think that she would do anything underhanded. He knew better of Bill and Beth.

"Of course not! Mrs. Marshall and her staff have been quite professional. They've never asked me to change anything."

"But have they fed you any information? Did they connect any of the dots for you or fill in any blanks? It's—it's not always a matter of just asking you to lie. There are subtle ways to change your story without you ever knowing it. Trust me, I'm a lawyer. I know how this is done," Bill concluded, picking up a napkin as if it were a piece of evidence.

"Quite honestly, I don't think that is one of the tools in her shed," Aiden answered, knowing that his belief in Keri's innate goodness would be chalked up to his Mormon outlook. "But, I have to say," he added, displaying the keenness of his Harvard insight, "it does appear to be one of the tools in *your* shed, since you know so much about it." Bill's mouth bowed into a Glasgow grin, too large to be spontaneous or real.

Aiden had no misconceptions about Bill's tactics. Over two long campaigns he watched him work. Bill's talent was getting people to say what he wanted them to say by making them believe it was their idea and not some idea he implanted in their psyche. It all came down to a matter of motivation, to helping them see that what they really wanted was the same as what he really wanted. More often than not, what they wanted was to keep their private lives private. To avoid the distractions of scandal that digging too deeply would invariably bring.

Bill would boast of his access to the most powerful companies, most powerful people, Aiden remembered. Access to resources he doubted even the FBI had. How he never asked anyone to lie — that would be unethical, and more importantly could subject him to criminal actions and disbarment. He didn't have to ask anyone to lie. First planting the seed of fear, he would lead them down a path of plausible testimony, showing the witness how some slight piece of evidence could make the difference between happily ever after and hell. Aiden now understood exactly how that felt. The agony of having to make that kind of choice.

"Listen, Aiden, I don't need to shape your testimony. We didn't call you as a witness here. I just want to make sure you have no ax to grind, that your testimony will not only be the truth but will be the complete truth — not just the portions that Beth's enemies want the jury to hear." The words hollowly tumbled over the open folio with his grandfather's news articles still showing. Chitchat, wholly disconnected from their actual conversation. The majority of Aiden's mind fixed on the folio and its implications, while some small portion tried to respond to their make-believe dialogue.

"Of course I have no grudge, no ax to grind," Aiden responded. "She helped make my career just as much as I helped make hers. Okay, she probably did more for my career," he conceded, seeing Bill's eyes squint in skepticism.

"I assume that they're limiting your testimony to the South American Free Trade issue?" Bill asked, looking directly into Aiden's eyes, never looking at the open folio.

After a long silence, Aiden responded out of a fog: "How the hell should I know? No one at Keri's office has told me anything about why they want me to testify. They've asked me questions over several meetings. I've discussed everything that I could possibly discuss with them — but that's it." He threw his hands up to his sides. "They haven't suggested that I say anything, they haven't told me anything about what they plan to ask me, or what they want me to say. The only thing that they've told me is to stick with the truth and it should go pretty smoothly."

"Uh-hum," uttered Bill, eyeing Aiden intensely as he nodded his head up and down. "And you believe them? You didn't think that they were trying to shape your testimony with that?"

"If suggesting that I tell the truth after taking an oath is a strategy designed to shape my testimony, then it is a strategy that I can live with very peacefully," he answered in frustration, but he felt the draw to go along with Bill, to wipe away the threat of public humiliation.

"Uh-hum," Bill continued in a softer voice. "Seems to me that they did something to get you on their side."

Aiden took the change of tone as a sign that Bill thought he had succeeded, or at least was at the point where Aiden had to make his choice. "I'm not on anyone's side. They ask me questions, I give answers — that's it," Aiden protested.

"Well, it seems to me that you're spending a lot of time defending Keri. Clearly she's done something to get you on her side."

"If you mean that I find Mrs. Marshall to be an honest public servant whose sole motivation is the good of the people — precisely what I used to believe about Beth — then yes, I'm guilty." He threw his napkin over the plate of food in front of him. Fear was turning to determination and his patience was almost exhausted.

He couldn't look at Bill anymore. He wanted space, distance, to think this through on his own without pressure. His body involuntarily shifted toward the open end of the booth. Bill mimicked the move, as if he would jump out and block him if he tried to leave. Aiden felt trapped.

"See, Aiden, that's the problem — that's where she gets to you. Let's face it, anyone looking at your face, looking at your background, knows that you're a sucker for the red, white, and blue, fresh-scrubbed face, yes I cut down the cherry tree line. Don't you think that is how she knows to get to you?" Bill asked.

"I didn't think she was trying to get to me," Aiden shot back. "I thought she was just trying to get to the truth. But clearly you, and I'm sure your boss and her pit bull trial attorney, have considered how to get to me, and that is apparently what this is all about." He felt crow's-feet forming at the corners of his eyes and his nostrils flaring. The confrontation made him uncomfortable, like a Quaker brought to violence by an insulting outsider. It wasn't him.

Bill propped himself up in his seat and leaned forward, his right hand stretching across the table. Aiden instinctively withdrew his hands and placed them under the table, beyond Bill's grasp.

"Our first concern is the security of this country. Not the president's reputation, not protecting her position or even her life." With the last suggestion Aiden's head shot up. The crow's-feet beside his eyes grew deeper as his eyes squinted.

"Oh yes," Bill continued. "We have every reason to believe that your Keri intends to go for the death penalty. But Beth would gladly forfeit her own life if that is what it takes to protect the security of this nation that she loves." His words were deliberate. Aiden took a long sip of coffee, as if its stimulating properties could give him the wisdom to separate truth from position. Bill backed off, remaining silent for several moments. Aiden calmed himself and pondered.

"What we need to know most," Bill resumed, "is, has the prosecution asked you anything about security briefings?"

"About what?" Aiden let out an incredulous cry. "I was only present during two or three security briefings. And — and I don't see what any of this has to do with them." The tremor in his voice betrayed the anger still lurking behind fear and frustration.

"It's a good thing that you don't understand what this has to do with security briefings. After all, the security briefings you were privy to took place before Beth became president and before many of the developments that make it related occurred. Obviously the situation with South America — the national security situation with South America — took an abrupt change just before the election, which is why the president had to change her position. I can't go into details since you don't have a current security clearance, but surely you understand that. You understand that it's why she couldn't fulfill her dream of opening free trade with South America — and you above all know that was her dream for at least eight years."

"I don't know any of that," he responded, shaking his head. "And I still don't understand what this has to do with the trial, with my testimony."

"Keri is trying to put Beth in a position where she would have to compromise national security issues, issues which you were partly privy to during the campaign, in order to defend herself." He held his hand up to stop Aiden from responding before he could finish the point.

"You may not understand how this involves national security, but that's precisely the point of having classified information, isn't it?" he asked. Aiden stopped trying to interrupt, puzzled by the potential connection and surprised by his own failure to consider the issue when talking to the prosecution. "They know that Beth will not threaten the security of the nation by allowing Paul to use the content of the security briefings to save herself." That part Aiden knew was nonsense. She wouldn't sacrifice herself for anyone or anything.

Bill sat back; he appeared to relax. But this made Aiden more tense, like a bird who dared to look in a snake's eyes. With an effortless twist of his hand, Bill asked, "Have they spoken to you about security briefings?"

"No," Aiden answered immediately, and then paused. "Well, only to remind me that they didn't want me to reveal any information from security meetings. They told me to let them know if I felt they were bordering on any national security issues or any security briefings I attended."

"I see," said Bill, pulling on his chin. "What they were trying to do, and I don't want you to feel bad for not having picked this up — what they were trying to do was to get you ready for the national security objection that we have to make. They were trying to plant in your mind an answer that you think is your own — that your testimony has nothing to do with national security even though you could not possibly know that. Nor could you discuss what took place in the security briefings to either defend that answer or refute it. A perfect paradox."

Aiden had trouble following Bill's logic. "But I agree with that. I don't see how my testimony would have anything to do with national security," he finally answered, trying to make it clear that he wouldn't be their pawn either. "I'm just going to testify to what I heard from Beth's own lips regarding her intentions with the South American Free Trade Act."

The waiter appeared and started to fill their water glasses from a metal pitcher, drawing a long, fixed stare from Bill. Aiden appreciated the interruption and how it seemed to annoy Bill.

"I'm not suggesting that you don't testify to that," Bill continued after the waiter left. "I would never suggest that you change what you believe to be the truth. But that's not the issue. The issue is preserving the sanctity of our national security and not letting a prosecutorial puppet of the president's enemies, the nation's enemies, put her in a position where she has to decide between her fate and the fate of our country. You would agree that is inherently unfair, wouldn't you?"

That style of questions — statements he would have to agree with in order to make him think he agreed with his hidden point — was Bill's calling card, his trademark. Aiden replayed memories of Bill hypnotizing opponents like a snake charmer, making them believe that they agreed with him, that it was their thought in the first place. Political opponents hesitant to support Senator Suarez, corporate executives reluctant to part with checks all fell prey to the same logic Bill was employing on him.

"Of course — of course I would, but I still don't see how all of this is related to national security," Aiden answered.

"That's the point. You have no idea of what you can be doing to Beth or to national security by giving an opinion without full information. And that's precisely what the prosecution is trying to do. They're trying to get you to give an opinion regarding national security when you couldn't possibly know. Don't let them bully you into it. For our country's sake, for Beth's sake, don't let them put words in your mouth — that's all we ask," Bill concluded, closing the folio shut with a thud.

Manufactured, Aiden figured, as Bill stood and left him sitting alone in the empty dining room. He slowly, deliberately caressed his coffee cup as diners started to fill the empty seats. What a performance, he kept repeating in his mind. But the points Bill raised worried him. The death penalty went against everything he believed in. So did turning from the truth to save his own reputation.

CHAPTER 7

Washington, DC, October 23, 2059

Bill sat clutching a half-empty tumbler of straight Scotch in a far corner of the presidential living room, hidden from the sparse beams of downward spotlights. No stranger to difficult days, he refused to smooth the edges of the countless crises he handled with alcohol. But as evening approached, he found himself on the outside of his personal crisis envelope. Beth sat uncharacteristically motionless at the other end of the room. She was dressed in her most executive suit and stared blankly at the door while shouting at him across the room.

It was a bad day, but he knew it could be worse. Keri had put on her star witness, Aiden Carroll. He was believable and worse, likeable, Bill lamented. Paul played their trump card, national security, before Aiden could tell the jury about the day he quit.

Judge Kneuaya didn't buy the national security connection. He wasn't going to preclude Aiden's testimony. Paul exercised the president's right to fully disclose the details of the connection to the chief justice of the Supreme Court, who could overrule the trial judge. The meeting would be just between Beth and Justice Currier. No Keri, no Aiden, no Paul, and no Bill. It was a presidential privilege Bill was counting on, to let Beth make the connection without any argument from Keri.

An hour of Beth screaming insults that felt like the sting of a thousand sea wasps wrapped around Bill's exposed flesh, while they waited for Paul, left him wondering. When did this happen? When did she start believing that she knew better than him? He had to put up with her ordering him about and demanding every ounce he had to give. But this was different. It wasn't just her need to act superior. She was starting to believe it, he worried.

Silently, Bill sulked in his dark corner. The cogs in his mind clicked as fast as hummingbird wings, playing out every move, every counter-move. How he could realign their positions back to the natural order, how he could wash the venom of her stings from his self-talk and stop self-pity and anger from getting in his way. A skill he forged in dark closets, hiding from his father's criticism as a child, building iron walls in his mind until his father became distracted by some other object to blame for his own failures.

She may be the president, Bill thought, but only because of him. On her own, she would never have risen past congresswoman or governor. Most likely she would have blown even that in one stupid rant if it weren't for him guiding her with the control of a master puppeteer.

"And what was that blue folder trick?" she shouted across the living room, mocking him. "Did you do that with your arts and crafts kit?" He knew she didn't understand the implication of the blue folio. Only a few outsiders would, not Paul, not Keri, not Judge Kneuaya, not the jury. Not even the media understood what it meant. But his handler would.

Aurelius was the only name Bill knew him by. Late forties, chiseled face, about 190 centimeters tall, always dressed in crisp business suits — he fit Bill's image of a CIA agent in the old government days. The type that listened more than he spoke and stared with eyes that needed no tattooed tears to signal that he had taken lives. Bill's relationship with Global Mundo gave him access to their resources. His position as the president's counsel gave him a high-level handler. The handlers always had Roman code names, very neoclassical, Bill thought. His use of the blue folio to intimidate Aiden, which Keri brought out through his testimony, could have repercussions, Bill feared.

He finished his Scotch in one gulp, ignoring Beth's shouts. Keri had exposed his meeting with Aiden to the world. She made it look like he was trying to manipulate him, to get him to lie. Her questions about the blue folio and Aiden's description of the seal raised suspicions. But the suspicion landed on *him*, not on Beth. It put a wedge between him and Beth, between his job of protecting her and his instinct to protect himself. There had to be a way to appear to protect Beth's reputation while protecting *his own* reputation. And he had to figure a way to explain the blue folio and seal to Aurelius. That, he feared, could be a matter of life and death.

Beth continued to shout at him from the front of the room. He had warned her not to drink in case the scent would be detectable later in the evening. She took his advice, but he paid the price. No intoxicant to restrain her anger, at least until she could target Paul.

Paul strolled into the living room as if the day had gone just as he had planned. Two steps into the room, an overhead recessed light lit up the top of his head, making his eye sockets look like dark canyons, evil abysses. He turned on the room lights without asking. The lights stabbed at Bill's eyes, bringing his mental machinery to a sudden stop.

He had insisted that she hire Paul because of his strength with powerful people. People who would pout in noxious ways, in offensive ways, when things didn't go exactly as they wanted in court. Bill never saw Paul cower; he never saw him give in to their rants, no matter who they were. He needed that skill right now.

"What the hell happened?" Beth attacked on Paul's first step into the living room.

"It's a trial, Beth! This is what happens during a trial," he explained, pausing between each word as if explaining banking regulations to a hillbilly. Bill enjoyed watching Paul put her in her place. It brought her sense of power down to earth, where he could reason with her, where he could control her.

"So the judge is going to let him testify?" she asked.

"Unless you can convince Judge Currier otherwise," Paul answered, without confronting her, staying a good two meters away.

Beth's grin suggested that she considered it a done deal, a sure thing. She had appointed Robin Currier to the Supreme Court only a year before. "She has to help me," Beth extolled with the confidence of an insider calling in a favor.

"No!" Bill shouted in exasperation, walking from his corner to the matching couches by the fireplace where Beth and Paul had moved, sitting across from each other. "She doesn't owe you a damn thing. You picked her for her reputation for honesty—that wasn't just PR." He sat on the opposite end of Paul's couch, afraid that sitting too close to Beth would make her defensive.

"Justice Currier is honest. If you try to tell her she has to pay you back for her appointment, she's likely to throw you in jail for contempt." He could see Beth's eyes squint in the way she did before her most vicious attacks. She leaned forward, but Bill didn't wait.

"You gave her a job for life. What card do you think you hold after that? She's free to do what her conscience tells her. That's why they're appointed for life," he added sarcastically. Only the Supreme Court justices maintained life appointments in the Second Constitution. All other federal judges now had to be elected to four-year terms.

Once she calmed down, Paul and Bill began the process of prepping her for the meeting at Justice Currier's home. They had her rehearse the arguments over and over again, like a schoolgirl learning her multiplication tables. She could repeat them word for word, but not with conviction, not with understanding, and not with sincerity, Bill feared.

"She'll be fine when she meets with Judge Currier," Paul assured, looking at Beth. But Bill wasn't buying it. He knew that she hated the idea of having to prepare to convince someone who, she felt, owed her. Someone who she felt was below her. That worried him, but not as much as having to explain the blue folio stunt to his handler. As the hour ended, Bill and Paul walked her down to the waiting motorcade.

As soon as the Secret Service whisked Beth away, Bill headed to the Hotel Monaco Washington on F Street. A late meeting with George Comstock. After Judge Kneuaya's ruling, George left a message suggesting that they meet, letting Bill know that he would be at the Monaco this evening. Coincidence? he wondered, given that Judge Kneuaya was letting Aiden testify. Soon his driver dropped him in front of what looked like an old post office.

Bill wasn't impressed by the hotel's trendy reputation with dignitaries who seemed embarrassed by their power or wealth, artsy types that flaunted a weird sense of style. Bill growled internally as he walked up the entrance steps covered by a garish eggplant-purple canopy underneath seemingly useless rows of Greek columns. What George saw in this hotel, he couldn't imagine. But anything different was good. He needed a change of scenery, a change of company.

Patterns and colors throughout the lobby assaulted his eyes, adding to the confusion in his mind. Bright green mixed with blood red, swatches of butterscotch plaids. It was as if he was looking at some modern piece of art that everyone but he pretended to get. Where did people get the time to care about this, to sit around and discuss these weird combinations? he wondered, trying to quarantine his fears of Aurelius. A rare few hours to do what he wanted and he didn't want to waste it racking his brain over colors and patterns.

George opened the room door quickly, grabbing Bill's hand. The powerful grip felt like a love affair compared to Beth's use of him as her punching bag. "Tough day?" George asked, ushering him through the doorway into the intimate living room. Highlighter-green walls, black and gray checkered chairs, and a deep golden carpet made Bill dizzy, not sure of where to stand. Strange sights that kept him unsettled.

"I can't remember any tougher," Bill candidly moaned. But within seconds he could feel the muscles at the back of his neck and down his arms melting. His face smoothed and breathing became easy, enjoyable. It was always this way around George, he realized. Even around such disturbing colors. Not just nostalgia, it was a parallel part of his life, as if he had continued on the ACLU path, the Second Convention path. As if *that* was the real Bill Waverly.

He followed George to the table in the small adjoining dining room, pleased to see colors that made more sense. He could have kissed the dark wood furniture, the gold-striped drapes in front of cream lace curtains, and the brass chandelier. At last a room that felt comfortable, familiar.

George joked as the two men took perpendicular seats, choosing to sit closer to each other rather than being separated by the length of the table. Bill's stomach rumbled. Some combination of the last seven hours with Beth and more alcohol than he was used to. But George's innate congeniality and true concern was reversing some of the effects of the Scotch. Getting right to the point, George began the conversation.

"I spoke to Mary and my partners. They have no objection to me doing this. It seems to me that the case is only a few weeks away from going to the jury" — George paused, waiting for Bill's nod of agreement — "and assuming that Beth doesn't pull off a miracle tonight, Mr. Carroll will fully testify tomorrow." Bill nodded again. He agreed with the miracle assessment.

"I don't know what Carroll's going to say — and I don't want to know," George said. "Just like I don't want to know whether Beth's guilty or innocent! It's not relevant to my job — I don't want any confessions from her, understood?"

"Understood," Bill readily agreed.

"I don't even want to know about the blue folder, at least not now," George added, staring directly into Bill's eyes, his face stern and tense. Bill's arm slipped off the dining room table.

There was a knock at the door. Room service. George let the waiter in with his cart of tea, coffee, and light snacks. Bill used the interruption to gather himself, afraid that George could read the reaction of his pupils and his reddening face. George was an outsider, he was sure of it. He couldn't possibly know about the blue folio, he told himself. But if he did? It would shatter his relationship with George. It would bring damnation from the only person whose opinion he cared about.

"So you'll do it?" Bill asked when the waiter had left, trying to sound optimistic. George didn't answer right away. It was clear that George had already made up his mind, even without an answer. Bill accepted the slower pace of discussion when he was in George's world. A more academic, cordial climate. Like playing a slow game of chess as a backdrop to interesting conversation rather than to crush your opponent. An exchange of ideas for their own sake, not to win. He enjoyed being in this world. He enjoyed this side of himself.

Bill yearned to be more like George. Now into his mid-eighties, George seemed to be enjoying the fruits of his lifelong work. Speaking engagements were like award ceremonies, where dignitaries of all kinds lavished him with praise for his work during and after the Second Constitutional Convention. He was held up as an American hero on par with Thomas Jefferson, if not George Washington. Apt comparisons, Bill believed. But he couldn't understand why George never accepted these comparisons, or any praise for that matter — publicly or privately.

George chafed at all of the praise heaped on him, like a lamb's-wool sweater that made him itch. It was an itch that Bill thought he knew. A nagging sense that he had left important work undone. The vision of what he did not accomplish overshadowed all that he did accomplish. His failure to eliminate the death penalty in the Second Constitution. It was the issue that bound Bill and George, that made Bill a part of this gentler, kinder fraternity.

Still waiting for a reply, Bill understood that George, more than anyone, knew the toll he would pay to take up this challenge, perhaps his final challenge. Would George be willing to spend the few grains of sand left in the top half of his hourglass trying to save the life of someone who he believed violated the very premise of the Constitutions, the exact protection he had provided for the American people? But sitting back and doing nothing, letting Beth be put to death, would be harder for George to live with, Bill figured. In Bill's mind, not getting rid of the death penalty and abortion made George feel like an impostor. It explained why he couldn't accept praise.

"I have conditions, Bill — and they must be strictly agreed to," George began. Bill sat silently, listening as he sipped a cup of tea.

"First of all, since I don't need any information from your employer, I don't want to meet her — I don't want to speak to her!"

"That won't be a problem," Bill assured, stopping short of expressing gratitude to every deity. Given Beth's disdain for George and her temperament, any meeting could be disastrous.

"I don't need a copy of the record since I'm only going to handle the death penalty issue. Have Paul argue for whatever sentence he thinks they can get away with. I want to limit my involvement solely to the issue of the death penalty and I want the president to know — I want there to be no misunderstanding by her — that my involvement has nothing to do with her."

Waiting for Bill's nod of approval, George continued. "I require a million-dollar retainer paid up front. And I need proof that it comes out of her personal money, not some slush fund or benefactor, not even Global Mundo. The money is to be paid to a charity that I designate within a week — and *it is not* refundable!"

Bill stopped himself from swallowing for fear that he might choke on the financial conditions. The amount was reasonable enough, but the insistence on proof that it came directly from Beth's personal assets, and that it was not refundable, would cost him at least an hour of humiliation. "Agreed," he responded.

"I have to clear up a few matters first. I won't be able to start on her case before Monday. That will give your client three days to decide if she wants me to proceed. I want the papers ready by the time of sentencing and to do that I can't wait to see how the jury decides."

Bill silently nodded his consent. Although Beth was sure to complain about the terms, he knew she would accept them. He envied George's insistence that the president not communicate with him in any way.

It was late when Bill left the Monaco. Visitors were leaving the Smithsonian American Art Museum and Portrait Gallery across the street, making the streets seem alive in the crisp late October air. He didn't know when Beth's meeting with Judge Currier would end, but he knew to expect her command to return to the White House as soon as it was done.

Alone on the street, he felt strangely at ease, like finishing Thanksgiving dinner and sitting down to watch a favorite movie. He dismissed his agent and walked the half mile back to his apartment, fluffing up his paisley scarf around his neck as he went. He would take whatever vile Beth wanted to spew in the morning, but he didn't want to talk to her tonight. Doing so would take him out of his parallel life, away from his fraternity.

He was barely over the threshold of his apartment when his celltop started to buzz. He didn't have to look to see who it was. A pang in his stomach reminded him that his other world would evaporate into thin air if he answered. Not yet, he thought. He wasn't ready to give up that world right now.

She would just keep calling back, he figured. She could even have the media company turn his celltop on from her end, and see what he was doing. She had done it before. At the very least, she could track the signal to find him.

He didn't know how to turn it off, he never turned it off. So he rushed to the kitchen in the darkness, opened a drawer, and threw the celltop onto a bunch of dish towels. Let it buzz, he said to himself, closing the draw. The towels would absorb the vibration. He wouldn't hear it in his bedroom.

He never thought of his apartment as a sanctuary. Just a place to sleep. He didn't like working there, preferring to sit at a desk in his office. Couches and easy chairs served no function for him. There was no such thing as sitting around watching on-screen shows. They rarely held his attention. How could fiction intrigue him when reality was so much more intricate, devious? News was about the only thing he would watch, but he knew that the trial would be on and he wanted to stay in George's world for as long as possible.

His on-screen started to flash. It was her for sure. She could override that as well, so he unplugged the entire system. It made the small apartment completely dark, a void. He liked that. Slipping between the sheets, he drifted off to sleep keeping to the world he preferred, replaying his discussions with George. Replaying his times at the ACLU. The happiest times of his life.

"Mr. Waverly, Mr. Waverly," he heard through the veil of a deep REM sleep. He couldn't put a face to the voice, it wasn't familiar. How did this fit into his dream? he wondered. He was arguing a death penalty case in front of the United States Supreme Court. All nine justices were asking him questions, like he was their best friend, like he was their professor. They wanted to know what he had to say on the subject; it made him feel important, relevant.

"Mr. Waverly, wake up," the voice commanded. Why would they want him to wake up? he wondered, starting to question whether the voice was in his dream. "Wake up, Mr. Waverly, wake up," the voice repeated, and a hand poked his left shoulder.

The touch startled him. He opened his eyes a slit, as much as the crust that had formed in his sleep would allow. The overhead light shocked his eyes. Instinctively, he pulled the covers tight to his chest, pushing his back against the headboard until he was in a sitting position, a defensive position. To the left of his bed stood a tall man in his early thirties, dressed in a dark suit with a dark tie. A bulge by his right hip, a gun? Bill cringed. A hit man sent by Aurelius because of the blue folio slip, he thought.

On the left side, there was a female, shorter, dressed in a black pantsuit with no tie. Her dark hair was pulled tight against her head and she looked serious. She scared him more than the man. Some of his handlers over the years were women, Octavia, Clodia. They were cold, all business.

"We need you to come with us, Mr. Waverly," the female ordered, her voice less kind, more authoritative than the male.

"What?" he uttered. "Where? Who sent you?" His mind wasn't fully functioning yet, but he feared that if Aurelius had sent them, he was dead. "On whose authority?"

"We're not at liberty to say," the female agent responded, pulling back her jacket enough to show a gun pinned to her left hip. "On our authority," she insisted.

They watched as he dressed. No opportunity to write a note or make a call. Nothing that could leave a trace of what was happening. His thoughts fixed on his two sons, fearing that he would never see them again, that he would never get the chance to tell them how he felt. He felt hopeless, scared as never before.

CHAPTER 8

Philadelphia, June 21, 2037

George arrived precisely at seven thirty. He was tired from worrying all night where Sebastian had gone for two hours before the vote on the treason clause. The ribbons of steam rising from a breakfast buffet on top of the antique walnut server, gracing the only wall without a window or door in the perfectly square dining room, was making him a little nauseous. The wait wasn't helping. He empathized with the intricate crystal chandelier looming over the oval walnut dining table, its crystal tassels dangling still, like a large glass wind chime just waiting for a breeze. Although a fireplace stood cold along the wall opposing the server, between two windows, its unpolished black slate facade and ornately carved white marble mantel made him feel unbearably hot even though it didn't add a degree to the sauna that passed for weather in Philadelphia in late June.

The dining rooms in the City Tavern, a few blocks east of Independence Hall, were small and intimately private. Secretive, George worried. Should he leave? Should he ask President Adee about the propriety of the meeting? Since they were meeting in an Independence Park building, as required, their conversation would automatically be recorded. What could be the harm? he reasoned, deciding to give Sebastian the benefit of the doubt and wait to hear what he had to say before deciding what to do.

A faint creak from the front door grabbed George's attention. He saw

Sebastian hesitate at the doorway to the dining room, beads of sweat ushering down his forehead, his cheeks flushed and red.

Sebastian meticulously blotted the sweat on his face as it streamed toward his crisp white collar. He wiped his hands with the handkerchief George always saw him carry, then waved his hands in the air to dry them before thrusting his right hand toward George as he walked to meet him.

"Thank you for coming, George. I'm sorry for the mystery, but I thought we should have a private meeting before the next set of arguments," he said, taking George's hand in his own inflated hand. His grip was surprisingly firm. George felt the outlines of muscles underneath the fleshy palm, which felt like dough.

"I was a little surprised — and curious — by your note," George answered, as the two men filled their plates and returned to their chairs, facing each other across the table. The more Sebastian ate, the less George wanted to eat. He piled chunks of sausage, bacon, and eggs into his mouth before fully chewing and swallowing what was already there.

It fit his reputation as a greedy power broker, gobbling up high-paying clients for his consulting firm as soon as he was appointed as a delegate. George stopped himself from making the judgment. He abhorred rash judgments — any judgments, in fact, about people. When Sebastian's consumption rate slowed, he looked at George, chewing and swallowing the half sausage he had last placed in his mouth, then broke the heavy silence.

"Now that the most important arguments are coming up, it seems to me that this whole thing is going to come down to just a few issues," Sebastian began, still chewing, small bits of food visible between his smacking lips. "I think there will be agreement on most of the language, thanks to such scholars as yourself. But it looks like there's going to be some real battles, too. Especially your treason clause, eminent domain, and the supremacy and commerce clauses."

George sat silently, waiting to hear the entire pitch before making any judgment or reply.

Sebastian was correct. The most contentious proposals were coming up for committee referral votes starting today. Eminent domain, the government's right to take property and increasingly give it to private interests, the supremacy and commerce clauses, the clauses that defined the split of power between state and federal government, that expanded or contracted the role of each, that favored local or national politicians and their friends, that brought out the most polarizing arguments and accusations from all sides. They were reaching a critical moment in the convention, George acknowledged to himself, fighting an urge to stand and pace as he waited for Sebastian to continue.

"I know you had your heart set on abolishing the death penalty, and I agree with you," Sebastian added, holding up his hand to stop George from interjecting. "But I think we both knew that couldn't happen. The delegates against it had marching orders. They would never let the new Constitution be signed if that were included. I'm telling you that as a friend, and as a politician with a great deal more experience than you."

The *friend* comment hit a sour note in George's ear.

Taking a pause to chomp another portion of egg, Sebastian continued. "I also think that several leaders have emerged. Obviously President Adee's opinion is given a great deal of weight, although she seems strangely quiet," he added with a doubtful look.

"She's waiting," George instructed, taking the opportunity to show that maybe he had more experience, or at least knowledge, than Sebastian. "She's letting everyone voice their opinions fully and come to their own consensus. She'll only speak when her opinion is most needed, when there is an impasse. It's the same thing that George Washington did during the First Convention," George said.

"You really think that's the reason?" asked Sebastian with a half wink, as if he knew something that George didn't, as if everyone knew something that George didn't.

"Of course," George responded indignantly. "It makes perfect sense. Historically—"

"I see," interrupted Sebastian with the attention of a student who just wanted class to be over. "In addition to President Adee," he continued as if George hadn't spoken, "I think that you and I have emerged as the clear leaders of the major factions. I have pretty good control over the *political* delegates, at least the moderate and conservative ones. Most of the *scholar* delegates, though, seem to look to you for all things constitutional."

George knew that Sebastian meant his words as a compliment, an acknowledgment of his status as a leading expert on the Constitution, sincere or not. But he felt his collar starting to choke from blood flowing north to his head in preparation for a fight.

"As to the *patronage* delegates, I think it's fair to say that Henri Ormond will do whatever President Adee does. The others will follow my lead," he concluded, without heeding George's building fire.

"How other delegates vote is not my concern," George responded with a crystal, icy edge.

"Well it really has to be your concern, and my concern, too," Sebastian answered. "We need to decide what is possible — what you and I can get done."

"It's not about *you and I,*" George erupted, a sliver of his anger slipping past his self-control. "I'm a delegate for a state that has asked me to vote my conscience — that has asked me to vote for what I think is right."

"Yeah, yeah, I know," quipped Sebastian. "Me too! That's what I'm talking about. Voting our conscience. But let's face it, we have to be practical. You and I have to be able to see what can be done and how best to get it done," he added, sidestepping George's forceful resistance. "We have to see what you and I can agree to — so we each get what we want most."

Looking across the table at the man who had helped to vote his treason clause to committee, George now saw only the backroom politician Sebastian was reputed to be. Images of him brokering deal after deal over meals just like this one floated through his mind. He began feeling like a fly dangling precariously in a finely-spun spider's web. Not sure of what Sebastian was proposing, George chose to dangle, at least a little longer.

"Listen — I know that this convention is one of your greatest dreams. That you, or at least your book, was one of the things responsible for making it happen. But as much as I know you idolize the original framers and their *naïve intentions,* I don't think that the First Constitution or the Second Constitution could be possible without compromise."

It was an argument that George had heard thousands of times on the way to the convention from people just as deaf as Sebastian to doing the right thing just because it's right. "The whole point of the treason clause is to guarantee the American people that its leaders, even its *politicians,*" he added sarcastically, "make decisions and cast votes based only on whether they believe something is right for the people." Holding up his hand to stop Sebastian from interrupting, George continued. "What you're proposing is to continue the politicians' loophole of casting votes as payment for something that they want in exchange."

Sebastian angrily waved off George's hand gesture and defiantly pointed his fork at George. "You make it sound like I'm selling out the people to line my pockets —"

"Not at all —" George began to calmly explain, but Sebastian cut him off again.

"All I'm doing is bringing your *childish* ideas, your grammar school version of the Constitution, into the realm of the real world. Showing you that in order for the government to function — to get things done, there has to be compromises."

The insult took George back, hitting his most exposed nerve, the feeling that he couldn't stand up to powerhouses like Sebastian, that he wasn't strong enough. That his arguments were *childish* and everyone else's were mature. He realized that Sebastian had been studying him, trying to find his weakness, the point in the ice where just a tap could crack an entire lake. The *childish* barb felt like that point, his fear and anger clogging his ability to react before Sebastian continued.

"A willingness to give the benefit of the doubt to each other. I'm not asking you to vote in favor of slavery. Let's face it, the issues we're discussing are close. It's just as likely that one side is right as the other. What I'm suggesting is that if we're all willing to work together, and just give a little deference to each other's ideas, trust in each other's judgment, then we will end up with the best of everybody's ideas. Isn't that what we're here for — isn't that what's best for the country?"

George painfully understood why Sebastian was so successful in his political career. With a single word, *childish,* he threw him off balance, like pulling a pit bull's hind legs in a fight, and then he attacked him with simple logic. George found himself believing, at least in the genuineness of Sebastian's motives. But bad ideas instilled with good motives are just as readily available to people with bad motives, he reminded himself.

"Let's be honest," George began in a deliberately calm voice, hiding his shaking leg, which seemed to absorb the strain of his anger, his hurt, his contused ego. "*Childish* to you means requiring politicians and business leaders to be honest, to play by the same rules as everyone else—"

"I mean no offense," Sebastian interrupted. "But you've lived in an *ivory tower* for most of your life." George's leg rattled nonstop under the table, but he refused to allow insults to mangle his arguments. "Those politician and business leaders you're so quick to condemn, they operate in the *real world*. They build the roads, the bridges, the airports that your wage earners, your wage burners, your welfare eaters take for granted."

"And they line their own pockets with billions of taxpayer dollars in the process," George jabbed, slapping his palm on the table hard enough to lift his silverware a fraction of an inch off of the table. He needed to remain calm, not to get into a brawl, he reminded himself.

"*In the process?* They *are* the process," Sebastian shot back. "Without them, we'd all be riding on dirt roads; inner cities would turn into piles of rubble; there'd be no jobs for your precious masses, and no payroll taxes to pay for their welfare." Sebastian was banging on the table with both fists, a deliberate show of greater force, George calculated.

Sebastian balled his fists into chalk-white hooves and planted them on the table, hoisting himself up. "You—you and your kind would throw away the smartest leaders in business and government and replace them with high school dropouts, just to ease your sense of social fairness. Well let me be the one to enlighten you"—he paused, walking around the table, to within a few feet of George—"they will be the first ones to hang you in effigy when unemployment skyrockets and they start losing their homes. As a messenger, Arthur Hanley may be a blunt sword, but he's right."

The room seemed hotter to George, at least ten degrees hotter. His neck chafed against his collar, swelling beyond the confines of its linen harness. He looked closely at Sebastian, who stood two feet in front of him, and took a moment to check himself, making sure his words flowed from reason and not his increasing anger. Sebastian's shoulders were awkwardly pinned back, as if he were trying to make himself look bigger, more menacing. Streams of sweat ran down both sides of his face. The neatly folded handkerchief unraveled as Sebastian tugged it from his breast pocket. It dissolved into a wet rag with the first pass over his face. George relaxed at the pathetic sight while Sebastian returned to his seat.

"Even if that were true, it doesn't mean you can rip off the people just because they're not looking—"

"George," a resonant female voice scolded from the open doorway, stopping him midsentence. When he turned and saw President Adee standing in the doorway, staring at him, eyes piercing, his leg shook more violently. He hadn't heard her enter the City Tavern. He had no idea where she'd come from. Had she been there the whole time? he wondered. Had she been listening outside? How long? His face grew dark with a different shade of red, a shade of shame, a shade of embarrassment.

"Satan's wings," she reminded him, dipping her head down so that her eyes peered out over the tops of her wire-frame glasses, the glasses she used to read, he noticed. To his surprise, she walked over to Sebastian and greeted him as if he were a dignitary higher than herself. "Good morning, always a pleasure to see you," she offered, shaking his hand with a touch of exaggerated decorum.

"I heard that the two of you were meeting here this morning, so I thought I would just drop by and say hi," she concluded, still standing next to Sebastian. She was looking across the table at George, who remained seated from fear that his legs would fail if he tried to stand.

"Would you like to join us?" George asked, hoping for an ally against the formidable Sebastian.

"This is a private meeting," Sebastian interjected, looking at George, not President Adee. A subtle hint that maybe this wasn't a casual visit, George surmised, then wondered if he was just being paranoid.

"Not at all," President Adee answered. "I'm sorry for the interruption." She nodded to Sebastian. "As I passed by I heard what sounded more like a heated argument than a discussion. I thought I would remind you that it is important to listen to each other. I think that Sebastian might have some things that we might all want to hear," she added, looking at George.

George was puzzled. She continued to stand next to Sebastian, her head barely equal to his while he sat, looking down at George as if she were trying to tell him to go along with Sebastian. Was she in his corner? It didn't make sense. She was the one who assigned him to shadow Sebastian. Her commitment to getting rid of special-interest control over the government was as strong as his own. He couldn't make sense of it.

"Of course," he dutifully whimpered, wondering if perhaps it was a political move on her part. His legs continued to rattle, but now they were venting fear instead of anger. Fear that he was doing something wrong, fear that he was playing to Sebastian's hand, that she wanted him to play into Sebastian's hand. When she left, George couldn't remember where he left off. He was still trying to figure out the purpose, the importance of her visit, when Sebastian picked up the argument.

"You see, even Chloe agrees that there has to be compromise," Sebastian triumphantly proclaimed. It snapped George out of his fog with a sickening jolt. It wasn't what he said, it wasn't even what he hinted at; the thought of Sebastian calling her *Chloe* seemed wrong. Like a lecherous old man putting his hand on a young girl's shoulder. He had so much trouble getting the image out of his mind that he failed to respond to Sebastian's outline of a proposed deal that would give him some portion of the treason clause in return for a lip-service change to the eminent domain clause, no campaign finance reform, and continued special rules for businesses that create jobs.

"What?" George blurted, more as a question to himself than to Sebastian.

"I know it's a lot to think about. But I need your answer sooner rather than later. If you're not the leader I'm looking for, then I need to find someone who understands how this is going to go down. Perhaps Dr. Alman, and her abortion clause."

"No! I'm not going to make a deal just to save some part of my treason clause," George answered in the sternest voice he could muster.

Sebastian stood and picked up the cordovan leather portfolio he used to take notes. As he walked around the table he slowly unzipped the portfolio. "Nothing — nothing could be accomplished your way." His voice had risen to a deep roar, but George couldn't tell if it was anger or acting.

"I would rather nothing got done than to keep open the sliver of malicious opportunity that exists between principle and expediency where the American people have been ripped off and usurped over and over," George answered, looking into Sebastian's eyes, which lacked any glimmer of understanding. Not even the slight upward deviation of a searching thought process. Sebastian reached into the folio and pulled out a blue paper folder, an unusual cobalt-blue folder, and placed it on the table in front of him.

"What's this?" asked George.

"I've joined the committee on the treason clause. This is a version that I'll ask be adopted." Without waiting for a response, Sebastian added, "Of course I'd love to discuss this with you in depth, but for now I have other appointments I must keep. It was a pleasure, if not productive," he concluded, briskly leaving the dining room without shaking George's hand.

George sat motionless, fighting a sense of despair. A poisoned apple like Sebastian, a greedy, self-serving leader who knew just where the dry reeds of discontent could be set ablaze to level an entire nation, could snuff the heart out of a Second Constitution. Leaving in place the old tools for corporate manipulation, political gain. Tools the corrupt could continue to hone for centuries more before the people realized that it was the same flawed document covered in a shiny new wrapper. A dangerous wrapper with pretty images of trust and hope and patriotism. Food for starving sheep being led to the shearing table.

He opened the blank folder and read Sebastian's proposed clause:

Committing a fraud upon the entire people of the United States of America for the sole purpose of financial or political gain, without cause.

George instantly understood that it was a useless clause. Although it sounded like George's own proposed clause, it threw in qualifiers, words that could be interpreted as limiting its application — *entire people, sole purpose, without cause* — making it virtually useless. An empty gesture — and worse, a gesture wrapped in hope, but with no hope of changing a thing.

Reading it over and over, a more sinister fear took hold. There is no way that Sebastian wrote this, George realized in a moment of horror. A professor's eye can always spot plagiarism, an instinct he grew to accept. There was a deliberate attempt to mimic his clause, but it had the sophistication of a constitutional scholar. Probably put together by a team of experts, he judged. But that raised serious and troubling questions. Had Sebastian come to the Convention with this in his briefcase? Or had someone handed it to him during his two-hour absence last night? It all violated the rules of the Convention.

George shuffled back through Independence Park, his eyes directed downward as if someone had dropped the answers to his questions on the pathway. The heat was oppressive; the humidity congealed the air. Each step took effort, like walking through water. By the time he reached Independence Hall, sweat covered his skin, his leg muscles had lost their oxygen, and he was exhausted, body and mind.

President Adee's admonition repeated in his mind. *Satan's wings*—why did she say that to him instead of Sebastian? It bothered him. He knew what it meant to her, someone who was so angry that they were keeping themselves from seeing reason. It was her most critical assessment, what she used to describe politicians who kept shutting down the government, pushing the country to default on its credit because they didn't like a law.

That wasn't him, he protested in his head. How could she think that was him? He respected her opinion above anyone. He couldn't stand the idea that she thought that of him. If she only knew what Sebastian was spinning, if she only saw his empty clause, she would have said it to Sebastian, not to him. But the stain hit a nerve beyond his fear that he wasn't up to this task, that he would be the undoing of the Convention. That Sebastian may have won her over. That maybe she supported Sebastian's clause.

CHAPTER 9

Washington, DC, October 24, 2059

Keri made a conscious effort not to rub it in when Paul entered the courtroom. After the news reports last night, the courtroom was bursting with soundbite-hungry media personalities and curiosity seekers. No one knew exactly what happened at Judge Currier's house, other than that it ended with US Marshals physically removing the president, against the wishes of her own Secret Service agents. The jurors wouldn't have seen the news coverage, so Keri needed a way to let them know that Paul's tactic failed. Justice Currier denied Beth's request with a short statement that the connection between Mr. Carroll's testimony and national security was *fabricated.*

"You may proceed, Counselor," Judge Kneuaya invited Keri, who was already standing and facing Aiden in the witness box. This was the moment, she thought. The moment of victory, where the eagle pounces upon its prey with thundering force to break it before it can react. The moment that exists in every contest, in every trial. Images she burned into her psyche from Sun Tzu's *Art of War.* She had trained herself to wait patiently for this moment and, when it appeared, to strike with the force of a grindstone thrust upon an egg.

Aiden wasn't the egg. He was the grindstone that she was about to heap on Beth. It would take a steady hand. A patient path. A skill she finely honed over a lifetime. Questions that would start slow and pick up momentum before reaching the egg, the final point.

"Continuing where we left off, Mr. Carroll," Keri began, thrusting a small dagger into Paul's side by reminding the jurors that the twenty-four-hour delay was both his fault and unsuccessful. "You were about to discuss your conversations about SAFTA with President Suarez during her campaigns?" It was an open-ended question. Not really a question, except for the raised inflection at the end of the sentence. A vehicle to let Aiden tell his whole story. Keri waited, anticipating an objection from Paul. An objection that could only heighten the jurors' suspicions that the president was trying to hide something.

"Yes," Aiden answered, without a sound from Paul. There weren't more than a handful of attorneys who wouldn't have made the objection, she estimated. Most wouldn't take the chance of being second-guessed for not being aggressive. But Paul was one of those who didn't care what others thought. He knew better than most. To Keri it meant that he was patient, that he was waiting for *his* moment of victory. No matter how much she felt she was about to crush Beth, she wouldn't underestimate Paul.

Aiden continued without waiting for another question. "Mrs. Suarez's support of free trade with South America played a prominent role in her senatorial race. During our conversations, she always expressed her belief that free trade — such free trade would benefit the people of Illinois as well as the United States as a whole. It would mean a steady supply of reasonable consumer goods, replacing the loss of reasonably priced goods which we used to enjoy from such markets as China and Mexico."

"What do you mean by prominent?" Keri asked in a monotone voice, being careful to keep the focus on Aiden's answers, not her questions.

"Something that she was wholly committed to. We talked about it every day during her run for the Senate. We put most of our focus on getting that message out. Position papers released to the media always started with the South American Free Trade Act. The same was true for her on-screen site and filed position papers."

"Did that continue through her entire senatorial campaign?" Keri wanted to show the jury how Beth's commitment before her abrupt change bordered on obsession. Anyone could change their mind, she realized, but a drastic about-face, out of nowhere, cried suspicion.

"Absolutely. It's what got her elected."

"Now, after she was elected to the Senate, did you continue to meet with her on a regular basis?"

"Not initially," Aiden answered, leaving the sentence dangling.

Without moving her feet or hands, Keri filled the pause. "Why not?" Their questions and answers were seamless, like a well-rehearsed scene in a movie. Where the most practiced exchange seemed spontaneous.

"I didn't take a position in Senator Suarez's office; I didn't work for her anymore. So except for running into each other at an occasional function, we had no communications until she considered running for president."

"When was that?" she asked without a pause.

"Well, she first contacted me after finishing her second four-year Senate term. During her break from politics, when she was back at Global Mundo. At first I was involved in the *feeling-out* process. To calculate if she had a chance of winning. Once we determined that she had a good chance of winning, she asked me to run her presidential campaign, and I agreed."

"During her presidential campaign — during your involvement with her presidential campaign, did you continue to meet with Mrs. Suarez on a regular basis?"

"I would say that during the feeling-out process, I met with her at irregular intervals. Only once every week or two. When she decided to run for president, I started to meet with her every day."

Keri stood silent, as if she were searching for the next question. It moved the jurors' eyes to her, refreshing their focus. In her mind it was like giving them a hit of pickled ginger between sushi courses.

"And during those times, during your daily meetings with her as she campaigned for president of the United States, did you discuss her position on the South American Free Trade Act?" Short pauses between the words painted them with an air of importance.

"Again, it was the biggest issue in her presidential campaign. We talked about it every day."

"Now, if you can, Mr. Carroll," Keri continued, her voice ever so slightly louder and more abrupt, telegraphing to the jury that they were getting into the key testimony. "Would you explain to the jury what the sum and substance of those conversations were during the early portion of Mrs. Suarez's presidential campaign?"

"Objection," Paul calmly interjected. Keri knew he was just trying to break the rhythm of the testimony. She didn't respond. She stood still, waiting for the judge to speak.

"Overruled," the judge answered with an air of resignation, acknowledging that he understood that Paul was simply doing his job.

"The same as when she ran for the Senate. She was quite excited about it and got everyone else excited about it, me included."

Keri moved back to the podium and placed her celltop in front of her. Choosing her words carefully, she relied on the notes on her celltop. Notes made questions seem mechanical, she understood. It could break the connection between her and the jury. But she wanted to make sure that the next series of questions were asked in precisely the right way.

"At any time during Mrs. Suarez's presidential campaign did she file any papers changing, amending, or altering her position regarding the South American Free Trade Act?"

"No — absolutely not," Aiden answered.

"At any time during her presidential campaign, did the marketing strategy for her position on the South American Free Trade Act change?"

"No, not while I was there."

"At any time during her presidential campaign, were any new, corrected, or amended position papers given to the media, put on her on-screen site, or given to the public in any form?"

"No — absolutely not."

"At any time during her presidential campaign, did she make any speeches or give any interviews where she explained that she had changed her position on the South American Free Trade Act?"

"Not that I'm aware of."

Keri's eyes stayed glued to Aiden, but she didn't speak. She could sense the tension grow in the silence. Once the room was silent enough for her to hear her own heartbeat, she knew it was time to continue, careful not to raise her voice above a whisper.

"At any time during the presidential campaign, do you personally know if Mrs. Suarez's position on the South American Free Trade Act changed?"

"Objection!" shouted Paul, in stark contrast to the softness and melodic tempo of Keri's questions. "This witness cannot possibly know what my client was thinking—"

"I got the gist of your objection, Counselor, no need to argue it," Judge Kneuaya admonished as Keri stood unmoved.

"Your Honor, I must argue it. This is precisely what the prosecution is trying to do; they're trying to put words in—"

"That's enough, Counselor," the judge angrily rebuffed as Paul edged toward the bench with a threatening stance. "I said that's enough, Counselor," the judge repeated. "I instructed you beforehand that any arguments must be made outside the presence of the jury and I have no intention of tolerating this now. Your objection is *overruled,*" he commanded. Looking in the jurors' cameras the judge added, "This witness will be allowed to give his testimony—now."

Keri knew Paul's reputation for standing up to judges tougher than Judge Kneuaya. He had often been held in contempt when he felt it necessary to protect his client or make a point. A contempt contest could muddy the testimony, Keri considered. But it couldn't stop her from dealing this blow. At most it could drag it out. She would find a way to use that, to make it more dramatic. Paul sat down without pushing the point, as if he could read her mind.

Remaining perfectly still, her hands lightly clasped behind her back, Keri acted as if she hadn't listened to the exchange between Paul and the judge. When Paul sat down, she continued as if not a moment had passed.

"Let me repeat, Mr. Carroll—during Mrs. Suarez's presidential campaign, do you personally know if Mrs. Suarez's position on the South American Free Trade Act changed?"

The long breath Aiden exhaled and drew back before speaking carried the weight of his frustration. It would resonate with the jury. Keri could feel it. They sensed the burden Aiden carried, waiting a long time to unveil a secret that only he knew, that only he could tell.

"Yes," he answered simply.

"Can you explain for the jury how you came to know this?"

"About three months before the election, in August of 2056, Mrs. Suarez and I were in her campaign office going over some position papers to be released. I asked her if she would, as president, propose the act as she initially introduced it in the Senate, or if she planned on incorporating any of the changes suggested by some members of the Senate."

"And what did she respond?" Keri interjected, and then took two steps back from the podium, making herself as small as possible to the jurors' camera so that they would see only Aiden.

"She said that she changed her mind and had no intention of introducing SAFTA when she became president, or even if she returned to the Senate." Keri stood still, looking down at the floor, as if she had just learned that someone had died.

"Did that surprise you?"

"Certainly! We built everything on her support of free trade with South America," he explained. "Every day I frantically tried to get that message out to every potential voter in the country, letting them know that if they elected Beth Suarez, she would fight to pass SAFTA. Now, she's telling me that she changed her mind. It blew me away."

Taking two steps back to the podium and pausing for effect as she slowly drew her arms behind her, Keri continued in her soft, low voice. "Did you ask her why? Why she changed her position?"

"Yeah," Aiden answered, then paused before continuing, as if he was trying to reel in an unseen anger. "She said that she was discussing it with her husband and—"

"Objection," Paul interrupted in a baritone voice, decibels higher than any previously used by him in the trial. "At the minimum, it's hearsay," he argued.

"It goes to state of mind," Keri argued without looking up.

"It would also be an admission," Judge Kneuaya responded. "Overruled. You may continue," he instructed the witness directly, to Keri's delight. It was *the* question. The question that would expose the president's deception, her true nature. She leaned back on her heels, letting her body relax, ready to enjoy the answer to a question she had worked for months to hear.

"She said that her husband told her that the free-trade act would cost his company billions," Aiden testified, and then paused to let it sink in, just as Keri had prepped him. The jurors' eyes widened and their bodies leaned forward, but Keri couldn't tell for sure what it meant.

"He told her that NAFTA, a similar agreement with Mexico and Canada in the last century, brought so much industry to Mexico that they could no longer hire Mexicans to work in their factories for minimal wages. As soon as these third-world areas became more affluent, and their workers gained some parity with American, Brazilian, and Mexican workers, Global Mundo would lose its best market for cheap labor."

Keri waited as Aiden took a sip of water from a paper cup perched on the rail in front of him before he continued. "How without free trade, his company could control the cheap labor force throughout significant depressed areas of South America, allowing them to sell products at huge profits. But that if SAFTA went through, it would eventually cost them their largest and one of their last sources of cheap labor."

Wrinkles of surprise bloomed on the jurors' foreheads, mouths opened in unison, Keri observed, as Aiden spoke. Juror number eighteen let a "Huh" jump through her lips. Open mouths quickly hardened into narrow, tense lips as juror number twenty uttered a "What the —" before he stopped himself. Keri expected the reaction, understating that none of the details of Aiden's conversation had been leaked to the media. This was the first time that the jurors, the audience, the American people, were hearing the reason for the president's abrupt change of position. The grindstone had landed on the egg and Keri let the force of the strike hit home before continuing.

"Did she mention whether or not her husband had asked her to change her position?"

"Overruled," the judge interjected as Paul started rising to his feet, forcing him to sit down before voicing his objection.

"No! No, she never mentioned it, and I didn't ask."

"What happened next?"

"Next?" Aiden answered as if the answer would be obvious to anyone. "Next I resigned. I told her that — that I couldn't take part in telling people to vote for her based on something she had no intention of supporting."

"And, how did Senator Suarez react?"

"She was rather nice about it," he answered, with his surprise at the time evident in the tone of his voice. "She thanked me for everything I did for her up to that point and told me that if there was anything she could do to help me in the future, to let her know." Keri knew this would help the president, help to humanize her, make her look nice. Bringing it out when she questioned Aiden was safer than letting Paul throw it out as some big surprise. She could sandwich it into a moment where it had the least effect. And the honesty made Aiden look more trustworthy, she calculated.

"She then reminded me that my work on her campaign was of course confidential and that she fully expected me to honor that."

"Did you?" Keri asked, knowing that this was an area Paul would attack. The jury could completely turn on Aiden if they felt he failed to keep a promise, failed to honor his word. But only if it was for a corrupt reason — money, power, revenge.

"No," he answered without a hint of regret or shame. "I felt it was wrong and I immediately went to the attorney general, Julius Stevens."

"Thank you, Mr. Carroll. Thank you, Your Honor," Keri abruptly concluded, silently walking back to the counsel table. Her pinpoint focus spread out and she could see spectators sitting in the back of the courtroom, the court officers' and the jurors' faces on-screen.

What she saw was mouths agape, eyes wide and glazed like they had all just seen a ghost. When news of the treason charge first broke, a few reporters speculated that Beth's veto was a gift to her husband's company. That speculation quickly died when the majority of reporters, who initially speculated that she supported SAFTA to help Global Mundo, pointed out that their cries of treason at that time were dismissed as absurd. They couldn't change their positions now, Keri realized. So Aiden's revelation came as a shock, one she hoped would turn the jury to anger, and to action.

Keri sat at the counsel table, allowing her mind to clear, to prepare for Paul's cross. Aiden's testimony dealt a crippling blow to the president, but Paul wasn't in the business of lying down or saying sorry. She had to be ready for his moment of victory, his moment of stealing victory.

■ ■ ■

She listened intently as Paul began his cross-examination with the deftness of a surgeon wielding a laser scalpel. He took his time attacking Aiden's possible motivation for turning on his former employer. His tone was gentlemanly and friendly. Gone was the sarcasm and grandstanding that he used on other witnesses. Keri had warned Aiden about this. Not to be beguiled by respect when he expected angst. Paul treated Aiden as if they were friends, taking him through the paces of his relationship with both Beth and Bill.

He sowed tiny seeds of bitterness from Aiden never having been invited to the White House or acknowledged by her after he left the campaign. But to Keri it didn't seem like Paul believed it, or at least that he thought the jury would believe it. Seamlessly switching topics, he kept the friendly demeanor.

"The conversation that you just testified to with then Senator Suarez took place I believe you said on August 8, 2056?"

"Correct."

"And you know that because that is the day you resigned from her campaign and the last time you spoke with her?"

"Correct."

Keri considered an objection. Not that it would be sustained, but she wanted to remind Aiden that she was there to protect him. Aiden looked fine, calm, she thought, watching him sit placidly, waiting for the next question, no anticipation or fear on his face.

"The ads and statements that she made during debates and public speaking engagements regarding SAFTA, those were all made prior to the date you resigned, correct?"

"The ones that I was present for, yes," Aiden answered.

"Those were all before the first time, as far as you know, Mrs. Suarez had changed her position on SAFTA?"

"I — I don't know. I only know when she told me she changed her position. I don't know when she actually changed her mind," Aiden responded. His puzzlement alarmed Keri. Witnesses act unpredictably when confused.

"So the only thing you can be certain of is that on August 8, 2056, Mrs. Suarez had changed her position on SAFTA?"

"Yes."

"You don't know if she changed that day?"

"No."

"You don't know if she changed the day before?"

"No."

"You don't know if she changed the week before?"

"No."

Paul paced around the small area next to the podium, arms crossed and his right hand tugging lightly at his chin. A gesture to give the impression that he was thinking of his next question, Keri assessed.

"When was the first time after August 8, 2056, that you heard Mrs. Suarez state that she was in favor of SAFTA?" Reverse psychology, Keri recognized. An assumption that President Suarez *must* have said she supported SAFTA after their conversation. The implication being, *Why else are we here if she didn't say she supported it after the conversation?* Keri saw the jurors' eyes squint with confusion. Precisely the reaction Paul was looking for. She respected the move.

"I don't know."

"You don't know when she said that she was in favor of SAFTA after the date you quit? Or is it that you don't know if you *ever* heard her say that she was in favor of SAFTA after you quit?"

Aiden looked over to Keri and then to the judge, as if he was looking for a hint of how to answer the question. The judge gestured to him to answer.

"I don't know!"

"You don't know which?" Paul quickly asked, with a little bit of acid dripping from the question.

"I don't know if she ever made a statement in favor of SAFTA after that day."

The rhythm of the cross concerned Keri. Aiden was under Paul's spell, answering questions immediately, without thinking about them first. If he grew even slightly paranoid he might change his testimony, adapt details of his story to try to defend himself. That would be the beginning of the onslaught. As long as he stayed with the truth, as long as he didn't try to stretch what he knew, change what he knew, he would be fine, she prayed to herself.

"Did you continue to follow her campaign speeches after you quit?"

"Of course. I had been very involved in the campaign and wanted to see how it went after I left."

"With your abundance of curiosity as to how they were getting along without you, wouldn't you agree that you watched most of the speeches that she gave after you quit?"

"I'm not sure about most of them; I didn't keep track of how many speeches she gave."

"Well, did you watch her every day?"

"I would watch or listen or read about the speeches most days."

"In any of those speeches *after* you quit the campaign, did you ever hear her say that she was in favor of SAFTA?"

"I can't remember one."

"Just so the jury understands this, Mr. Carroll. You can only tell the twenty-three good members of this jury that you know for sure that she changed her mind on SAFTA on August 8, 2056, *but* you cannot tell them that she ever made a statement in favor of SAFTA after that day. Isn't that correct?"

Stick with the truth, Keri repeated in her head, as if she was speaking with Aiden.

"That would be correct," Aiden answered, without any hint that he was trying to hide his ignorance, or that it changed anything. Keri exhaled.

"Nothing further, Your Honor," Paul concluded, returning to his seat.

The end surprised Keri. He hadn't touched Aiden's conversation with Beth. No attempt to suggest he misunderstood, that it was what he wanted to remember and not what was actually said. As if he was conceding that Aiden's recollection was true.

While the courtroom emptied, Keri stayed behind. One of the best days in court of her career, but something irked her. Something that Paul knew, something that she didn't see. He was too pleased with his cross, too confident.

CHAPTER 10

Annapolis, Maryland, October 24, 2059

Keri found the streets of Annapolis as comforting as a warm blanket on a cold night. She needed a break from the goblin bugging her since Paul finished his cross of Aiden earlier in the day.

"We had a wonderful time, didn't we?" her husband Clay asked softly as they slowly rambled down proverbially quaint Conduit Street, past Duke of Gloucester, toward Main Street in downtown Annapolis. Late October and still not a single day of frost. Seventy-degree temperatures over the last two days rekindled summer, but the evenings quickly cooled into the fifties, making the light hand-crocheted shawl draped over her shoulders a welcome accessory.

It had been fourteen years since they lived here. Four years which felt like forever back then, but now seemed like a blip. So short, it didn't seem real. She was stronger then, she thought. At least more idealistic, confident. The type of confidence that experience chips away at. A small fish ready to swim with sharks and whales, ready to take on anyone and anything for the commitments she made, the promises she made. Age bought clarity, she thought. The clarity to see what she was and what she was up against. The wisdom not to underestimate.

"It was a wonderful time," she answered, squeezing Clay's hand to confirm her words.

Clay skipped a few paces ahead, thrusting his arms to the royal-blue evening sky, turning to face her. "I wish I shared your fountain of youth," she joked.

She never saw her position as the first elected attorney general under the Second Constitution as anything special. Just a job she did because she had to, because she could protect others who couldn't protect themselves, because God gave her that gift. She thought of herself as a simple lawyer, a student of law, always trying to learn, searching for that one more thing she could understand. Not even the most routine case failed to intrigue her. It kept her mind young. As much as she loved being a lawyer, what she cherished most were her roles as mother to her two now-grown boys and as wife of Dr. Marshall.

They met in the last year of his fellowship in pediatric neurology at the Children's Hospital in Phoenix, Arizona. Keri Eversley had just finished her second year of law school. They married two weeks before he opened his practice in his hometown of Cheyenne, Wyoming.

Originally from Florida, she took to the clean air of the Rocky Mountains. Week-long horseback trips through the Medicine Bow Mountains; fly-fishing and skiing were so natural to her that they seemed like things she grew up with. The people of Cheyenne took to Keri as a native daughter. She found a large community of evangelicals, people proud to proclaim themselves as *born again.* But Clay's Methodist church, where his family had been members since its founding in the late nineteenth century, welcomed her and her views. They listened to her. She became a bridge, an ambassador among Cheyenne's many denominations. She was happy to call it home.

"Don't you wish it could be like this forever?" asked Clay, allowing her pace to bring her fully within the grasp of his outstretched arm as they continued without missing a step.

"I thought it was," she answered, pressing her body into his side. Interruptions didn't seem to have the same effect on her that they had on him. She could separate her personal life from her professional better than him, focusing one hundred percent on him when they were together, and one hundred percent on work when she was working. He had more trouble pushing out the thoughts of the day.

But something was different tonight. She couldn't silence the suspicion that Paul was up to something. On the drive home she called a private number George Comstock had given her sometime after she stepped down as the US attorney general. She left a message on his voice mail, explaining some urgency. Her mind kept drifting to her celltop, expecting it to ring.

Professor Comstock's speech at the rally of five million changed her life. He was the answer to the Marlen Hilds of America, she thought. Throughout her last two years of law school she devoured constitutional classes like a black hole swallowing galaxies. Her commitment to Marlen, her promises to God, commanded her to be part of the Second Constitution. Her heart soared each time it looked like the convention would be a reality. It belly flopped every time negotiations broke off.

After her first son was born in 2029, she started her own blog, the *bleatosphere.* It provided a voice for everyday people who were tired of feeling like sheep. It hit a nerve. She became the people's pandit for the convention. When the Second Constitution was ratified in 2040, she announced her candidacy for US attorney general, realizing that God required more from her, perhaps a lifetime. Her signed declaration of intent to leave public service after only one four-year term as the first head of the new Justice Branch, jettisoned from the Administrative Branch by the Second Constitution as an added check and balance, made people trust her.

Turning off of Main Street in the direction of their home, Clay became quiet. She knew he felt her slipping away, preparing for the night's work. Her glances to her celltop didn't help. Why wasn't George calling her back? she fretted.

Once inside the front door of the federal-style, colonial-era mansion, she put her arms around Clay and drew herself close, holding him tightly for a long embrace. Their lips met briefly and she looked deeply into his eyes before letting him go. She watched him take the stairs up to their spacious apartment on the top floor. The main floor and basement were dedicated solely to her work, to her mission.

■ ■ ■

"Congratulations, Mrs. Marshall," "Great job, Keri," members of her team howled — with the confidence of a pit crew whose racer was three laps ahead — as she walked into the conference room.

"Thank you all, but we're not here to discuss what went right. We're here to figure out what can go wrong," Keri soberly instructed, deflating the celebration.

"You all saw Paul's cross. Where's he going?" she threw out to the fourteen people seated around the large conference table.

"Where's Mike?" she absently asked, looking around the table until her eyes landed on the leader of her witness team seated three chairs to her left. "Did you get hold of those two witnesses?"

"Yeah, but their people wanted to know what it was about. Eventually I had to tell them who I was calling for," he apologized.

"Don't worry about it," Keri assured him.

"They had some concern about why you wanted them to testify. Do you want me to prep them?" Mike asked.

"No. I'll meet with them myself. I'm not going to ask them to testify to anything they haven't already said publicly," Keri explained without giving further details. "Are they available on Sunday?"

"They'd prefer tomorrow, early if possible."

"I can't. I have to go to New York in the morning."

"New York?" shrieked Roger Dalton, the head of the memo team, from the other side of the table.

"Just a little paranoia. A little insurance," Keri cryptically responded. She knew her trip would raise some questions that she didn't want to answer. There were no witnesses, no evidence in New York. The staff would wonder why she was going.

"Memo team?" she asked, looking across the table to her right at the four team members — two middle-aged associates and the two youngest associates on her team. "I want you to stay after we break to discuss some memos that I want ASAP. We should be resting this week if everything goes okay, and I want everything prepared for Paul's motions to dismiss.

"Before we break into groups, any questions?" she asked, searching for hands that never raised. Team members seemed more focused on whispering to each other. She kept strategy close to the vest, concerns too.

Once she was alone with her memo team she closed the conference room door. "I don't want this to be general knowledge to the team, or anyone else," she instructed, her voice hushed. The team members glided their chairs over until they were directly opposite Keri. "I want you to start working on a memo about the *knowingly false when made* requirement for fraud in the treason clause."

It was something they had discussed from the beginning of the case. Keri would have to prove that Beth made a statement that was false, and that she knew it was false when she made the statement. It's what made treason cases based on fraud so hard to win for prosecutors. Keri had successfully proved it when she was the attorney general. She showed how automakers marketed collision-avoidance systems as AutoDrives, cars that could drive themselves, to increase sales at the cost of thousands of lives. Only Lorimar Petite, with Paul Gordon as his attorney, beat the treason charges. The case went to trial after Keri left office. Technically it wasn't her loss, but in her heart it was.

"Paul's cross today makes me think he'll argue that we have to show that the president made a statement supporting SAFTA after her conversation with Aiden."

"That would assume that the president changed her mind right before she spoke to him," Singh Munindar, the youngest member of the memo team argued. "Can't the jury infer that she changed her mind long before that? It wasn't like she ran to her campaign manager and said that her husband just told her to change her position. She waited until Mr. Carroll asked about her position. It had to have been long before."

Roger, the team leader, leaned into the table and spoke in a firm but low voice. "Her *statement* can also be her decision not to divulge her change of position. We have case law on that." The four associates shook their heads in agreement.

"Well, that's part of what I want in the memo. But beyond that," she continued as the associates turned their heads slightly to aim good ears at her words, "I also want you to look at whether or not her signing the *veto* itself could be considered the misrepresentation, the false statement."

They leaned back in their chairs. A few eyes drifted up and to the left, searching for precedents they could pin to the logic. "It may be nothing; it may be something. I'm not sure. But I'd like to pursue it," she concluded.

"Brilliant!" Roger replied. "Never thought of that. How do you intend to prove it? Are there any cases on this?"

"I'm not sure," Keri answered. "I don't think so. I think you're going to have to patch together the pieces of the argument. Cases that show an action can be a statement, a misrepresentation." She hesitated, weighing what cards to reveal.

"I made a call to George Comstock on the way home from court today," she finally said. From their expressions she saw that they understood the depth of her alarm. "I'm going to try and meet him in New York tomorrow to discuss it. If anybody knows whether or not we can make that argument, he'd be the one." The mood was somber as the team left the conference room to start their research.

Keri had met George Comstock after the Second Constitutional Convention from her position as the primary blogger supporting the convention, and later as the attorney general. Mostly bumping into each other at ceremonial functions, they expressed a mutual admiration. Several years after she finished her term as attorney general, George expressed his admiration for her use of the treason clause. He was quite proud that it could be used to save tens of thousands of innocent lives.

Of all the awards and honors she received, Keri cherished none higher than George's heartfelt compliment. He extended his personal contact information to her with an offer to help, if ever she needed him. She never used the number and wasn't sure that the offer still stood.

She closed the conference room door and left another message for George, hoping he would pick up or at least call her back quickly. While she waited, she poured a cup of herbal tea and settled into a chair in the center of the conference table, facing the displays on the wall. Room lights dimmed to bare existence when she pressed a button on her celltop. Another tap and all thirty displays jumped to life in her preferred pattern. The twenty-three jurors huddled around the center four panels that held the images of the witness, the judge, herself, and Paul. Jurors she was most concerned about were arranged closest to the center panels.

The system was quite efficient for conducting such a large trial. On a treason trial, the president was entitled to a grand jury—twenty-three jurors instead of the usual twelve. It kept attorneys general from bringing treason charges for political reasons, but made a conviction infinitely harder.

Rather than having twenty-three people from around the country come to a central location where they would be hounded by the media and protesters, they each attended the trial by on-screen display at work, home, or other locations. Strict laws and security protected their identities. Even their bosses would only know that they were on *a jury*, not which jury. The secure rooms employers would provide or portable booths the court would deliver to their jobs or home meant total secrecy.

Each booth had a display with five screens, for the witness, for the judge, for the questioning attorney, for the non-questioning attorneys, and for any exhibit being used. A camera captured each juror's face during the proceedings. When the on-screen system was first adopted, this camera was supposed to ensure that each juror was present and paying attention. Lawyers could demand the disqualification of any juror who was not present or participating in the trial and they could prove this with the on-screen display.

Lawyers quickly turned this feature into an important tool, using the playbacks of the jurors to divine their reactions to the testimony. Heads cocking back, eyes widening, brows raising or lowering all became part of a new language that lawyers used to decipher jurors' thoughts. Within a few years, this became a legitimate purpose of the cameras. While the practice had its detractors, no one doubted its efficiency at predicting the outcome. It certainty bred more settlements and plea bargains than under the old in-person jury system. But Keri knew not to waste even a second on the possibility of a plea deal.

In the dim lights Keri deftly moved her hands in the open space in front of her, controlling the thirty screens. Swiping her right hand twice to the right, she skipped large portions of the day's testimony that she knew too well to have to review. Pushing her hand forward, like a cop stopping traffic, the testimony froze on the screens. Alternatively swiping to the left to back the testimony up, or gesturing once to the right to restart the playback, she reviewed critical segments over and over, focusing on only one screen with each replay.

She spent hours going over Paul's twenty minutes of cross-examination. Carefully studying every facial tick on the jurors, the witness, and Paul, she pointed the index and middle fingers of her left hand to drag captured portions of testimony to their proper place in the outline on her celltop.

It was a three-dimensional experience for Keri, living inside the testimony, being part of it. She lost all sense of time and place. She lost her ghostlike fear, at least until she finished the transcript when it slowly crept back.

Climbing the stairs to join Clay in their apartment, Keri stopped on the landing where the stairs angled up to the left. She sat and looked out of the window glowing violet blue with the beginning of dawn. In the distance, Chesapeake Bay was as still and dark as death. So was she. Why hadn't George returned her call?

■ ■ ■

An early riser by nature, Keri was up within an hour. She opened the refrigerator and pulled out leftovers of the cheese and pâté she and Clay shared last night. She spread a little pâté on a freshly cut slice of French bread and then sat, sipping tea and looking out the window. Before Clay joined her, she left another message for George, explaining that she was taking the 11:47 maglev to New York and would very much appreciate the opportunity to see him sometime today.

In the middle of her long warm shower, she heard the soft rapid pulses of her celltop, which she had left in the bedroom. "Honey," she called to Clay. "Can you bring me my phone?" she asked, shutting off the water and quickly drying herself.

"Got it!" Clay shouted back. "It's from Bitterman, Tao —"

She grabbed the celltop and immediately answered. "Mr. Comstock?" There was a brief silence on the other end, then, to her surprise, a female voice.

"No, Mrs. Marshall. I'm sorry, this is Mrs. Tinsley, Mr. Comstock's secretary."

"Of course, Mrs. Tinsley, I'm sorry I just assumed it was Mr. Comstock."

"Not a problem, Mrs. Marshall. Mr. Comstock asked me to call you as soon as I got in this morning. Unfortunately he's not going to be able to return your phone call and he's not going to be able to meet you today. He wanted me to let you know as soon as possible."

Taking a moment to digest what the female voice was telling her, Keri responded, "I understand. It really is, however, very important that I speak with him this weekend. Can you please let him know that I won't need much of his time? I'd just like to ask his opinion on something."

"I understand, Mrs. Marshall. But I believe that Mr. Comstock will not be able to speak with you for some time. Certainly not until after your trial. I hope you understand. He was of course very concerned and wanted to let you know that he got your messages, but that he is unable to speak with you at this time."

Slowly the implication of what Mrs. Tinsley was telling her sank in. It wasn't a matter of scheduling. Something was preventing him from being able to speak with her. The thought made her brace her free hand against the dresser, not sure how steady her wet, shaking legs were.

"I perfectly understand, Mrs. Tinsley. Please thank Mr. Comstock for getting back to me so quickly and let him know that I look forward to seeing him in the future," she managed to say in a clear voice.

"Certainly. I know he looks forward to seeing you in the future as well," Mrs. Tinsley added.

Hanging up the phone, Keri started calculating the pieces of the conversation, arranging and rearranging the pieces as if it were some jigsaw puzzle that could be fit together. Does he think the president should or should not have been prosecuted? He could just tell her that. He has to know his advice would be welcome. Is he not following the trial? Does he not care what happens? Couldn't be, she thought. He devoted most of his adult life to ensuring the personal freedom of every American through this clause. It would be like asking an astronaut not to watch the first human landing on Mars. Impossible.

It bothered her most that he didn't call to tell her himself. That was the one piece that she couldn't fit. Why? As the day wore on, the nagging question pulled her mind from each task, from every conversation.

Returning to the large conference room after her walk with Clay in the evening, she kept replaying the last fifteen minutes of Paul's cross-examination over and over. It wasn't the strategy that bothered her, she realized. It was something in Paul's demeanor. Not touching on the conversation itself, not pressing the motivation angle. There was too much he could have done but didn't. He was content, confident, even cocky. What did he know that she didn't? What did he have in his briefcase that she didn't know about?

Like a moment of revelation for a believer, it came to her as a clap of thunder: "They have George Comstock," she muttered out loud, as if hearing the words could protect her from the horrible reality. That's why George couldn't talk to me. That's why he didn't call me back himself. It would be a conflict of interest, a breach of client confidentiality for him to even speak to me. "Oh my God," she muttered out loud again. "How do we argue against George?" It was Paul's moment of victory, she feared.

CHAPTER 11

Philadelphia, July 21, 2037

Sebastian sat by himself at one of the round tables — away from the table square — in the Bourse. His stomach growled louder than the delegates arguing only a few feet away, and they were pretty loud, he happily observed as he picked at the food in front of him. President Adee had pushed the session two hours past their usual dinner break. He half expected her gavel to shatter into splinters from the constant banging during the session. She dismissed them until the next morning, out of frustration, he guessed.

Hostilities flared over the clauses that divvied up power between the federal government and the states, the supremacy and commerce clauses. Passions burned white on either side. Each side accused the other of being the evil that exalted corruption over democracy. Industries that monopolized access to Congress. Land developers who made local politicians dance with tethered purse strings. Both clauses were to be argued together. There was no other way to address them, Sebastian knew. That played perfectly into his plan.

At the table square, Javier Mulero, the political delegate from New Mexico, ripped into Raju Sunderam, the scholar delegate from Nebraska. Sebastian hadn't seen the two say a cross word to anyone until now. A sign that the clouds had gathered for a perfect storm, the storm he counted on.

"You're trying to turn the federal government into a monarchy — what about the states?" Sebastian heard one of them ask, not looking over to see whom.

"You're just using that as an excuse to keep money in the pockets of local politicians!" the other yelled back, as if his opponent had single-handedly caused all of the problems in the country.

Sebastian listened less for what they were saying than for their tone. Sophisticated ladies and gentlemen pointing fingers while they screamed at each other created a unique sound, like banging a palm on a piano keyboard instead of forming harmonious chords. The most discordant tones would come from words meant to wound, rather than explain. Those are the words he listened for.

Any hope of the convention falling apart would come on these clauses. That's what Sebastian told his clients, the industry heads who flocked to him once he was appointed as a delegate. They had grown fat from institutionalized governmental corruption. The Second Constitution would put them on a starvation diet, he warned, increasing their fear and his fees leading up to the convention.

Corruption always existed, Sebastian observed as if it was his stock in trade. People were indifferent to it. Everyone knew that politicians had their hands in everything and that special interests owned the politicians. But no one wanted to do anything about it. An occasional scandal, someone being too direct or too greedy, could stir up the people, but never for long. One or two scapegoats, a sacrificial lamb, is all it took to quiet them down. But that had changed.

Ironically, what changed it was institutionalizing it, making it legal, he lamented. Only suicidal politicians took bribes. The rest took handouts for their political action or leadership committees. Money flowed like Niagara Falls from high-paid lobbyists and corporations protected by Supreme Court rulings that granted them a higher degree of freedom of speech than people, citizens.

"A strong central government is efficient. It'll eliminate waste and corruption," a female voice broke through the chaos of a dozen delegates vying to be heard.

"We can deal with corruption without having to take away state sovereignty!" a new male voice shouted. "The treason clause, an independently elected attorney general, and term limits will stop it," the same delegate continued without giving anyone a chance to answer. Sebastian peered over at Hanley and saw him fidgeting in his seat, ready to jump. Not yet, Sebastian repeated to himself.

"*Hitler* had the most efficient form of government!" the female voice roared. "Is that what you want us to become?" Some snickered, others gasped. Sebastian smiled. He looked over to see that the comment came from Melissa Gould, a scholar delegate who was Jewish. It came off as an accusation of being un-American and anti-Semitic, punctuated by her storming off toward the rest rooms. Daggers to wound, *at last,* Sebastian thought. He made eye contact with Hanley.

Barely hushed groans spiraled up the vast atrium as Hanley slowly rose from his seat at the corner of the table square. His reputation for argument ad hominem, attacking the person when he didn't like the proposal, could limit his effectiveness, Sebastian worried. Even delegates who agreed with Hanley's basic logic detested his methods and sought to distance themselves. But Sebastian judged him a perfect recruit for his plan. A sniper, an assassin in a room full of policemen. Policemen are trained to shoot to protect, while soldiers, snipers are trained to shoot to kill, Sebastian thought as his sniper began the attack.

"Here we go again," Hanley mocked. "Is it just me, or has the purpose of this convention changed to *let's see how far we can go to weaken the United States*? Let me see if I have this straight. First, you want to handcuff our elected leaders by threatening them with treason. Then you want to take from them the ability to stop one person from blackmailing society by taking away the power of eminent domain. You want to diminish the power and prestige of the presidency of the United States by creating a new Justice Branch of government; you want to guarantee that our country will only be led by amateurs, by forever eliminating the possibility of career leaders; and *now* you want to revert back to the days of colonialism when we were a scattering of independent colonies by allowing there to be fifty rules of law on every issue when all we need is one."

Eyes rolled so uniformly that it looked like a single eye tumbling round and round the table. Few tried to hide their disgust. It was a sign that courtesy was breaking down as tempers grew hot, Sebastian thought, content to let his soldier rant.

"There has been so much talk during this convention about the legacy we will leave to the generations that follow us. If we are not careful — if we are not realistic," he added, casting a fiery gaze at Comstock, "the day that we sign the Second Constitution will be heralded as the day that America fell from its position as a great world power for the romantic notion of *simpler times.*" He ignored cries to "Sit down!" and took a few seconds to compose his words.

Sebastian beamed with a general's pride at how well Hanley was following his orders, delivering the speech calmly as they had prepared and practiced at the City Tavern in the morning. He laid off the personal attacks, except for his glance at Comstock. Enough to ignite the zealots on both sides without it being perceived as just a bizarre personal position. Anything could happen.

"I may not be the most educated among you. I can't quote chapter and verse of the inner thinking of each of the original framers of the Constitution," Hanley continued, rolling his own eyes. "It doesn't take a constitutional Einstein to realize that our citizens move through the states with the same speed and ease that colonial people used to visit their closest neighbors. Why shouldn't we accept this and acknowledge that we have become one nation — undivided — and avoid the confusion and unfairness of subjecting every citizen to fifty different laws? That is the purpose of the supremacy and commerce clauses, and to weaken them is just plain stupid!"

"Soundbites!" cried the incredulous voice of Melissa Gould from across the marble floor as she walked back from the ladies' room. "Is this what we're going back to?" she asked, referring to the public outcry against soundbite politics that dominated the political scene for the first two decades of the century. "Instead of spewing the bits of your pet peeves, why can't you just discuss the merits of each proposal, Mr. Hanley?" she shouted, walking to within a foot's length of his face.

Sebastian watched as Hanley's face grew red, seeming to swell out of proportion. His fists clenched, his mouth pursed, he was struggling against his native instinct to retaliate. The reptilian instinct that Sebastian relied on to get what he wanted.

"There's no need for that," Javier Mulero calmly chided. He started to rise from his seat with a majority of delegates muttering approval. But the words pushed Hanley beyond the limits of his self-control. Exactly where Sebastian wanted him.

Gould was violating Hanley's private space, her screaming face almost touching Hanley's chest. Sebastian watched with delight as Hanley, out of instinct, reached out with both hands and shoved her squarely on her shoulders. Sebastian could clearly see that the shove was not intended to inflict injury, only to push an aggressor back, beyond the limits of personal space. But he knew it would not be perceived that way.

Although small, Gould was as aggressive as any prizefighter, Sebastian thought. Were she not so liberal, he might have recruited her as one of his weapons. Reacting to the shove, she planted her right foot back, bringing with it her right clenched fist, cocked and ready to release a blow. Hanley's right hand floated up and behind his right shoulder. His clenched fist began a forward motion toward Gould's head. More than Sebastian could have hoped for.

Delegates shot to their feet upon Hanley's initial push and now the gentleman from Kansas, seated to Hanley's right, quickly locked his arm in Hanley's elbow, preventing him from hitting Gould. From the effort it took to restrain Hanley's arm, Sebastian could tell that Gould would have been seriously injured had the blow landed.

Shouting voices immediately bounced off the marble walls. Sebastian jubilantly bathed in the curses flowing from the mouths of stately old gentlemen and gentlewomen with the same ease of hardened sailors. The high and mighty were stooping to the gutter, he beamed, to his turf. Some protested the social breach of striking a woman, others the use of violence to pursue a point in a matter of such importance. Some even accused Gould of having ignited the flames of violence. Within seconds all of the delegates were on their feet. Whether out of disgust or fear, many rushed through the exit from the Bourse. Sebastian continued to sit at the round table, content to watch.

Jack Connors, the tall, muscular preacher from Arkansas, was one of the first to help restrain Hanley, but Sebastian saw the preacher's face flush with fire and brimstone. Hanley's unmanly physical attack on Gould clearly offended the preacher's Southern sense of chivalry, and he let Arthur Hanley know it in no uncertain terms. Pushing his ballooned chest against the much smaller Hanley, he forced him to back up in small steps to avoid being knocked down, verbally attacking his status as a man.

The brash assertion of male dominance threatened to erupt into a more vicious brawl as the preacher's forward motion continued to back Hanley into a corner of the atrium against the thick drapes covering the storefronts. Sebastian spotted the wide-eyed panic, fear, and desperation on Hanley's face. He looked like a trapped rat. It could fall apart in a moment, Sebastian crowed.

Still standing near the table square, Sebastian saw Mulero seize a plexiglass saltshaker and feverishly bang it on the wooden table in front of him, shouting "Order, order!" at the top of his lungs. The echoes of his cries reverberated above the sound of the saltshaker, which was muffled by the tablecloths. His shouts added fury to the combatants, now spread throughout the atrium. Sebastian stood by the round table, watching Gould shouting at Hanley, calling his manhood and his morals into question as she kept pressing closer and closer to him. Her tongue held an edge as sharp as a freshly stropped straightedge razor, he thought. Perfect.

"You're such a big man—you have to push a little woman to try to make your point!" She heaved toward him. "Why don't you throw another tantrum, little boy," she taunted, lunging against the barricade of arms set up by Paulina Childs and Brian Han. "Try it again, little man. Your punches are weaker than your arguments."

Almost fully against the drape covered storefront, Hanley seemed torn between the approaching preacher and the poisonous barbs from Gould. He had apologized immediately, but now anger was overcoming his remorse. His innate nature was rebounding.

The diminutive Anaihyia Alman jumped in front of the preacher, stopping his advance. Connors' attempts to circumnavigate her to either side were met with quickly shuffled sidesteps, creating an impenetrable barrier between him and the caged Hanley. "Go help Melissa and take everyone out of here. Now!" she commanded in a soft but unquestionably firm voice.

Connors, still heated, dutifully walked over to the delegates surrounding Gould and declared, "He's not worth it. Let's get out of here."

"Fuck him!" yelled Gould, keeping up her barrage.

"Don't argue with an idiot," Connors responded. "He's not worth it. Let's leave and address this in the appropriate way." The delegates surrounding Gould all headed toward the exit, with Gould shouting insults the entire way.

Once they exited through the doors, Mulero walked over to Dr. Alman, who was still protecting Hanley, and asked if she was okay.

"Yes. Just leave," she responded firmly.

As Mulero walked toward the exit, the visibly relieved Hanley turned toward Dr. Alman and started to say "I know I was wrong, but—"

"Don't but me. There is no but!" She was as forceful as Gould had been in berating him. It stopped him from uttering even another word. "There are no excuses—there are no justifications for what you did. Personally, I don't think a person like you should even be allowed to be part of this," she concluded, abruptly walking to the exit herself.

Sebastian followed her out. Hanley would have come to him for comfort, and he didn't want anyone to associate him with Hanley's outburst.

After leaving the Bourse, Sebastian walked to the park at the south end of Independence Square. Street lamps glowed with a visible halo from the ninety percent humidity and ninety-degree temperature. Twenty of the delegates gathered under the lampposts. He stood at their edges. Not speaking to any of them, he would at most nod or shake his head in response to their comments.

One by one they threw out plans of action to deal with Hanley's inexcusable conduct. *Expulsion, arrest, censure.* A vivid image of them forming a noose and lighting torches to track down the villain popped into Sebastian's head. Things were out of hand. Just what he wanted. He looked around to note who was not here, who was not calling for Hanley's head.

Comstock, Sebastian thought with surprise. He overheard someone say that Comstock went up to see Adee. Sebastian climbed the stairs in Tower Stair Hall up to Adee's office. Her door was open. Adee, Comstock, Ormond, and Seth Canova were standing at her conference table. Sebastian walked in without announcing himself. Adee nodded to him, but returned her eyes to the official Rules of Order laid out on the table. She was angry. On the table were a stack of sealed envelopes with the name of a delegate handwritten on each one.

"Thank you, gentlemen," she offered to the men standing around the table. "But I don't want to discuss it now." Handing the stack of envelopes to Ormond, she directed, "Please personally deliver each of these this evening. And let Mr. Hanley and Ms. Gould know that I will be visiting them at their residences in a short while. Ask them to remain there."

Ormond acknowledged the request with a slight bow and left her office with the envelopes in hand. It was hitting the fan, Sebastian realized with the contentment of a spider spying a fly in its web.

■ ■ ■

Sebastian walked to the Bourse, arriving before 9:00 a.m., as instructed in Adee's handwritten note. Everyone was there, everyone except Hanley, Gould, and Adee, he noticed. The delegates sat around, somber, like someone had died. Hushed gossip circled the atrium. Speculation about why they were meeting at the Bourse, why Hanley and Gould weren't here. Some opined that Adee had kicked them out of the convention based on reports of delegates who saw her walking toward their residences after midnight. Sebastian eavesdropped on all the conversations he could hear.

"Come to order," cried Ormond, banging the table square with the wooden cylinder he brought with him. Delegates stood straight and silent as Adee slowly walked across the marble atrium floor. The seriousness of her gaze caught Sebastian's eye as she stopped six feet in front of the hushed group. Pausing for a few seconds, she neither invited nor permitted the standing delegates to sit. Sebastian stayed to the back of the crowd.

"I have decided to meet today in the Bourse because I cannot bring myself to stain the sanctity of Independence Hall on the childish and selfish actions that occurred here last night," she began, her voice strained with anger.

"I know that most of you think you had no part in what happened last night. But those things do not happen in a vacuum. It can only happen in an atmosphere of mistrust, self-dealing, and disrespect," she said, emphasizing each word slowly as she looked around the room into stunned eyes. She paused the longest at Sebastian's eyes. He didn't flinch.

He knew she suspected his backdoor politicking since the eminent domain discussions began. Maybe she suspected that he had something to do with last night's fight? He didn't care. His chin erect, his eyes squarely looking into Adee's, he showed no sign of remorse or guilt.

"I have decided to begin our break three days early. GO HOME!" she shouted, shocking them all. "Go home and think about your part in this. How each and every one of you contributed to this disrespect of the great purpose we were sent here for."

Fantastic! Sebastian thought. The early break would send a message. Media pundits would speculate why, each coming up with a theory that foreshadowed the convention's unraveling. Security would be too tight for him to speak with his clients. But this news would send them a clear message: *The plan was on track, their money well spent.*

"Before you come back," Adee continued, "I want you all to take responsibility for making the Second Constitution a reality. Think about how you can help build an agreement on what is right for the people of this country and not how you can sabotage each other. Now get out of here!"

Before her last words finished echoing in the atrium, she turned and stormed out of the same exit. Sebastian could sense the guilt of the motionless, speechless delegates. He would have preferred anger. One by one they slowly slithered out of the Bourse without a word.

CHAPTER 12

Washington, DC, October 24, 2059

Bill flicked off the on-screen display just as Paul finished his cross-examination of Aiden, knowing full well what was coming. The walls of the Lincoln Sitting Room, in the presidential residence, seemed to agree, turning dark, oppressive. Too early for sunset, he thought, even for late October. Through raindrop-speckled windows he watched heavy, rain-laden clouds move in from between the Jefferson and Lincoln Memorials. The bigger storm, however, would come any moment from Beth. After she'd sent the FBI to drag him out of bed the previous night, he frankly didn't care.

Irony blared as he looked around the room. The most prestigious living room probably in the world and it looked like a pigsty. Furniture covered with sheets, piled with papers and celltops. Coffee cups and glasses, all more than half empty, littered every level surface.

There was a time when he viewed the White House as a different world. A world of class and prestige. Sitting alone on the couch, he didn't feel classy or prestigious. It felt like he just woke up in a cheap motel room after a raunchy bachelor party.

Because of the importance of Aiden's testimony, he tried to watch it with Beth. As Aiden revealed the details of his last conversation with her, Bill saw her temper rise as fast as the mercury in a thermometer plunged into lava. Her shouts at the display and nonstop rants on her celltop were more than he could take. Either she would have to go to another room to watch the testimony or he would leave the White House and watch it at home, he demanded. To his surprise, she watched the rest of the testimony from her bedroom suite on the other side of the Yellow Oval Room of the residence.

It was 4:00 p.m. when Paul began his cross-examination. Bill thought it a good time. An hour of cross and then Paul could break and continue the next day, after they had a chance to review the testimony. Surprised by the gentleness of the cross-examination, Bill nearly swallowed an ice cube when it ended moments before 4:20. He moved to the couch facing the South Lawn and sipped his cup of tea. Whatever moments he had left before Beth came into the room, he meant to enjoy them.

"I can't believe you talked me into hiring this asshole!" Beth shouted, pushing the living room door open so hard that it nearly broke the panes of glass. "My hairdresser could've done better than that!"

"Was there anything Aiden said that wasn't true?" Bill asked.

"What does that have to do with anything? I didn't hire your high-priced buddy so the two of you could sit around and marvel at how truthful Aiden is. I hired him to make Aiden look like a liar. What's the point if my own attorney gets in bed with my accuser?" She marched back and forth in front of him, shooting dagger glances.

"His testimony was simple and believable. You can't just lawyer around that. Paul would lose credibility with the jury. Right now Paul's credibility is the only thing you have on your side. Just wait until he gets here and ask him what his strategy is before you go crazy."

"You better watch your attitude," she threatened. "Remember you're just as much a part of this as I am."

"No, I'm not," Bill responded emphatically. "I told you *not* to veto SAFTA."

"You told me not to make any statements regarding SAFTA. You never told me not to veto it."

"That's bullshit and you know it! I specifically told you that if you vetoed SAFTA without coming clean on the reasons, you were risking—you were setting yourself up for a treason charge." Bill was growing angry in a way that he rarely showed.

"So I have one lawyer who's siding with the enemy and another who's trying to stab me in the back."

Bill didn't respond, afraid he would lose control of his anger. Emotions or personal feelings should never get in the way of strategy, he reminded himself. But her last comments made his antenna rise a little higher. Was she setting him up? he wondered. He knew his boss well enough to know that grinding him under the wheels of a bus wouldn't cost her a moment of sleep. Especially if it meant saving her own skin.

The two sat in the room like prizefighters in their respective corners, awaiting the bell for the next round. Occupying themselves with celltops, they neither looked at each other nor spoke.

Paul strolled through the open single French door panel, sporting a smile and the confidence of a lion fresh from battle with a goat. "Good evening," he chimed to the two stoic occupants sitting on opposing couches in the dim room.

"What do you have to be so pleased about?" demanded Beth, rising from her chair and charging toward him like a silverback gorilla faced with a rival male.

"Whooooaaaaa," Paul ordered, putting his hands out as if to fend off the approaching beast. "Did you watch? It went well," he explained, holding his hands out to his sides, palms up, as if to show he had no weapons. It didn't matter. She jumped right in front of him, pointing her finger in his face.

"What the hell do you mean it went well? He made me look like a liar and you didn't lay a hand on him. You just let him tell that bullshit story and you did nothing to make him look foolish."

"Do you think that there's anything I could have done to raise any doubt, let alone a reasonable doubt, about whether he was telling the truth?" Paul asked. "What he said was one hundred percent believable. I guarantee you that every person in that courtroom, and every juror on-screen, and probably every American in the entire damn country believed him. To attack him wouldn't have dented him in the slightest. It just would've made them hate us and make them believe his testimony more."

Bill agreed with Paul's assessment completely. But he also knew that it would take a miracle to convince Beth that leaving negative testimony unanswered was better than a vicious, if not effective, attack on Aiden.

"So you admit it! You agree with the prosecution. If you agree with the prosecution how the hell can you represent me? Why didn't you tell me this up front? I would've gotten somebody else — somebody who would've fought for me."

"I am fighting for you!" Paul bellowed, his frustration peeking through his polished exterior. "At this point our best bet is the technicalities. My job is to keep you from being convicted of treason, not to make sure you get elected for a second term. I'm not your public relations manager, I'm your *criminal* defense lawyer. The chances of you being convicted of treason are a lot higher right now than they are of you ever being reelected. And if I were you, that's what I would be focusing on."

Bill saw Beth's face fill with blood and her skin lose all elasticity. Her expression grew harder than stone, eyebrows dropped in the center, mouth pulled tightly back hiding all but the thinnest line of lips. She was swallowing Paul's honesty as if it were drain cleaner, harsh and deadly.

"So you think I'm guilty of treason?"

"Absolutely not. You're not guilty of treason unless a jury of twenty-three finds you guilty of treason. And my job is to make sure that never happens!"

Bill sat on the couch through the entire conversation without saying a word. It was useless, he knew, to try to help Paul explain the realities of the case to the president. It's just who she was. A bull in a china shop, no remorse, no possibility that she could ever be wrong. Why would this be any different?

For a rational person, the threat of a treason conviction, the threat of a possible death sentence, would make them reevaluate. Not Beth Suarez. Bill knew that her only hope was Paul's *technicalities.* She would never be reelected; she would never hold any public office, no matter how small. It made her little use to Bill's future. Damage control was the best possible outcome he could hope for. He didn't want to go down in history as being the personal attorney for the only president ever convicted of high treason in the history of the United States.

"So what are these miracle *technicalities* that can save me?" Beth asked, calming down enough to listen.

"There are two. The Constitution requires *two* eye witnesses to the alleged act of treason. Aiden is one. Who's the other? Marshall still has a couple of witnesses left, but I don't think any of them are going to say that they were part of your conversation with Aiden. It will be difficult for the jury to fully understand, but we stand a pretty good shot at getting the case dismissed on the two-witness rule."

Beth paced around the room with her head down for a few moments, then asked, "What's the second?"

"The second is the one I think gives us the best shot. They haven't shown that you made any statements that you supported SAFTA after that conversation with Aiden."

Bill perked up at the explanation and looked over at Beth, trying to catch her eye. It was his way of reminding her of his advice not to make any statements in favor of SAFTA after she changed her position. She adroitly ignored his glances with a familiar indifference. But he sensed that she was beginning to understand the implication of what Paul was saying.

"For this one, we get two bites at the apple. First we might get the judge to dismiss the case after the prosecution rests. Second, it's something that I can get the jury to understand, to hold on to. But for me to sell this to the jury, I have to be realistic. I had to acknowledge that Aiden had no ax to grind, no reason to lie."

Bill saw Beth's eyebrows dipping down a little and her anger building. Paul continued: "But that even if he was telling the truth, it's not treason because you never made another statement supporting SAFTA after that, and the prosecution hasn't proved when you changed your mind."

"Then shouldn't I testify? Shouldn't I tell the jury when I changed my mind? That it was only days before that conversation, and the reason I never made a statement after that was because I didn't want to break their trust? Put me in front of the camera, put me in front of people and I can convince them of anything. How do you think I became president?" It was Beth's answer to every problem, Bill thought. She truly believed that she could fool anyone, anytime. Obviously she could fool more voters than her opponents during a campaign season, he jokingly mused.

"No, no, no!" Paul frantically shot back. "Testifying is the absolute worst thing you could do in this case. You don't want to open yourself up to cross-examination by Keri Marshall—"

"Keri Marshall? She's a country bumpkin!" Beth shouted. "I would eat her for breakfast. She's a lacrosse mom who dabbles in the law. Even worse, she's an idealist. Nobody is easier to tie up in knots than an idealist."

"Don't underestimate her," Paul instructed. "She's one of the best trial attorneys I've ever come across, and she's not an idealist, she's a patriot. Somebody who truly understands what the treason clause is all about, and knows how to use it. Your testimony is absolutely out of the question." Bill felt Paul's frustration. He wasn't alone.

"Don't tell me what is or is not out of the question. I am the president of the United States," she growled. "I didn't get here by being stupid or weak. I don't know how *you* got to where you are, but I don't sit down and play possum for some second-rate *patriot.*"

Bill chuckled under his breath, making sure that she couldn't hear. It was typical Beth swagger. But he knew she meant it, and no one could convince her not to shoot herself in the foot, if that's what she set out to do.

There was silence in the room as Bill watched his boss digest the raw meat thrown out by Paul. Paul stood still, just within the entranceway, looking intently at Beth's face as if he were waiting for a moment to drop a bomb on her.

"What?" she demanded, coming to a halt and responding to his gaze.

"Well, Madame President. Our argument that the prosecution would have to show statements made by you in support of SAFTA after the Carroll talk calls for a new interpretation of the treason clause. There aren't any precedents, no cases on point since the Second Constitution, at least not with the treason clause. So we will be asking Judge Kneuaya to take precedents from civil cases of fraud and establish a new rule of law for treason cases."

"Great! So this wonderful technicality that is going to be my savior doesn't even exist, and you have to ask a judge who clearly hates me to create it for me?"

"It's a matter of legal interpretation, Madame President. The civil case precedents strongly support this interpretation. But we can't guarantee that Judge Kneuaya will see it the same way. If he doesn't, we will appeal it all the way to the Supreme Court, and I'm confident that we will get the interpretation we want."

Paul's shoulders were back in their straight alignment, forming a cross with his torso. Frustration gone, confidence restored, Bill estimated. He could see that the argument was starting to penetrate Beth's rocklike head.

"What I prefer to do, however, what I think is in your best interest, is that we try to get the treason charges thrown out immediately after the prosecution finishes their case. It puts us in a better position as far as the appeal and puts you in a better position with the American public."

"I agree," she responded, seeming surprised that their thinking was identical. "So what do we need to do to make sure this happens? I don't know Judge Kneuaya, and I can imagine he wouldn't be happy if I tried to reach out to him."

"Absolutely. That's not the way to handle it. But I do have an idea," Paul concluded.

Bill stood from the couch, piqued by the possibility of a solid strategy. As he searched the room for a clean cup, and poured half a cup of tea from the still warm carafe, he felt Paul's eyes following him, as if he was expecting an answer. Beth stood silent, staring at Paul, waiting for him to finish his plan.

"What?" asked Bill in response to Paul's stare.

"Well, Bill, it's simple. There is only one person alive today who could definitively convince any judge, even the Supreme Court justices, that the facts of this case do not fit under the meaning of the treason clause."

"No! Absolutely not!" Bill replied as Beth's eyes switched focus from Paul to Bill.

"It makes perfect sense," Paul beseeched. "You've written these types of briefs before; you know it's true. I have the greatest faith in our memo department, just like I did when you headed it, but why take the risk? If we got Comstock on board —"

"Oh, so it's back to *His Majesty,*" Beth interjected.

"Why take the risk?" Paul repeated, ignoring the president's outburst. "We wouldn't be asking him to try the case, just make the oral argument on our motion to dismiss, to let us put his name on the brief. He doesn't even have to write it."

"We had a deal," Bill protested. "He agreed to help us with the death penalty issue, and not because he wanted to help the president. It was only because he's opposed to the death penalty. He made it absolutely clear that he had no interest whatsoever to help her get off."

Bill instinctively moved to the far end of the room, looking for someplace to hide. Paul and Beth followed him, blocking him into a corner, cutting off any chance of escape. He felt put upon, uncomfortable. Peer pressure to do something he knew was wrong. Something he knew would hurt him somehow, would hurt his relationship with George.

"Of course!" Beth ranted. "The president of the United States doesn't rise to the level of the great and powerful Mr. Comstock. We should all kneel and thank the gods that he has agreed to descend from Mount Olympus to keep the world from injecting me with poison."

"Cut it out, Madame President," Paul demanded. Beth halted her rant, something Bill hadn't seen her do since she was a senator. "He could very well be your get-out-of-jail-free card. A simple argument from him that a conviction for high treason would require proof that your statements were false when you made them could end this case before we even have to get to the question of whether or not you'll testify."

"There is no question about whether I'll testify. Of course I'll testify—"

"Not the point, Madame President! The point is that a one-hour argument from the man who wrote the treason clause can end this case in the court and in the public eye once and for all."

Probably realizing that Bill was more likely to be persuaded by Beth, Paul said his good nights and left without ever having sat down. Beth seemed to ignore Paul's exit, pressing forward toward Bill, who was now able to maneuver out of his corner.

"I'm not doing it!" Bill responded, trying to avoid Beth's insistent stare. "I know George well enough to know that he wouldn't consider this. And you risk the possibility that he will pull out on the death penalty argument," he added, plopping down onto the center of the couch and stretching his arms out along its back. "Leave it alone. Take what he's given you and leave it alone."

"Easy for you to say, Bill. You're not the one whose neck is being fitted for a noose, are you? Although maybe you should be," she added, snapping Bill back to the reality of what he had created. "You know I'm a survivor.

I'll survive nuclear winter. I'll survive this. I'll even survive Your Majesty's refusal to help me. But I can't say the same about you."

"Don't threaten me," snorted Bill. "I know where enough skeletons are hidden to make it impossible even for George to save you. Don't you dare threaten me. You got here because of me—"

"Precisely! I'm in this trial because of you. It won't be my head that rolls."

Bill's anger was rising to where he feared it would overtake his better judgment. Lashing back at her wouldn't solve the problem. It would only make it worse. The thought of traveling to New York City, to visit his old professor, quickly became attractive. It would put time and distance between her demand and what he knew was right. Anything was better than trying to talk sense into a senseless egotist.

"Fine," he barked. "I'll go see him tomorrow. But don't be surprised if I come back and tell you exactly what I'm telling you now. He won't do it!" he yelled as he grabbed his celltop and started toward the living room door.

"Where are you going?"

"I'm going home and then in the morning I'm going to New York to see George Comstock."

"I mean tonight," she demanded. "You can't just leave. This place is a mess. Call the cleaning staff and stay with them while they clean," she ordered, as if he were some busboy. Without waiting for a response, she left Bill standing in the living room.

Like his office, the presidential residence was off-limits for surveillance. They could talk freely and leave papers around without worrying about the prosecution snooping. In his paranoia, Bill put the presidential living room off-limits to everyone. No staff, no Secret Service, no cabinet members, no family—nobody was allowed in the living room without Bill or a member of Paul's staff present. Beth trusted him only and thought nothing about making him supervise the cleaners.

Bill paged the cleaning staff, and for two hours he impatiently paced the floor until they finished cleaning under his watchful eye. On his way to his cold, empty condo, he stopped at a local bar where he was sure nobody would know who he was. The type of bar where people drank to escape their pitiful lives, where people were too wound up in their own problems to ever know who was who in Washington.

The on-screen was set to some sporting event. Two stiff drinks and no conversation. Just what he wanted. Being around people, without being with people. A safe place to lick his wounds before walking the two blocks to his apartment and passing out.

CHAPTER 13

New York City, October 25, 2059

Bill was glad to be off of the train and in a Secret Service car on his way to Greenwich Village. He suspected that the passengers' snarls were more the result of Aiden's testimony than his taking over two rows of the train car. They didn't diminish during the ride from Washington to New York. He read them as hate, mistrust. The way a jilted spouse looks at a cheating partner after learning the truth.

On the sidewalk, looking up at the three ears of Indian corn hanging from the twelve-foot-high wood-and-glass front door of the West Village brownstone, Bill tried to quarantine the sensations clutching his breath. He had called ahead to warn George that he was coming, without telling him why. There was no good reason he could give him, he thought. Nor could he justify the personal risk of asking George to do this. The risk that he would be driven out of their shared world.

"Oh, I was hoping it was a trick-or-treater," George joked as he opened the door.

"Thanks for seeing me. Thanks for letting me barge in on your weekend," Bill responded, heartily shaking George's hand. The two stepped inside. His agent remained on the stoop of the brownstone.

"My old students are always welcome, no matter what the date or time," said George. Bill knew that was true.

"Mr. Waverly," Mary Comstock offered, walking from the kitchen to the foyer, just outside a sitting room. "It's so good to see you. I know your duties make it difficult for you to make social calls, but I hope you can stay for lunch at least?"

"I wouldn't miss it for the world," Bill responded. Mary was that type of effortless beauty that transcended time. No pretense or guile. Bill thought of her as the personification of truth. She appeared to be exactly who she was. Such honesty could be intimidating. But no one could ever be uncomfortable in her presence.

He pondered how Beth would react to Mary. Would her innate bulldog clash with the angelic Mary Comstock? Would it change Mary's unyielding genuineness? Throughout his career, he met all manner of wild beasts dressed in human garb. He didn't think any one of them could make Mary change who she was in even the smallest measure.

"I hope you like Korean?" Mary asked as she turned and walked back toward the kitchen. "It's my latest. Especially kimchi."

"If you make it, I'm sure I'll love it. Whatever kimchi is," Bill said politely as he watched her return to the kitchen. Her long legs gliding on the highly polished wooden floor complemented her smooth, wrinkle-free dark orangish-brown skin, with her naturally gray hair, streaked with small remnants of black, framing her smiling face.

"It will be a while until it's ready. Why don't we sit and chat?" George cheerfully suggested, inviting Bill into the sitting room. Except for the electric lights, the sitting room could equally suit a framer or a reframer, Bill thought. Twelve-foot walls accented by meticulously restored nineteenth-century molding. A large bay window protruding out toward the street, neatly dressed with layers of cascading white lace curtains. Antique red printed linen drapes, brought from George's beloved Colonial Williamsburg, framed the upper half of the windows.

"So you came to check up on me? Make sure I'm earning that retainer?" George joked.

Bill laughed. "No, I'm actually here to talk to you about something else. To ask you for another favor." Bill's head turned toward the floor, his eyes diverting from George, until his focus fixed on the valve of the antique metal radiator by the window. George patiently waited for Bill to continue.

"We think" — he hesitated — "Paul Gordon thinks, that we might have one shot at getting the case dismissed after the prosecution rests."

"Let me stop you there, Bill. I have no intention of getting involved in any part of the case other than the death penalty. I thought I made that clear." George's tone left no room for negotiation, not even discussion. Bill had never seen that side of his professor. He could go back and forth for hours with a student, a judge, or an adversary, always leading them to the right conclusion. This dead end shook Bill.

"I know," Bill continued. "It's just that Paul thinks that you could really—"

"I really hate to interrupt you, but honestly it's not something I want to discuss," George responded. "I will not help her on anything other than the death penalty issue. I won't even discuss it with you." The finality in his voice was turning to annoyance.

"If you just look at his brief, I think you would find the issue interesting. It—"

"No, Bill," George insisted, putting up a traffic cop's hand. "And please don't mention another word about it. I don't want to know what you or Paul or President Suarez plan on doing. I don't want to know what the strategy is. I don't want to know what the arguments are. I don't want to discuss the case other than the death penalty." Annoyance was turning to anger. Bill felt like a small child being yelled at by a parent for the first time. Afraid that the next words would be that he'd be put up for adoption or given to gypsies. Irrational, but terrifying.

Bill sat silently, thoughts running through his mind. How could he get around the wall that George erected? How could he keep this part of his life intact while getting what he needed for the other part of his life? It wasn't his professor talking. He could deal with that. It was the reframer talking, and there was no easy way around that.

"Don't feel bad," George consoled, dropping any sternness from his voice. "Over the years I've turned down almost every major political figure. Presidents, attorneys general, senators, half the governors and members of Congress. It's not personal. Certainly not personal to you. Not even to your boss."

Bill's eyes stayed fixed on the dull metal valve of the radiator hypnotizing him into inaction. How uncomfortable it felt to ask George to do something he knew was against the code in this parallel world. People like him and George didn't surrender their beliefs at the call of the rich and powerful. They were purer than that.

Moving his head into the line between Bill's eyes and the metal valve, George asked, "Are you okay? I know you're under a lot of stress. How are you doing?"

It struck Bill that no one had asked him that question, while actually looking for an answer, for decades. "What's wrong with you?" was the closest thing anyone ever asked. It wasn't the same. His wife asked him that before they got divorced. His kids asked him that before they stopped calling or visiting.

"I still remember you as a law student," George reminisced. "The convention was coming up and you were so eager to work on it. Your research on the death penalty was invaluable," he said, drawing Bill back to the comfort of their shared world.

"It may not have won that battle, but everything that you did is still in the official record of the Constitution. Someday! Someday! I still have faith in the humanity of the people of this great country. Someday they'll get it, and we'll win that battle, you'll win that battle. You'll see. In your lifetime. Maybe not in mine," George added.

"I would really like to live to see that; it would make me feel like I did at least one thing right," Bill concluded, showing more of his inner feelings than he had exposed to anyone since he left the ACLU. His eyes drifted back to the metal valve as his mind drifted to the last time he felt valuable. Not important, valuable.

"You've had quite an illustrious career," said George. "I hope it's brought you happiness?"

Bill's eyes swelled, but he couldn't tell if it was from the question or from keeping them open and fixed for too long. He was afraid to blink. Afraid that it would squeeze a tear. A telegraph he wasn't willing to send to his old mentor, the person he most respected in the world. The champion of his alternate universe. Not moving his head or eyes in the slightest, he responded, "What's that old lyric, *life is what happens to you when you're busy making other plans*?"

"Life's not over yet," George reminded him. "You have a bright mind and a passionate heart. A lot can be done in a short period of time. You're still young."

Snapping himself out of his hypnotic stare, Bill shook his head slightly, as if to clear the sentimental cobwebs that stood in the way of him pressing for what he came for. He was frozen. Suspended between each of his worlds.

"How are the kids? Do you find time for them?" asked George, Bill picking up on the obvious attempt to change the subject.

Bill laughed. "Not working for Beth Suarez. I'm lucky if I have enough time to eat a meal. Do you realize that I haven't seen my children since her presidential campaign started, let alone since she took office? I don't think I've talked to them more than once in the last year."

"No, I wasn't aware of that. That's very sad," George answered, standing up from his chair and opening the sitting room door. He turned to Bill. "Now at least I have the pleasure of your company for a few hours. Let's talk about the kids over lunch."

Bill stayed seated, abruptly turning his eyes to George. The cobwebs cleared and he was off the fence, standing on the side of his life as the president's counsel. "With all due respect, George, I think that as the president's attorney I at least deserve the respect of discussing this matter. I know her office does." It came out as if he was offended. Friendship and respect weren't working; maybe indignation would do the trick, he calculated.

George hesitated for a moment. "You are always welcome in my home," he began softly, still standing at the sitting room doorway. "But I'm afraid if you insist on trying to talk about the case, I am going to have to ask you to leave."

"But I only need —" Bill began, before George cut him off.

"I'm sorry, old friend. I don't know what happened to you, but as far as I can see you're just flapping Satan's wings. I have to ask you to leave," he ordered, walking into the foyer and opening the large wooden front door. A cold blast filled the foyer as Bill walked to George's side, not sure of what to do or say. He studied the professor's eyes for a hint that he would relent. Some small break in his ultimatum. There was none. His feigned indignation didn't work. It now became real.

"I'm sorry to have bothered you," Bill snapped as he brushed past George on his way out. When the door closed the pangs of regret immediately took up residence in his stomach. He told his Secret Service escort to leave. He wanted to walk, by himself.

He was edgy, walking in no particular direction. Some demon crawled inside of his skin. His heart was racing like he was plugged into an IV of caffeine. He tried and tried to clear the emotions, to quarantine them so he could calculate his next move. But it wasn't working. George had never spoken to him like this before. He was used to Beth, but not George.

On 7th Avenue, by Vesey Street, he headed north, mind racing, heart pounding with each step. In his pocket the dull vibration of his celltop went on and off so rapidly that it felt like she was sending him Morse code. It could only be Beth. It annoyed him. It spurred him to walk faster and with more anger, but without direction.

What happened to me? Satan's wings? he kept repeating in his head. *What did he mean, what happened to me? Who is he to accuse me of flapping Satan's wings? Who is he to judge the president's attorney?* George may have been great once, but his bed of laurels had kept him out of the loop, out of what was really happening, Bill reasoned. His head would buy it for a few moments, but his stomach couldn't digest the grimy feeling that made him want to wretch.

"Watch it!" a young man snapped as their shoulders brushed along the busy street. Midafternoon and 7th Avenue was as crowded as the Easter Parade. In the crowd, Bill could get lost. He wasn't the president's counsel. He was just some schmuck aimlessly walking on the sidewalk. He blended in, he became invisible. A relief.

Can't you give me a goddamned minute, he frantically shouted in his mind, ready to explode over the *buzz buzz buzz buzz* of his celltop. He yanked it out of his pocket and looked for the power button to turn it off. He rarely ever turned it off and couldn't figure it out. He held each button down for a few seconds, and the law of averages prevailed and it went dark. It looked odd with no glow, like the dark side of the moon. It seemed so inanimate, useless, just as he felt.

The emotions tearing at his belly erupted and pulsed through his veins. He was mad at Beth, he was mad at George. But he was used to being angry and keeping it under control. What was different? he asked himself.

It wasn't anger, at least not toward them. A phantom obstacle that he couldn't see clear enough to fight. He felt like bumping into someone in the crowd on purpose, hoping that an argument could clear it all away, the way that lightning discharges a storm.

The one thing he couldn't do was go back to Washington and listen to Beth. The image of her face made him sick. Thousands of people on 7th Avenue insulated him from Washington, from that universe. They also checked his irresistible urge to turn around and run back to George's house to apologize. There was comfort in the crowd, but their eyes worried Bill. All it took was one pair to recognize him. One person to report his presence to the media, and he would be trapped. He started looking in the eyes passing by and thought they were looking to blame him, judge him. Desperate, paranoid, he needed someplace to be alone. Where she couldn't find him.

Above 23rd Street, pedestrians on the sidewalk were spaced far enough apart to avoid shoulder scrapes. He didn't have to keep his eyes up to avoid inadvertent confrontation. Glancing down, to avoid stares he couldn't decipher, loosened the grip his paranoia had clamped on his wit. Enough to think of a destination. The sharp burning sensation in the ball of his right foot reminded him that he hadn't walked this far in years — decades. More than two and a half kilometers from George's brownstone, he had exhausted his ability to steal privacy by walking.

Chelsea was more residential than the West Village and Meat Packing District he had just traversed. The night she had the FBI pluck him from his apartment provided enough reason to believe that she would send the FBI or Secret Service to George's house when he didn't take her calls. Trains, planes, his apartment, Paul's office would all be monitored by her orders. They would check any purchases he made with a credit or bank account. If he checked into a hotel using his real name, they would be knocking on his door within fifteen minutes. He still kept some cash in his billfold, just in case. This was that just in case.

He stopped by one of those boutique hotels in Chelsea more popular with corporate executives for liaisons than with tourists. Cash payments wouldn't raise an eyebrow, or leave breadcrumbs for the Secret Service to follow.

The room was modern romantic. Clean lines, sustainable fabrics and materials. Reclaimed weathered wooden floor and an abundance of a deep plum color. Just enough to make him feel foolish, checking into a notell in the middle of the day, alone. He immediately took advantage of the well-stocked minibar, pouring himself a tall, straight Kentucky sour mash that he sipped repeatedly. After each sip, he gauged the status of the knot in his gut, looking to see if he'd done with alcohol what he couldn't do with his finely honed mental tools. Five ounces consumed and he still couldn't shake it. He continued to sip.

What happened to you? What happened to you? kept repeating over and over in his head. George had always been that fatherly voice he wished he had throughout his childhood. Encouraging, praising, teaching. Instead of criticizing and minimizing — the actual voices of his youth. Nothing was ever good enough for his father. Not when he got full scholarships to Yale undergrad and William & Mary Law. Not when he was at the top of his class or when he made the Law Review. Those were the voices that spurred him to success, to get perfect grades, perfect scores on the college and law school entrance exams.

When George entered his life, the professor's voice drowned out his father's, at least for a while. George saw him as a top student in a top school. He chose him to help with abolishing the death penalty, and getting ready for the Second Constitutional Convention. The trust, the words of encouragement, seemed to erase the scripts implanted by his father. He felt vital and for the first time in his life, that he could accomplish something worthwhile.

As George became wrapped up in the Second Convention and Bill graduated, their contact waned at least in frequency. George had helped him to get his first job with the ACLU and he knew he was proud of his work. Without his constant presence, however, the scripts from his youth crept in stronger and stronger. Instead of seeing the value of the work he was doing, he started to question it, constructing the comments he knew his now-dead father would make. *If you were at the top of your class, then why do you make so little money? Why do you have to volunteer your time for people who can't afford a good attorney? Look at your friends, look at your classmates, see how good they're doing?* He pictured every detail of his father minimizing his work, minimizing him, as if he were standing in front of him.

Those voices grew too loud to ignore. That's when he opted to leave the work he cared about, that gave value to his existence, and find a good-paying job. One that even his father could not minimize. He vowed never to let anything or anyone ever get to him again. Nothing would stop him from climbing to heights where everyone had to look up to him.

He pulled the curtains shut. They were dark, sun-blocking curtains. He left all of the lights off and unplugged any device that gave a glow. A towel crammed against the bottom of the room door blocked light from the hallway. Total darkness, like the hiding spots of his childhood, dark closets. He found solace in total darkness. A feeling that no one could get to him here. That he could resurrect the rules of his world — worlds. Establish order within. Expel thoughts or emotions which weakened him, stopped him.

That's very sad. That's very sad. George's words kept popping into his head. Were they the emotional phantom he couldn't define? They didn't hit a chord. No part of him felt that he had not been good to his ex-wife or children. He provided for them, even after the divorce. Most of his money went to them. He lived modestly, so they could live well. He never criticized the children. He always supported their dreams, at least financially. Why is it *very sad* that he hasn't spoken to them or seen them? he wondered. Nothing. No answer in his head or in his stomach. That wasn't it.

What happened to you? The question stung. Looping over and over in his head, it morphed into *What's wrong with you?* An old nemesis. One that he could recognize. But still it didn't fit. It didn't relieve his sense of dread, the paralyzing panic that left him powerless. "What is it?" he cried out loud in the darkness, clutching a pillow against his belly and rocking gently back and forth. "What is it?"

George didn't think that there was anything wrong with him, he figured. That is why he felt so comforted in George's world. In his ACLU world. The grimy taste came from realizing that his parallel worlds were about to collide, which could only cause cataclysmic repercussions. Like crossing two plasma energy beams. That was the venom pulsing through his veins, threatening his worlds.

The two worlds could not coexist, he reckoned. Beth could no more understand the rules of honesty, honor, and patriotism in George's world than George could understand the concept of power for power's sake. Each world had its own set of rules. Both were part of him. He thrived on power and the position it gave him. But honesty and justice from his early years in law provided his sense of self-worth. One without the other was like living with only arms or only legs.

Now that he could see the problem, his panic ratcheted down a notch. He could fight anything he could see. How to keep both parts of his life intact — that's all it takes, he thought.

There was only one possible solution. One way to get George to help Beth without destroying his relationship. Everyone had a price, even George Comstock. Whether it was something he wanted or something he feared. There had to be something he valued above his determination to stay above politics, his determination to only take the side of the people. But it couldn't come from him. George could never know he had anything to do with it, or it would destroy their bond.

He resolved to speak with Aurelius. He would know how to do it without involving Bill. It was his only hope. It was Beth's only hope. He shuttered at the thought of what they would do to George. He was more afraid that they would make George compromise himself than hurt him. Bill reluctantly turned on his celltop. There is no other choice, he tried to consul himself, then sent a message to an untraceable address to set up a meeting not sure of how much danger he himself was in for using the blue folio to try and intimidate Aiden Carroll.

CHAPTER 14

Philadelphia, July 29, 2037

From his perch in the third pew, Sebastian analyzed the delegates one by one as they entered the Supreme Court room after being dragged back to Independence Hall without explanation. Their conversations, facial expressions, the steadiness of their walk — all had meaning to him. He sensed his plan congealing, although secrecy over why their break was cut short caused his ample breakfast to churn a little in his stomach.

Had Adee discovered his instigation of Hanley's push? he wondered. Hanley wouldn't discuss their meeting because he believed that they belonged to the same brotherhood. But would he try to shift the blame? Sebastian worried. If so, he would have to recalculate, to figure a way to keep the gains his careful strategy had already reaped.

Hanley was an easy recruit, Sebastian thought. Not because of a lack of intelligence or commitment. He had brains and the passion of a pit bull with its teeth locked. But his passion boiled over into emotion, into rage. And that could be manipulated.

"We could sell communism to a group of evangelical Christians by convincing them that the other candidate insulted Jesus," he would explain in political strategy sessions with his fellow New York power brokers. In a Southern drawl laced with a New York accent he would deliver the punchline, "and *e-van-gelical* Christians are very partial to democracy," to raucous laughter. Knowing what people hated was much more powerful than knowing what they wanted. They would always choose hate over want. It's how smart politicians got elected.

His private meeting with Hanley the morning before the blowout with Gould proved his point. Little suggestions here and there that liberals were trying to weaken the United States worked like a bellows to a fire. Anecdotes of his own fights to keep New York liberals from shuffling wealth to the lazy poor added fuel.

He would just as easily push images of Patriot Party conservatives requiring Christian prayers in public schools, or taking away a woman's right to her own body when working on a liberal. Condemn meat eaters to vegans and leaf eaters to carnivores. It was his stock in trade. What did he care, he was an omnivore. A little hate and the convention could fracture into little pieces that he could digest one at a time.

Seeing Comstock walk into the chamber lightened his mood. His gait reminded him of an Opie, a wide-eyed country rube, an idealist. Idealists, even passionate idealists, were easy to discourage. Don't attack them, attack their support. Easily roused, they could just as easily be discouraged when their support faltered.

"How was your vacation?" Comstock asked, walking into the pew and sitting down.

"Short," Sebastian joked, drawing smiles from the delegates closest to them.

Once the delegates were seated, Adee stormed into the room. She quickly motioned for the delegates to stop their applause and took the platform instead of her chair behind the judicial bench. She bore a deadly expression in her eyes and it worried Sebastian.

"There is a possibility that one of you did not take my lecture last week to heart," the elderly justice pontificated. "You were all instructed at length on the need for secrecy, so there can be no excuses." Unaware of where her anger was leading, Sebastian felt a little relief. It didn't sound like it was about his meeting with Hanley.

As she explained that the fight between Hanley and Gould had leaked to the newspaper, which is what brought them back so abruptly, his focus switched from her to the delegates. They were shielded from news, so it shocked them. He sensed mistrust, betrayal. Perfect, he crowed. His clients would be ecstatic.

"I have already notified your governors to get their alternates ready. If I find that any one of you is the source of the leak, you will be expelled from this convention," she said, her fiery stare seeming to gravitate toward him. All of the delegates turned to look at him. He knew enough not to react. Not to make an insinuation grow by offering a defense. But mere suspicion could hinder his plan by making delegates reluctant to speak with him in public and especially in private.

"I don't know who is responsible for the leak. I don't want any speculation or gossip," Adee ordered, apparently realizing the implication of her glare. "We will continue with the convention while the FBI finishes its investigation. We'll take the rest of today to get ready to resume our discussions of the supremacy and commerce clauses tomorrow."

Just as everyone stood and began to leave the pews, Sebastian's attention snapped back to Adee as she loudly called his name.

"Mr. Irving, if you don't mind, I would like to see you upstairs in my office in five minutes," she ordered, without waiting for an answer or an argument. The chamber filled with hushed "Oohs."

Was she playing his game? he wondered. Was she trying to undercut him by calling him out in front of everyone? Either way, he feared that it could take its toll.

"I'm sure it's nothing. Just came out wrong because she's so angry about the other thing," Comstock consoled.

"You're probably right," Sebastian responded, never showing fear or anger.

Delegates hovered in the vestibule and Tower Stair Hall, pretending to examine the historic documents. They separated for Sebastian, busying themselves with conversations and activities that brought their eyes away from him. Whatever she was up to, he had to put a stop to it — now.

When he walked into her office, she seemed less angry, signaling him to a large chair by the window. "Thank you for coming, Mr. Irving," she began.

"Please call me Sebastian," he offered as he plopped into the deep upholstered chair.

"I prefer to call you Mr. Irving." Her coldness snapped him back to his reality, generating a deeper evaluation of her. She stood, while placing him in a chair from which he would have great difficulty standing. Her higher position was designed to assert power, he assessed. Last names meant that he would have to call her either President Adee or Justice Adee, giving her a superior standing. She was good, damn good. But when it came to a fight, he still put his money on the street kid. And that was him.

"I hope that you don't think I'm as stupid as your actions would suggest," she began.

"I had nothing to do with that leak—" he began, before she interrupted him.

"This has nothing to do with the leak, Mr. Irving. But that doesn't mean I don't know what you've been up to."

"I'm not up to anything," he pleaded, tilting his head down slightly to puff up his chins and cheeks.

"Please, save it. I've talked to a lot of the delegates you've been going to behind everybody's back. They're concerned and so am I, with your motives and your methods."

"Are private meetings forbidden?" he shot back with more frost than respect.

"You know they're not prohibited. That's not the point. I know what you're doing, trying to make deals while nobody's looking. You don't get what this whole thing is about. That's what's so sad," she lamented. "Do you understand how important this is?"

He looked her straight in the eyes, gently nodding assent, having calculated the futility of any verbal response.

"I wouldn't mind these meetings if you were taking part in the discussions. I understand you haven't been to the Bourse meetings. And you hardly ever speak up in the hall anymore."

"I've only missed one public session," he protested. "Other delegates have missed more sessions than me, yet I don't see you calling them out in front of the whole convention. With all due respect, what is *your* agenda, Madame President?" he mocked.

He paused to see if his accusation was having any effect. When she gave no reaction, he continued.

"I know I never sat in Congress, I never sat in the White House or on the Supreme Court. I never lectured to legions of students or millions of people at rallies. I'm just a public school kid—"

"Don't give me that shit!" she blurted, stunning him into silence. "I came from a poorer background than you. Nobody paid my college tuition or law school. So don't give me your toe-in-the-sand, I'm only a street urchin crap."

Not sure whether it was her words or her coarseness that stunned him into inaction, Sebastian found himself unable to reply.

A soft rap on the door broke the momentary silence. Seth Canova, the convention secretary, crept into the room. "Sorry for the interruption. Deputy Director Brummet would like a word," he whispered.

"Excuse me for a moment," she said, then left him alone in the room.

A lion, Sebastian thought, conducting a postmortem of their exchange. In his pecking order a lion was a powerful and virtuous leader. The former a compliment, the latter a weakness he could exploit. Not by overpowering her. But by putting her in a position where she would have to be unfair to stop him. Her virtuous nature would check her. He could use that to checkmate any interference from her.

Her intuition surprised him, though. She saw through the first part of his plan: divide and conquer. But did she figure out his part in the Hanley-Gould matchup? His plan to break down the convention? If not, they lose and he wins, he happily concluded.

His mind turned to his next moves. One by one he scrutinized every detail of the scholar delegates in Independence Hall from today, searching for weaknesses. Little tells revealed their growing fear. Silly jokes that they laughed at harder than appropriate. Avoiding Hanley and Gould. Going out of their way to be friendly to political delegates. He could taste their fear. Fear that the convention could fall apart.

Comstock's mannerism in the hall replaying in his mind, he wondered, is *he* up for grabs? What a coup. Delegates respected the professor, but he wasn't a leader. He wasn't a lion. All virtue, no power. There was no counterpart in the animal world. No animal could survive without being able to overpower or being willing to surrender for secondhand scraps. Purely human — the rarest of creatures, the weakest of creatures.

The high road was easy to take when it was dry and well packed, he thought, comparing Comstock's tells today with those from their breakfast meeting at the City Tavern. But when dry earth turned to mud and the road started to slide down the hill, even the most committed take the low road. He wouldn't sell out for his precious treason clause, but for the whole enchilada? For the convention?

"Sorry for the delay," Adee offered as she walked into the room and resumed her position in front of his chair. "The FBI found the leak. It was a food worker who stayed behind in the Bourse. He'll be held until after the convention. So will the reporter and editor who printed the leak."

"So I'm off the hook?" he exclaimed, trying to plant a seed of guilt in her mind.

"I never thought you were on the hook," she quickly reminded him.

She poured him a cup of coffee and handed him a small plate of cookies before sitting in a higher, more formal chair she dragged from the end of the conference table.

"It dawned on me that you and I have never spoken," she pointed out. "I understand you're from the Bronx?"

"And I understand you're from Idaho?" he replied, trying to regain the upper hand by taking hold of the questions.

"Yes. But that's kind of boring. I'm fascinated by the Bronx. What was it like growing up there?"

"Have you ever been?" he asked.

"A few times. I used to make appearances occasionally at Fordham University. Beautiful campus, the botanical gardens and zoo and of course Little Italy just a few blocks away," she answered, clearly remembering great restaurants he knew well. "I have friends in Riverdale. I try to stay with them when I'm in New York."

"Yeah, Riverdale was always pretty nice. Elite, even in the seventies when I was growing up. I lived walking distance to Riverdale but they were the rich kids, and I wasn't."

"Where did you live?"

"Fort Independence, literally on *the other side of the tracks* from Riverdale. My grandparents moved there in the forties when most of it was new. My grandfather ran his painting company out of the garage."

He rarely talked about his childhood. It made him feel uncomfortable, like when his mother tried to set him up with friends' daughters and then asked if they kissed. She could never accept his sexual orientation. But he knew she loved him. And he loved his parents, especially his father.

"When my grandfather died, my father took over the business and the house. I was the only white kid by the late seventies. I was always the only Jewish kid," he added, stopping to stuff a cookie into his mouth and taking a sip of coffee to soften it. Sometimes he used his life story to make a point or make himself appear more human. But he wasn't quite sure why he was telling her.

"Sounds rough. I didn't have any Jewish kids where I lived either," she revealed.

He could sense her searching for some common bond before getting to her point. Being Jewish was a common bond, but not the type that could make him alter his course. She would've known that, he thought.

"What brought you into politics?" she asked. He weighed what version to reveal, choosing the truth on the assumption that it would yield the best advantage.

"About ten years after my father took over the business, he stopped getting government contracts. They all went to minority companies. Our local politicians were very sympathetic but told us that there was nothing that they could do."

He stopped short of telling her how that is when he decided to never be on the wrong side of politics. If you don't control the power, you're powerless, he determined at the time. "I saw it break my father. At only fifty-seven, he died considering himself a failure even though he was one of the hardest-working men I have ever met." Silence remained for more than a minute, as if in honor of his father.

"Given your history, I'm surprised you're not a bigger supporter of George's treason clause," Adee posed.

"Why is that?" he asked, not seeing any connection between the two.

"Had there been a treason clause like George's when that happened to your dad, it would've been treason. It might have stopped it," she offered.

It made him think for a moment. "I don't think anything could have stopped it," he concluded. "Those types can't be stopped by goody-goody laws. No offense, but I've even seen your buddies on the Supreme Court do it. That *Hild* case, just one of thousands. You know how it works." She got him to expose more of his thoughts than he wanted, he realized.

"Oh, you are so right," she sighed. "I've seen it time and time again. But isn't that what this is all about? Changing how things have worked to how they should work?"

"In the best of all possible worlds! In the best of all possible worlds," he droned, rolling his eyes in contempt of the promise of utopias hawked by liberals and idealists.

"No, not in an ideal world. In a practical world. In this world," she argued. "If we don't find a way, then we can be certain that money politics, polar politics, politics based on hatred will never change. Right now we are the only force that can change that."

"Seems to me that the only thing you're trying to change right now is my mind," he responded.

"Not at all, Mr. Irving. I don't want to change your mind in the slightest. I do, however, wish to change your method."

"What?"

"In the last half hour, I've gotten to know more about you than any delegate over the last two months. How can we understand your ideas if we don't know what you're proposing and why?" She paused and took a sip of tea.

"I may disagree with Arthur Hanley's views, but at least I know what they are," she added. "I hope that you will give us the same opportunity. Share your thoughts with the convention as a whole. It's the one thing you're not doing. You're not taking part in the process." This is where she was leading him all along. He admired her skill, how subtly she got him to the point she wanted to make. He would never underestimate her again.

"So you don't want me to stop the private meetings?" he asked. Her stamp of approval on his meetings would be a great calling card.

"Not at all. I've even signed the petition to rename your favorite dining room at the City Tavern to the *Irving Room,*" she gleefully replied.

"The what?"

"You didn't know about that? Seems you've become a bit of an icon, at least your breakfast meetings."

"No, I wasn't aware of that." And he wasn't sure he liked it. How did it fit into his plan? How did it affect his ability to manipulate? He would have to recalculate.

"Well, I think it's a tremendous sign of respect," she added. "One you can return by taking a greater part in the discussions, both in the hall and in the Bourse," she concluded, standing and dragging her chair back to the conference table.

By grasping first one arm of the chair and then the other, Sebastian shifted his weight back and forth and slowly pushed himself out of the crevasse and stood. "I will become a fixture at the Bourse," he promised. It was an easy promise. It's how he planned on capturing the converts, the ones who would flock to his compromises rather than risk leaving Philadelphia empty-handed.

At the door, she offered her hand. "If you'd agree to call me Chloe, I'd be quite honored if you would allow me to call you Sebastian."

"Thank you, Chloe. The honor would be all mine," he responded, shaking her hand. First names were a great way to get to people. But in his mind, she remained just Adee, impersonal, an object to be conquered.

At the top of the stairs, he saw about ten delegates still hanging out in the Tower Stair Hall. "Sorry to disappoint!" he bellowed. "The busboy did it."

Laughter ascended to the top of the tower with such force that he thought it might ring the Centennial Bell. The small joke undid any suspicion cast by Adee calling him out in front of the delegates. Time for the coup de grâce, he judged, on his short walk to his office in Philosophical Hall. His constituents, his clients would be pleased.

For the remainder of the day his mind drifted back to memories of his father. He pictured his father looking at Irving Hall with pride, a vindication. It made him happy.

CHAPTER 15

Washington, DC, October 31, 2059

Keri arrived at court two hours early. She couldn't sleep. The last two witnesses would take the stand today. They would be easy. That wasn't what was causing her eyelids to droop. That honor belonged to the inevitable motion to dismiss after she rested the prosecution's case. More particularly, the possibility that George would argue that motion. His argument would carry more weight than any precedent, especially since there were no decisions on this precise issue. Without a precedent, George's interpretation would be the best authority available to the judge.

Senator Nath and Congressman Lynn were her hedge against losing that argument. The president's statement that she believed it was in the best interests of the country to veto SAFTA could be taken as a false statement when she uttered it at the veto ceremony. And these were two eye witnesses to that statement, as well as the video of the ceremony.

They were the ones who ended up looking foolish after SAFTA was defeated. They were the ones who called for the investigation that led to the treason charge. Keri had prepared them for Paul's cross-examination on these issues. But she sensed that the fire had left their bellies. That they were not looking to hurt the president if they could avoid it. They wanted the political climate to return to normal — to get the country off of the treason trial and back to work. No danger of them changing their testimony regarding Beth's statements, Keri thought. Not with a videotape. But on cross-examination, reluctant witnesses could say unexpected things. And at this late stage of the trial, even a small slip could turn the cards against them.

She meticulously arranged the exhibits on the counsel table and on her celltop, testing to make sure that they displayed correctly. Then she sat alone, composing her thoughts, preparing for the battle, especially for the motion. Deep in thought, she barely heard the courtroom door open and the footsteps of two men.

"Good morning, Keri," Paul chirped, a little too cheerfully for her liking.

"Good morning, Paul," she answered, turning and looking at the companion at his side. "Mr. Waverly, what a surprise."

"I hope you don't mind if I sit in today, Mrs. Marshall," Bill asked, as he sat at the far right of the defendant's table.

"Not at all," Keri answered, knowing that she had no hope of stopping the president's personal attorney from at least sitting in on the proceedings. He was not listed as a witness so there would be no reason to exclude him. A space large enough for a seat still remained between Paul and Bill, she observed. The motion would most likely come after lunch. It could still be filled by George. Then she would have Paul, Bill, and George to deal with.

Paul left the courtroom with fifteen minutes remaining before the trial would resume. Keri stood, stretched, and walked over to Bill. His presence worried her. He was a well-known friend of George. Would the empty space be filled this afternoon? she wondered.

"You had George Comstock in law school didn't you?" she casually asked.

"Yes," Bill answered.

"How was he?" she continued with an air of natural curiosity.

"He was everything he's cracked up to be. Brilliant! Creative! Caring! An amazing human being," he rattled in staccato succession.

"Do you ever get to see him?"

Bill's face contorted. His eyes peered sideways, taking in her expression. "I just saw him last weekend. The same old George, full of fight, just as smart as ever," he concluded matter-of-factly, turning his head forward again but letting his eyes stay fixed on Keri's face.

"Glad to hear it. I met him a few times," she responded as she walked back to her counsel table and sat. Her eyes pretended to review her notes while she was calculating the damage George could create, and what she could do if he showed. Why would they have met the same weekend she tried seeing George if not to go over the motion to dismiss? she worried, struggling to keep her fear from reaching her face. It explained why he couldn't talk with her until after the trial. When had they hired him? Would he have helped her if she'd called a week earlier?

The courtroom door opened again but Keri was too afraid to look around. She felt a gentle hand rest on her right shoulder and turned to see Michael, the head of her witness team. He often hung around the courthouse when witnesses were getting ready to testify. He could ease last-minute jitters by staying with the witness, hand-holding. He leaned down closer to her face. "Can we talk for a moment?" The seriousness of his voice pushed her fear farther up her throat.

Outside of the courtroom, the two found an empty attorney room. Attorney rooms had no recording devices and were soundproof. The only openness to the room was a small porthole window.

"After our meeting on Sunday I got to thinking about the false-when-made problem," said Michael. Keri listened patiently with half her mind still in the courtroom and a quarter of her mind still on the possibility that George would show up this afternoon. "I did some checking on my own," he added, "and I may have come up with something."

"What?" Keri asked, more of her attention drifting toward him.

"I found a witness that may fill in the missing piece."

"What do you mean?" Keri asked hurriedly.

"Do you know Congresswoman Aines — Cordia Aines?"

"I don't know her. I've heard of her. I know that she's a Democrat from Ohio. I believe she's serving her first term."

"Well, it turns out that she spent a fair amount of time campaigning with President Suarez in the last election. They did a lot of rallies and fund-raisers together."

"And?" Keri asked impatiently, aware that the judge would be on the bench in less than five minutes.

"And, she's willing to testify that they attended a Knights of Columbus dinner two months after Aiden Carroll left the campaign, and that Suarez made a promise to the group that she would strongly support SAFTA."

Convenient witnesses at convenient moments in a trial always raised Keri's paranoia. Lawyer paranoia, she called it. But she learned to trust that instinct. "Any recording of the event?" she asked. Virtually every political event was recorded. She knew that and Paul knew that.

"No! I checked. No audio or video recordings. Not even some drunken Knight recording it on a celltop." Michael's answer seemed too ready and too happy for Keri's comfort.

"Do you believe her?" she asked, looking for more than the words he was about to say to test her suspicions.

"I'm not on the jury. I think the more important question is, will the jury believe her?"

Keri's face turned a shade of red rarely displayed to her staff—or to anyone. "No," she said in a loud voice, shaking her head side to side. "The most important question is whether or not *we* believe her." Her anger was visible, palpable.

"I have to get back into the courtroom," she added. "We're about to begin. I don't have time to deal with this now. I'll meet with her after I finish with these two witnesses and make my decision then. But I'm not putting on a bullshit witness," she commanded, before bursting open the door to the courtroom and returning to her place at the prosecution's table.

Good to her word, Keri kept the witnesses on the stand for only fifteen minutes on direct examination. Just the facts. No attempt to elicit emotion or personal feelings about what Beth did. Through them she established that Beth had actively campaigned on support of the SAFTA agreement during the primary and campaign. And that the first time they heard from her lips that she had no intention of signing it was at the veto ceremony. She coordinated the video of the veto ceremony with their testimony, highlighting her statement that she believed that SAFTA was not in the best interests of the American people.

During this testimony, she kept a close watch on Paul and Bill from the corner of her eye, looking for whether they understood her strategy. If they did, she couldn't detect it. Then again they were experts at not telegraphing their thoughts or strategy.

On cross, Paul started with the collateral attack, the attack on their motivation for requesting the initial investigation and for testifying. Where

Keri stayed away from emotion, Paul poured salt on their wounds, like a poultice to draw out their anger.

"And that made you mad, didn't it?" he demanded of Senator Nath, who tried to sidestep the question.

"I was surprised," the senator tried to explain.

"You were mad? Weren't you?" Paul insisted, walking right up to her in the witness box. Keri anticipated this and prepped her witness accordingly, laying a land mine that he just stepped on.

"Of course I was mad," the senator replied with authority. "She lied to us. She lied to the American people."

Without missing a beat, Paul continued. "Oh, it couldn't possibly be that she saw some harm coming to the American people from the legislation that *you* drafted — that would be impossible, of course." It was the type of question that great trial lawyers like Paul could always pull out of their bag of tricks. It didn't matter what the answer was. The question made any answer seem suspicious.

"If that were true, counselor, then why didn't she discuss this with us long before it was put to a vote in Congress?" the senator asked Paul, following Keri's preparation. Ignoring the question, Paul smoothly slipped into the direct attack on Keri's position. The attack Keri feared.

Over and over, he made both witnesses agree that they had never heard Beth utter a statement in favor of SAFTA after Aiden Carroll left the campaign. It hit Keri where it hurt, in her confidence. He found different ways to make the point, keeping each on the stand for almost forty-five minutes.

Keri feared that the point he now got to repeat through three cross-examinations — of Carroll, Nath, and Lynn — was sinking in. The videos of the jurors' reactions could help her see how much damage he did when she viewed them later. She feared it may have been enough. She realized that her only argument at the end of the case may be Beth's statement at the veto ceremony, the weaker argument. One that she could not be sure she would win with the judge or the jury, especially if George showed up.

It was 11:00 a.m. by the time Paul finished the cross-examination.

"Does the prosecution rest?" Judge Kneuaya asked, looking at Keri.

"Before resting, Your Honor, I would request a one-hour adjournment."

She gave no explanation, fearing that if she said she was considering a witness, the jury would take it as a sign of weakness if she didn't call the witness.

"We will reconvene at twelve sharp," Judge Kneuaya ordered. With that, Keri left the courtroom and took the staircase at the end of the hallway. Attorneys often used attorney rooms on other floors during a trial. Mostly for privacy. Michael kept Congresswoman Aines squirreled in a room on the 8th floor, two floors down, for fear that Paul or Bill would see her and figure it out.

Keri exited the stairwell first at the 9th floor, and commandeered an empty room. A few clicks on her celltop and she pulled up a screen split into four. Each quarter screen held the video of one of the most crucial jurors. A few more strokes and she advanced to the last five minutes of Paul's cross-examination of Senator Nath.

She studied each face with the eye of an art connoisseur examining an original Rembrandt, looking for the slightest hint of reaction. A raised eyebrow, parsed lip, direction of the eyes, curl of the mouth. What she observed didn't ease her butterflies. Same reaction when she looked at the last five minutes of his cross-examination of Congressman Lynn.

They understood his argument, she thought. Whether they agreed with it or not, they understood it. Her gut told her they wanted proof of a statement supporting SAFTA after Suarez spoke with Carroll. With it, she was safe, she thought. Without it, the odds tilted in Beth's favor. Please let Michael's witness be real, she prayed to herself, heading for the staircase down to the 8th floor.

"Sorry for making you wait," Keri offered as she cupped Cordia's unwrinkled hand between her own and looked her directly in the eye. She was young, so young, Keri thought. Not more than a year or two older than Keri's oldest son. Statuesque, she could be a runway model. That could explain Michael's giddiness, she thought. But not Cordia's excitement, overexcitement. A flag went off in Keri's head. Most witnesses are nervous. Excited witnesses aren't natural. That is, unless they're experts who make their living testifying.

"I have about forty minutes before I have to decide whether or not to put you on the stand," Keri explained. "So please forgive me if I come off blunt or offensive." The congresswoman nodded, folding her hands in front of her like she was trying to behave in church.

"Why did you wait until now? Why didn't you bring this up to us sooner?"

"I didn't know that what she said at the dinner was important," the congresswoman answered.

"When did you realize it was important?"

"Only the other day. Sunday or Monday, I think. I was talking with some of my colleagues about the trial. One of them mentioned that the case may come down to when Suarez said she supported SAFTA."

"What friends — excuse me, what colleagues?"

"Some of the other representatives, a few of our state legislators, and members of our chamber of commerce. We were at a luncheon together. I don't see what this has to do with my testimony?" the congresswoman snipped.

"You can be sure that Paul Gordon will see what this has to do with your testimony. If you testify. I need to figure out if your testimony would outweigh the damage that he will do on cross-examination." The explanation seemed to put the congresswoman's nose back in its place. "Why were you all having the luncheon?"

"We were discussing SAFTA. We were discussing how to eventually have it passed."

"So SAFTA was important for you and your state?" Keri asked, knowing the answer. Ohio had the most to gain by SAFTA. Once a huge manufacturing state, it transformed into exporting logistics and technology to countries with cheap labor. They could supply cheaper goods for the United States and the world, and Ohio industry could make it happen.

"If the president was convicted, would the vice president sign it into law?"

"What are you suggesting? How dare you suggest —"

"I'm not suggesting anything," Keri interrupted. "But Paul Gordon will. You must admit it all looks just a little too convenient. How did you come to talk with Michael?" Keri saw equal shades of plum growing on the faces of the congresswoman and the head of her witness team. A long pause before answering made her suspicion blossom.

"I'm—I'm not sure. Someone at the luncheon knew someone at Michael's firm. Next thing I knew we were meeting." Most of Keri's staff were volunteers who worked at private firms. Michael was a senior associate on a partnership track at a large Wall Street firm with a heavy presence in Ohio. The fish were starting to smell like they had been sitting in the hot sun for too long.

Another ten minutes of questioning and she was positive the congresswoman was lying. No explanation for how she remembered that the president's statement was from *this* dinner instead of the many others they attended together before the president's talk with Carroll, unable to remember anyone else who was at the dinner except herself and Beth. And especially her reaction when Keri pulled up the names of the other politicians at the dinner and offered to call them for confirmation. What a shame, she thought as she left the room.

"At the very least it will defeat their motion," Michael lobbied her as they walked down the hall. "Let the jury decide if she's telling the truth. If you don't believe her after she testifies, then don't include it in your summation. But at least use her to get to the jury."

"Interesting," was Keri's only verbal response. She bolted up the two flights of stairs, followed by Michael. He waited outside the courtroom as she prepared at the counsel table.

"Back on the record," Judge Kneuaya directed his clerk. The screens filled with the jurors' faces as all cameras turned on for the proceedings to continue. "Does the prosecution rest?" he asked, looking at Keri. She stood to address the judge. Her hands fumbled with her celltop, as if she was looking for the answer there. She turned to the courtroom door, looking through the long vertical glass pane on one half. Looking at Michael. A simple nod and he would go and get Congresswoman Aines.

She locked eyes for a moment with Paul. He had a puzzled look. Like he knew she had something up her sleeve that he hadn't anticipated. Every possibility ran through her mind with the speed of light. Every outcome calculated in seconds until only one question remained: *Then what? Then what?* she repeated in her mind.

Her eyes drifted to the bench and, after drawing a deep breath, she answered, "The prosecution rests." Judge Kneuaya dismissed the jury until the following Tuesday and instructed the attorneys to return at 2:00 p.m. for argument on the defense motions.

■ ■ ■

Keri returned to the courtroom when it opened at 1:45 p.m. She never left the floor. Instead she stayed in one of the attorney rooms, reviewing her memos and going over each argument in her mind. If the only thing left after the motion was the statement at the veto ceremony, she would have to live with it. Make the most of it, she consoled herself. Two wrongs don't make a right. Even good results don't justify dishonest tactics. Isn't that what the treason clause was all about? she reminded herself.

For fifteen minutes she tried to concentrate on the memos in front of her, but the part of her brain that always stood vigil, looking for danger, kept its focus on the door. How many would walk in? Who would walk in? Would it be George Comstock? The slightest creak from the hall shot through her brain like a high-speed bullet through a watermelon.

When the door opened, she fought the urge to turn around and look. It would signal fear, weakness. A lone pair of footsteps, heavy thuds on carpet. From the corner of her right eye she saw a large silhouette, unmistakably Bill. She cringed as he picked up a chair from the back of the room and placed it at the defense counsel table. Three chairs now. Paul, Bill, and George. Her courage wavered. But not her conviction in her choice to forgo Aines' testimony. It is what it is, she thought, accepting what was to come.

Just before 2:00 p.m. the door opened again. Two sets of footsteps. One lightly throbbing the carpet, the other barely audible. As Paul reached his table, she stood to greet Mr. Comstock. She could not censor the respect he was due. But when she turned, she saw the childish stature of President Suarez taking the seat between Paul and Bill. She looked small, but gave off that aura of power that accompanied her title. The appearance of power, perceived power, Keri thought. No match for real power. No equal to the power that George Comstock would have brought to this contest. Her relief bordered on light-headedness.

CHAPTER 16

Washington, DC, November 12, 2059

When Bill arrived at the courthouse and saw Keri, every fiber of his being told him that today was going to be a disaster. An earthquake that would topple the walls of the White House. That would strip away the last vestiges of privacy into the inner workings of the presidency.

Since Judge Kneuaya denied their motion three weeks ago, Bill watched from the White House as Paul plied his craft with the skill of a brain surgeon. Today Bill had to be in court in case Beth testified. The judge denied part of their motion, *without prejudice.* It meant that they could argue again that Carroll's testimony wasn't enough at the end of the case. Bill had watched Paul drive that point home with every witness over the past weeks.

Witness after witness testified that Beth never spoke in support of SAFTA after Aiden quit. The jury might discount testimony from the president's fellow Democrats, expecting them to help each other, Bill knew. But the witnesses included Patriot Party, Republican Party, People's Party, and Conservative Party members. That would be hard to discount.

Paul asked each exactly the same questions with exactly the same answers for every public appearance after the Carroll meeting.

"At any time during that meeting did you hear the president tell the audience that she supported SAFTA?"

"No."

"Did she even suggest it?"

"No."

"At any time when you were with the president that day did she tell *you* that she supported SAFTA?"

"No."

Bill took pride in this. He insisted that SAFTA not be on the agenda after Carroll resigned. It was an easy sell. Most candidates, regardless of party, supported SAFTA. Without controversy, why include it in a debate? No one ever suspected his strategy.

On cross, Keri mimicked Paul's questions, one for one, substituting "Did you ever hear her say that she no longer supported SAFTA?" to make her point and ended each cross with the question Paul didn't ask.

"Would it have been important for you to know that she changed her mind?"

"Absolutely," each witness answered.

Tacit agreement. Support by silence, by implication. A little damage, Bill thought. Not enough to derail Paul's point.

As the witnesses stacked up, Bill tried to persuade Beth that Paul's strategy was working. It would be impossible for anyone to think that she made any statement in favor of SAFTA after the Carroll meeting. But she wasn't having it. She insisted on testifying, ignoring their dire warnings.

"I know better attorneys than the two of you combined," she yelled in the attorney room before court began. Nothing could change her mind. It was her right. Her right to shoot herself in the foot, to jump off the cliff if she so desired. To stab herself in the back. And Bill was certain that was precisely what she was about to do.

Paul scheduled the entire day for her testimony, whether that would be needed or not. He estimated that her direct examination would only be about an hour. Bill wanted to make sure that Keri's cross didn't carry over to tomorrow. Why give her a clear night to review the videos and come up with more cross-examination questions? Beth would do fine on direct. It was Keri's cross that he foresaw as the poisoned apple.

Beth sat at the counsel table, between him and Paul. He would be there for her, even if she refused to take his help. He pushed his premonitions into quarantine and prepared for the inevitable as Paul rose to the podium.

"May it please the court," Paul elucidated with a hint of a British accent.

"At this time the defense calls the president of the United States, the Honorable Beth-Roche-Suarez." The words rolled off his tongue with a poetic cadence, summoning every advantage available from the office of the president. Framing her in a picture of power, prestige, and American presidential integrity. Chills climbed Bill's backbone up to the follicles along the sparse swatch of hair encircling his head as Beth stood and walked to the witness stand. Things rarely affected him.

Her direct examination was flawless. She looked at Paul as he asked each question but, after a moment's pause, turned her nocturnal eyes directly into the camera in the center of the twenty-three faces on-screen. It's what she was good at. Making each juror think that she was looking directly into his or her eyes. Speaking directly to his heart or her soul. That each of them was the only one that mattered. It was a conversation, a dialogue between her and each juror.

She made her conversion away from SAFTA seem like an agonizing decision. A decision she didn't want to make. Compelled only after weighing every advantage and disadvantage to the people of the nation. Everyone laughed, even Keri, when Paul asked her about conversations with her husband.

"When we were able to get some time alone," she answered in a low, secretive voice, "I can assure you there wasn't much talking." Bill watched her lap up the laughs. It was her drug, her addiction. The ability to make others believe what she believed. To make people love her. It even made him forget for a moment what would happen once Paul sat down.

Paul ended his direct examination just shy of an hour. After a fifteen-minute break Keri was ready to hike Beth down a different path, Bill worried.

Keri began the cross-examination standing perfectly still behind the podium. No hand gestures, no facial expression, no pointed inflection in her voice. She was friendly, as if she believed what Beth had just said on direct examination. Constantly referring to her as "Madame President" and "Your Honor," she wouldn't lose any brownie points for disrespect, Bill figured.

He followed as Keri carefully painted Beth into a corner. Trial lawyers called it *closing the doors*. A long hall with doors on both sides that had to be closed before reaching the end of the hall, before asking the final question. Cutting off all potential for escape. He had warned Beth about this. But he couldn't tell if she saw it coming.

"In the last year of your first term as senator, you personally proposed SAFTA in the Senate, correct?"

"That is correct, Mrs. Marshall," Beth responded, keeping her voice calm and remembering to use Keri's name. Bill was cautiously optimistic.

"In each of the four years of your second term in the Senate, you personally asked for an open vote on SAFTA, correct?"

"Yes."

"When you announced your candidacy for president of the United States on June 7, 2055, more than a year before the election, you filed position papers supporting SAFTA?"

"Yes."

"From June 7, 2055, until the election on November 7, 2056, you never withdrew those position papers?"

"No."

"You never filed amendments saying that you had changed your mind on SAFTA?"

"No." Beth was falling into Keri's rhythm, answering immediately, before she had time to think. Bill saw her ears blooming red, a signal that she was irritated. But so far, she was staying on script.

"You expressed your support for SAFTA at political rallies and meetings after you announced your candidacy?"

"In the beginning."

"In the beginning, you expressed your support for SAFTA to potential voters at *every* rally and meeting, isn't that true?"

"In the beginning."

"When you say *in the beginning,* you did that from June 7, 2055, to August 3, 2056, wouldn't that be true?"

"That sounds about right." Beth fidgeted slightly in the witness seat. Imperceptible to most, Bill thought. But every movement, every facial expression was exaggerated under a jury's microscope.

"You would agree that on August 3, 2056, three months before the election, you told an audience at the Cox Convention Center in Oklahoma

City that if elected, you would sign SAFTA into law within your first one hundred days as president?"

"That's correct."

"And your campaign manager, Aiden Carroll, resigned from your campaign after a discussion with you five days later, on August 8, 2056?"

"I believe so."

"So, if I understood you correctly, you changed your mind within five days before your conversation with Aiden Carroll, is that correct?" Bill braced himself, knowing that Keri had reached the end of the hall. All of the doors were closed.

"To the best of my recollection, yes," the president responded, looking directly into the camera. She had to accept the timeline — Bill and Paul had knocked that reality into her head. The prosecution had already proved that she spoke in its support on August 3, 2056. She had to own it, show no fear or hesitation.

"Well, Madame President. Was that decision like switching on a light? What I mean is, did you just wake up one day and say to yourself, I no longer support SAFTA?"

Beth paused before answering — a good sign to Bill. It focused the attention back on her, away from Keri. Still following the game plan.

"Of course not. It was a process. The more information I reviewed, the more doubt I developed."

"How long?"

"I don't know," Beth snapped back, making Bill cringe. It was an easy question, not one that should have switched her from Dr. Jekyll to Mr. Hyde.

"More than a week, less than a week?" Keri probed, trying to pry open Beth's skin.

"More than a week. Much more than a week," Beth answered, more composed, but slipping from the script that it was just a short time before Aiden quit. Bill's blood pressure rose a few points.

"More than a month or less than a month?"

"More than a month."

"Much more than a month?" Keri cast the bait, trying to elicit an exaggeration.

He had rehearsed this with Beth, warning her over and over to never testify that she considered changing her position on SAFTA prior to August 3, 2056, her last recorded statement in favor of SAFTA. But she had to know where this was going, he reassured himself.

"I would say closer to two months, certainly nowhere near three," her controlled, Dr. Jekyll persona answered, confidently looking straight into the camera. Bill winced.

"And when you became aware that *you were no longer sure of your support for SAFTA,* two months before you spoke to Mr. Carroll, who did you tell? Who did you discuss it with?"

A most dangerous question, Bill realized, as Beth's eyes darted from Keri to him. The worst place for her to look. She looked like she was afraid to answer, that she wanted her attorney to tell her what to say. Rather than returning her look, he put his head down and pretended to look for something on his celltop, praying she would see the problem. The question *assumed* that she questioned her support two months before Aiden quit. If she didn't address that, the jury would assume it was true.

"No one," she answered, ignoring the assumption.

"No one?" Keri repeated, hurling her stare into the air and spinning around to look at the camera. "Not even your cabinet members? Your advisers? An old college professor, perhaps?"

The glibness of the question irritated Beth. Bill could feel it. "I spoke with Mr. Waverly," she said, looking over at Bill.

"Your attorney?" Keri asked with utter surprise. Bill poked Paul's leg, causing him to shoot to his feet.

"Objection!" Paul shouted. "Privilege."

"Overruled," Judge Kneuaya responded.

When Beth sat silent, Keri asked it again. "When you started to have doubts regarding your support for SAFTA, the only person you spoke with was your personal attorney?"

Another objection, same result, continued silence.

"You can answer," Keri urged, with the gentleness of a mother coaxing a timid child.

"Yes, I spoke to my attorney. Why, am I not allowed to speak to my attorney?"

"Were you afraid that you were doing something illegal?"

"Objection."

"Overruled."

"Nooo," she bucked. "I just wanted his advice."

"His advice as your attorney? An adviser? A friend?" Keri prodded.

"Objection," Paul spurted, standing. "The prosecutor is trying to trick the witness into waiving her attorney-client privilege by suggesting that they spoke as friends or as a nonattorney adviser." It was a speaking objection, which Judge Kneuaya had warned them against. Arguing in front of the jury to make a point. All objections were limited to one or two words, such as "hearsay" or "irrelevant." The jurors' camera would be turned off for any further discussion. It risked Judge Kneuaya's anger but Bill agreed that Paul had to take the risk.

Rather than issuing a stern warning, Judge Kneuaya's mouth broadened into a sinister smile. "Overruled. After all, there would be no point to the objection now that you have told your client how she should answer the question."

The jurors laughed. They understood Paul's dirty little trick, but Bill didn't care. The chance of her waiving the privilege outweighed everything.

"As my attorney, of course," she responded, appearing annoyed at the judge's suggestion. She hated situations that she didn't control. But Bill knew she hated being portrayed in a bad light even more. That is when she became most unpredictable, he feared.

Keri shifted one step left of the podium and a half step closer to Beth. To Bill it looked like a cat positioning for the final pounce. Beth edged forward in the witness box, her determination tangible. The mouse ready to jump into the cat's mouth, he envisioned.

"Let's just make sure the jury understands this," Keri began, pointing to the twenty-three faces on the screens facing Beth. "After campaigning for years — shouting at the top of your lungs that you wholeheartedly supported SAFTA — you'd completely changed your mind in less than three months, and the only discussion you had about this miraculous conversion was to ask your personal attorney for his legal advice?" It was the type of question designed to make the witness look foolish no matter what the answer. Worse, Bill realized, it was the difference between a trial lawyer's common sense and a politician's obsession.

"Yes, but how dare you insinuate that I should not have talked to my lawyer," Beth shot back through her Mr. Hyde face. Bill hung his head in frustration, hoping that she would realize just how deeply she stepped into Keri's trap.

Keri grew cool. The lines around her mouth smoothed. She turned and brought herself back behind the podium and slowly raised her head and looked at Beth, who was still too hotheaded, in Bill's view.

"I apologize, Madame President. I apologize if I gave you the impression that I thought you should not have spoken with your attorney," Keri began. Beth sat back with an air of victory that Bill knew was premature. "Obviously it was prudent for you to find out whether your change of heart — your drastic change of position on SAFTA — could be treasonous."

Beth shot back to the edge of her seat, gritting her teeth like she was going to physically attack.

"What I want to make clear to this jury," Keri continued, "is that after such a drastic change of position, you never spoke about SAFTA again except to ask your lawyer if you were committing treason?"

"Objection," snarled Paul, jumping to his feet. "This is beyond —"

"Sustained," Judge Kneuaya ruled, turning to Keri. "You can ask if she had a conversation, but you know you cannot ask what the conversation was about."

"My apologies, Your Honor," Keri demurely responded.

"You didn't speak to Congressman Lynn about your complete change of position, isn't that correct?"

"Yes, but —"

"You never spoke to Senator Nath about your flip-flop, isn't that true?"

"Correct, but can I explain?" Beth tried to add.

Keri continued asking the same questions down a list of members of Congress, foreign-aid advisers, treaty negotiation team members, and media personalities, one by one. She ended the string of questions with, "You never told even one of the voters whose votes you wanted, isn't that true?"

"Yes, but you make it sound —"

Bill saw Beth reacting to the jurors' faces. He knew that in her eyes she was losing points with voters and that was all she cared about. It was her Achilles' heel.

"As a matter of fact," Keri interjected, "the one and only discussion you ever had about your change of position was to ask your attorney if you were committing treason, isn't that true?"

"Sustained," Judge Kneuaya angrily responded. But Keri had made her point with the jury and with Beth.

"Yes, I asked him if it would be treason and he told me *absolutely it would not*!" Beth shouted while she looked at the twenty-three faces on-screen.

Every quarantined sensation regurgitated into Bill's mind in an instant. She has no right. How dare she? he fumed, frozen with shock.

"Objection, there is no question!" Paul shrieked.

"Your Honor, the witness has made a statement to the jury and I believe I have an absolute right to follow up on her response," Keri replied slowly. A choking silence filled the courtroom. Judge Kneuaya hesitated.

"Perhaps this is better discussed outside the presence of the jury," Paul interjected. But the judge continued to remain silent as Bill focused on the pulsating veins on Beth's neck.

"We don't need to discuss this outside — we don't need to discuss this at all," Beth spat. "They want to know what Mr. Waverly told me, let them know."

Shut up, Bill commanded in his mind, trying to focus on Paul's reaction.

Speaking over Paul, Keri instantly asked, "Are you waiving the attorney-client privilege?" She dangled the question like a shimmering fly fastened to a hook, twisting and bobbing it up and down until the witness had to jump and bite.

In a flurry of movement and voices, Bill, Beth, and Paul all moved and spoke at the same moment.

"Yes — absolutely — I have nothing to hide," Beth challenged, her voice ringing out above Bill's.

"Don't answer that!" Bill commanded in a shrill voice, a second behind Beth, as he vainly tried to stand. His seat was so far under the counsel table that when he tried to stand, his belly hit the edge of the table, causing him to flop back into his seat. By the time he pushed his seat back enough, Beth had already spoken and Paul was on his feet voicing his objection.

"Clearly the witness is not aware of the implications of the question. I would request a brief adjournment to explain her rights before answering," Paul pleaded.

But Judge Kneuaya's eyes, wide with fury, fixed on Bill now standing by Paul's side. "Mr. Waverly, you are only here as an observer. Nothing more. You have no right to object and certainly no right in *my courtroom* to instruct a witness. I suggest that you sit down and remain quiet or I will have you removed from the court."

Bill obeyed, sulking back into his seat — an automated submission from a childhood of paternal rebukes. He felt weak.

"If I may," Keri began softly. "As Mr. Waverly may now be in a position to give testimony in this case, I think it would be appropriate to have him sequestered." Bill looked at her as if his gaze could pierce her heart, unable to hide his anger.

"That would only be an issue if Your Honor overrules the objection and if the witness answers it in the way Ms. Marshall is clearly hoping," Paul responded. "If I may have a few minutes with my client, I am certain that it will not be an issue."

Sequestered? It sounded foreign to Bill, like an old Latin word tucked into deeds whose meaning attorneys had forgotten for centuries but were too afraid to do without. He knew what it meant. But why, how could he be removed from the courtroom? He was the president's counsel and she needed him more than ever right at this moment. The strategy was too diabolical to him. Even a jury would understand that. Remove the president's attorney so that he can't advise her not to waive her attorney-client privilege. A catch-22, a gold-plated bear trap with no escape.

Bill leaned over and tried to whisper into Paul's ear, but Paul's right hand physically blocked him. His eyes were focused on the judge, who seemed to be looking to heaven for inspiration.

"We will give the jurors a short recess," Judge Kneuaya at last responded, instructing them to return in ten minutes. He clicked off the juror cameras and turned to the uniformed officer sitting at the back of the courtroom. "Please take Mr. Waverly to a witness room until we send for him."

"But —" Bill started to argue, pushing his chair back and standing as quickly as he could.

"Not another word, Mr. Waverly. I am going to sequester you. I will, however, give Mr. Gordon a few minutes alone with the witness to discuss her rights."

The uniformed officer took Bill by the arm and led him out of the courtroom, down one hall, and then another and into a four-meter by four-meter room. Muted shades of green, a plush soft couch and chair, and some reading material—all of which Bill figured was designed to keep a witness relaxed. But he wasn't relaxed. He paced the floor like a wild animal caged for the first time.

Pulling out his celltop, Bill tried to review Beth's testimony on-screen. No signal. He couldn't make calls or send messages. Nothing. The lack of contact with the outside world made him pace faster.

He set the timer on his celltop, looking for something he could control. The adjournment should be up by now, he thought, visualizing Beth walking into the courtroom and emphatically stating that she would not waive her attorney-client privilege. If she did that, it would be only minutes before he was called back in the courtroom.

The minutes on his timer ticked off one by one. Ten minutes. There could still be reasons why they hadn't come for him. They may have been late starting. Keri may be trying to pressure Beth into waiving the privilege on the stand. Paul could be objecting and the judge taking his time on rulings. *She must claim the privilege,* he begged.

Twenty minutes. Why had they not come for him? His pacing resumed, mostly along one wall that let him look out of the small square window in the door. It would give him a second or two of notice that someone was coming. Or signs that anybody had left the courtroom. Anything—Christ, anything.

Thirty minutes came and went. As did his hope that Paul had got through her thick skull, that she understood. She shot herself in the foot, he knew. Now she was probably aiming the gun at him. Would she use him as a scapegoat? Try to say that he told her to do it? Or would she just expect him to back her up on whatever lies she was now telling her potential executioners? Either way, it put his nuts in a vise.

No use in wallowing on about all he had done for her. It didn't matter to her and it didn't matter to him. They were both out for themselves. No illusions. One con artist could never really trust his accomplice. If she could sacrifice him to keep her job, she would.

But what was his outcome? he questioned. What did he want at the end of this day? Suddenly, intensely, what he wanted was to call his children. To let them know something he had failed to admit to himself for most of their lives. That they were important to him. Calling them after she threw him on the altar of sacrifice would seem meaningless, desperate. He wanted them to know that he was thinking of them, before his life was destroyed.

The vision of his children made him spiral into a state of depression that calmed him in a way he rarely experienced. He sat on the couch without looking at the timer, without looking through the square window, without moving. Reflecting more on the past than on what was about to happen. Is this what it's like when your life flashes before your eyes? he wondered. Self-judgment before judgment day. He didn't like the way he was stacking up.

The door opened with a crack, startling him. The court officer poked his head in. "They're breaking for lunch. You have to remain here." The officer closed the door quietly and Bill hit the resume button on his self-judgment, hoping to find at least one thing his children could be proud of.

CHAPTER 17

Philadelphia, August 19, 2037

"Heavenly Father," Sebastian prayed, grasping the hands of the delegates on either side of him. Careful never to use "Lord" or "Jesus," he uttered Christian-style prayers with the ease of a Baptist minister sitting down to Christmas dinner. After his meeting with Adee, he had enough tables put together in his dining room at the City Tavern to hold his own court every morning over five to ten delegates. Rather than calling it the Irving Room, he named it the Jacob Irving Room, after his father. A private caucus room, sanctioned by Adee.

Good to his word, he took a greater part in the formal discussions and became a constant presence at the Bourse. But he rarely put forth ideas. Instead, he backed surrogates tempted into fighting his battles, keeping himself in reserve. Different delegates for different issues, he mulled.

His stalwart Christian conservatives — Arthur Hanley, the influential Reverend Jack Connors, and like-minded delegates from Wyoming, Alabama, Texas, Missouri, Utah, South Carolina, and South Dakota — filled out the table today. Without their support, he couldn't get what he came for. Already resigned to the fact that he couldn't break up the convention, he had to deliver a toothless Second Constitution to retain the respect and resources of the most successful people in the country, his clients. They would pay any price to be able to continue to control the business of the country, even for one more generation.

As a unanimous "Amen" issued at the end of the prayer, defeat hung over the room like a cloud of impenetrable smoke, choking all hope. Pessimism seemed the only thing shared by the entire convention. A belief that bridges could not be crossed, chasms could not be filled, fragments could not be reassembled. He wanted to widen the chasms, just a little, so that he could appear to be the only one able to close them.

The division of state and federal powers arguments didn't disappoint him. Delegates hacked at each other over the supremacy and commerce issues incessantly for three weeks. Scholars against political delegates, scholars against scholars, intellectuals against conservatives, conservatives against each other. A free-for-all. In the Independence Hall arguments, the square discussions, and even the committee meetings, communications and consensus deteriorated.

If he could deliver a compromise on states' rights, he plotted, a majority of the delegates would give in on his counter-proposed treason clause, the most important step to maintaining control for his clients. Without Comstock's clause, there was room for friendly Supreme Court decisions like the ones they had built over the last 250 years. Sebastian sat back and let his guests whimper for over an hour, until their frustration boiled over to desperation.

"Ladies and gentlemen, we have fought the good fight," he interjected, the conversation ceasing and eyes turning to him. "*They,*" he bellowed, pointing toward Independence Hall, "want total victory, total surrender. The scholars, the liberals, the *atheists,* will not give an inch."

"Never," spat Hanley, patting the table.

"We must be realists," Sebastian continued, the eyes on him turning suspicious.

"What exactly do you mean?" Connors demanded.

"We need to take a step back and regroup. Recalculate what we can accomplish, pool our resources in one direction," he explained, as he brought the bluish glow from his tablet to life.

"I can deliver enough votes to block any mention of abortion," Sebastian boasted. Groans of dissension rose. He didn't care one way or the other about abortion. It was a tool he could use to polarize or unite delegates.

"I totally agree," he answered the groans, acknowledging their unrealistic hope to have abortion outlawed in the new Constitution. "But this way we can continue to fight it in the Supreme Court until *Roe versus Wade* is overturned." Their vigor returned. He knew abortion would never be outlawed, even if *Roe versus Wade* was overturned. But as long as this group never saw that reality, they could be played.

One by one he cut through each group member's *asks*, the changes they wanted most. Comparing the hopeless to the hopeful, he made defeats look like victories. Like he alone could guarantee their best outcome.

"We can hold them tight on the right to bear arms," he boasted. "At most we'll lose assault weapons and have some stronger licensing in urban areas, but we can hold on to our God-given right to bear arms." Even though the cherished right to bear arms had nothing to do with Christianity, or even conservatism, he knew this group held it sacred. It symbolized independence, self-sufficiency, the pioneering spirit that built the United States. For Sebastian, it was a great bargaining chip. Small concessions on assault weapons, major victories on gun ownership, and he could call in the marker he needed.

Forty minutes of shuffling the deck in his favor and the telltale beacons of trust glared. Relaxed postures, an occasional hand over a heart, each delegate looking at him when they spoke, the group waiting for his response after each speaker. They were ready.

"I know that many of you knew Arnold Tolbert," he solemnly began.

"Hear, hear," cried several of the delegates, expressing their admiration for the founder of the Patriot Party. Even those that didn't switch to the Patriot Party held great respect for him.

"I'm sure you all recall how he transformed the conservative platform to support stronger federal authority. What you may not know is that he intended to reverse that. Here — at the convention." Some eyes widened with surprise while others smiled a knowing smile. It wasn't true, but Sebastian counted on the egos of delegates wanting to seem like they had the confidence of the Patriot Party founder. Those knowing smiles told him which delegates fell into that trap.

"He hoped to get more delegates like us appointed to the convention, so that we could return the Constitution to our founding principles, to Christian principles," he continued, looking into the eyes above the pseudo-knowing smiles and nodding vigorously. They nodded back as if they had all sat in on the same fictitious meeting.

"And it would've worked that way had it not been for Justice Adee and that *Hild versus Town of Hamelin* case." He could sense the climate rise with frustration.

"For us to continue the fight, we must switch back to stronger state powers. That is where we will have the best chance. Get the best deal we can with the Second Constitution, and then make our gains state by state, just as Arnold Tolbert planned."

He gauged the delegates' reception to this 180-degree switch of the Patriot Party's platform. What he sensed was confusion. That was good, he thought. It wasn't anger; it wasn't disagreement.

"You know that's what he would've wanted," he prodded Hanley and the other knowing smiles. The seed planted, he sat back and let the surrogates pick up the battle. One by one they jumped on the bandwagon, all claiming to have the same intimate knowledge of Tolbert's mind. Connors was the only person neither claiming to know Tolbert's mind nor seeming to care what he would have thought.

"There will be a Second Constitution," Sebastian announced, rising from his seat. "We can't leave here without it. The people are too united on that. If this convention doesn't work out, they would call for another one every few years until it does work. Our strategy has to be to make what gains we can now and to lay the foundation to continue making changes in the future."

"You can count on us!" a delegate shouted, and they all followed suit, jumping to their feet and surrounding Sebastian. Sebastian's mission a fait accompli, he marched the nine delegates to Independence Hall for the continuation of the discussions.

■ ■ ■

"Thank you, George," Sebastian cheerfully offered, patting the back of his arm as he shuffled past him into the pew. He had toyed with the concept that George could still be turned. Not bribed, just given enough hope that some good could come out of the convention. That he could claim a legacy, for the smallest of concessions.

The two exchanged jokes and details of their private lives over the last three weeks. Sebastian dangled the possibility of support for the treason clause with questions designed to make George think he was becoming a convert. Questions could be so much more persuasive than promises because they weren't viewed as lies. It was a tool he used effectively over the years. At the same time, questions could sow seeds of fear. "I sure hope this supremacy clause doesn't end this whole thing," he had confessed to George, planting doubt.

"I'm certain that we'll be able to come to an agreement," George had replied at the beginning of the debates. Now, three weeks further along and no closer to agreement, his replies carried less certainty. "I hope so too. It would be a shame to lose this over states' rights."

He let Hanley and the other delegates carry the argument on the floor while he chipped away at Comstock. But Comstock sported his annoyance with parsed lips at any interruption, anything that diverted his attention from a speaker—and nothing annoyed him more than private conversation. Sebastian waited silently when a delegate spoke, pressing his arguments on George in the few minutes between speakers. Not to get Comstock to agree to what he wanted, just to get a sense that he would come to the table to talk, that he would negotiate to save the convention, the Second Constitution.

"What you're saying is great," interrupted Comstock. "I think everyone in this chamber would love to hear that there is hope for an agreement on state rights. Why don't you ask to be recognized? It would be great news."

"It's not something that should be discussed in front of everyone, not yet," Sebastian answered, seeing Comstock's forehead wrinkle in puzzlement.

"Why not? What could be better than having everybody discuss it?"

"No. I don't think it would work that way. It would just end up in a stalemate. If you have a couple of the scholars come to the Jacob Irving Room tomorrow morning, we might be able to hash something out."

"Hash something out? We can hash out the details right here," George responded with a red face.

"It's more complicated than that. There are things"—he hesitated—"things that the *politicals* will want to hash out on other unresolved issues." He could see that the phrase *hash out* didn't sit well with Comstock.

"I thought I made myself clear," Comstock answered, looking directly into Sebastian's eyes and raising his voice just loud enough to catch the attention of the other delegates before the next speaker mounted the platform. "This is not about making deals. If that's all you want to discuss, there would be no point in meeting at the Jacob Irving Room," he concluded, with no hint of sarcasm at the name of the room.

During the remaining four speakers, Sebastian silently pouted. Comstock seemed unaffected, participating in the discussions as if they hadn't spoken. It angered Sebastian. He would have to go through another scholar delegate. Comstock was a dead end who could, at best, be neutralized.

Rap rap rap! Ormond signaled the supper break. The delegates stood to head for the Bourse.

"You're joining us at the Bourse, right?" Comstock asked.

"I wouldn't miss it," said Sebastian, the words rolling defiantly off his tongue as he stayed in his seat and watched the delegates exit.

Still angry, he walked down the stairs from his pew and turned the corner of the jury box to head for the vestibule. In one of the narrow archways between the Supreme Court room and the vestibule, he saw Comstock talking to Alman. Passing through the archway, Sebastian brushed against Comstock a little too harshly for it to be considered innocent.

"Excuse me," Comstock responded, taking a half step back and using his hand to point out the open pathway with what seemed like a slight bow.

"You're such a Boy Scout," Sebastian snarled. It drew shock from the delegates, who slipped back to surround the two, as if to watch a cockfight.

Without raising the temperature of his tone, Comstock responded, "And you think that's an insult?"

"It's not an insult. It's a fact," Sebastian replied, standing directly in front of George without so much as blinking. "For all your education, you're just a weak, bleating sheep who holds on to fairy-tale ideals. Too weak to get it done, to do what's necessary," he added, pouring salt into what he divined as Comstock's most open wound.

It took a moment for Sebastian to realize that he used the bleating sheep analogy out loud. Part of his pecking order, the part that described most Americans, but one he would never share. He would make the best of it, he determined. He had to get his barbs in quickly, he thought, seeing Adee and Ormond among the spectators coming to watch.

"You all wonder why the *people* feel so powerless. Why businesses and politicians seem to control so much," Sebastian continued, looking around at the delegates. "It's not because they're smarter or have more money. It's because they have the balls to stand up and do something. We all know that's true." The insult intended for Comstock landed on the *people,* collecting harsh stares from even his most conservative delegates, even from Hanley.

"They are weak because *you* hold your ideals higher than their needs," he continued, looking at Comstock, trying to bring the attack back to him. "Because *you* refuse to com-pro-mise, leaving the sheep alone to be devoured by wolves."

"What does that make you, the wolf?" George asked, drawing laughs and applause from the crowd in the small dark vestibule.

Sebastian's chest pumped high with pride at the suggestion that he was a wolf. It's exactly how he viewed himself. All power, no virtue. Closest to original human instincts. The strongest of creatures.

"And you think *that's* an insult?" Sebastian mimicked. "Between being a bleating sheep or a wolf, yeah, I choose to be the wolf. That's why I've been able to get it done, not just lecture about high ideals and utopian concepts, but get real things done — through compromises."

Comstock took a step closer to Sebastian, close enough that he had to look down to speak to him directly. "Of course the Second Constitution cannot be completed without compromise. Everyone would agree to that. The problem is that you use the word *compromise* like it's a four-letter word." The comment drew pugilistic approval from the crowd. But Sebastian knew exactly how to turn the comment to his advantage. Make it appear that Comstock was being unfair and he would back down, apologize. And Comstock had just given him the opening.

"A four-letter word?" Sebastian questioned with feigned insult. "What four-letter word, Mr. Comstock? Please, enlighten us all." His voice turned from mocking to demanding. "Be a man! Tell us what four-letter word you think I am guilty of using."

The challenge echoed off the plaster walls of the packed vestibule as Comstock stood silently for a moment. His face showed no strain. His eyes glistened, his head gently angled to the side as his mouth expanded into an almost imperceptible smile. Sebastian watched as the audience followed the gestures like an orchestra following a maestro. Terror at the bluntness of the challenge, the affront, the audacity, filled them. Conjecture at the composure of the prey. Anticipation at what lethal blow lay beneath the most modest of smiles.

"Deal," Comstock whispered. "You use *compromise* when what you mean is *deal.* Your four-letter word is *deal.*"

The gasp from the audience sent shivers down Sebastian's spine. Comstock's a fucking lion, a lion in hiding, waiting for his prey, he realized. *Why didn't I see this before?* he chided himself. No turning back. His only option was to keep swinging.

"So you admit there must be compromises," Sebastian replied with a little unintended vibrato. "If the convention fails, it will be because of you!" he barked. Delegates took a step back, their bodies relaxed, arms unfolding. They were no longer watching an entertaining fight, a schoolyard battle. They were listening, and that worried him.

"Perhaps you don't know the difference," Comstock instructed. "What we've been trying to find is compromise, consensus. Not the quid pro quo — the something for something — that you've been trying to pawn off as compromise. We're looking for common ground."

The comment seemed sarcastic to Sebastian, but he didn't read that in the reactions of the delegates, some of whom shouted "That's right, you're trying to make it all or nothing!" His mouth went dry and the skin beneath his suit steamed like a sauna as he struggled to cross his arms in front of him. Skin clung to his suit in odd spots, restricting his motion.

"You're such a Boy Scout, you're such a saint," was the only response Sebastian could utter, like a bully looking for that one nerve that would hurt the most.

"And what are you?" Comstock replied. "A profiteer? Do you believe in anything other than profits? Do you believe in anything but yourself?" Comstock challenged, like a therapist trying to get his patient to make a breakthrough.

"It's not about what I believe—" Sebastian began.

"Of course it's about what you believe. It's all about what you believe," Comstock interrupted.

"It's about what I can get—what I can get done," Sebastian corrected himself. "You live in a fantasy world. I live in the real world. And in the real world, it's about what we can get done." Comstock had pushed Sebastian into a corner. He was defensive, desperate. The street fighter was swinging, but this wasn't a group of street fighters. It was separating him from the other delegates, setting him apart from them, making him seem like he was out of sync.

"That's just some line you fed yourself on years ago," Comstock scolded, like an angry father. "It's your way to justify giving up any conviction you ever had to get what you want. Without beliefs, you're nothing. You're a profiteer—a pirate, set to pillage the very people who trusted you to protect them."

Sebastian knew he had to stop this. His support was disappearing in front of his eyes. All the fear he had sowed was being washed away by some rube, a wide-eyed altruist. He had to make them see danger in following silly ideals.

"Well at least with my way we will leave this city with a signed agreement, something that we can present to the people!" Sebastian yelled. "Your way, we'll leave here with an example of how not to get things done," he concluded, pushing his way through the ring of delegates and storming out of Independence Hall. The crowd followed him onto the street in front of Independence Hall. He didn't know which way to go. Where to go. He turned left and walked straight as fast as he could, west on Chestnut Street, away from the Bourse, his legs burning as he depleted their short supply of oxygen.

Two blocks on he turned the corner, collapsing against the gated storefront of one of the diamond exchanges, gulping air between hoarse curses. "Mother fucker," he wheezed. "Who the fuck does he think he is? I have beliefs." Utterances as spastic and frenzied as his thoughts.

Slowly his heaving chest settled. Tears formed crooked streams down his cheeks. Not sure if they were from crying or suffocating, he abruptly wiped them with the sleeve of his expensive suit jacket. A pestilence that branded him. Coward, child, fragile. Everything he despised, everything that he saw demoralize his father. He had beliefs. He believed in strength.

Looking around at the shuttered storefronts and empty streets, he felt foolish. Like his thoughts were absurd, abnormal. George had got under *his* skin. It plucked a nerve that set him off and he couldn't figure out how. All might be lost, and he didn't know why.

CHAPTER 18

Philadelphia, August 23, 2037

Ever since his argument with Sebastian, George woke up several times a night, replaying their exchange over and over. No regrets, just concern. Calls and e-mails weren't returned. Handwritten notes George personally pushed through Sebastian's mailbox left unanswered. Nothing. Not even a sighting by a delegate. Speculation slipped from every tongue.

George took to eating breakfast at the City Tavern, hoping to see the Jacob Irving Room stocked with a buffet. After today's breakfast, he waited outside Independence Hall on Chestnut Street, facing the mall, the Liberty Bell, the Constitution Center. Searching for any sign of Sebastian.

A moment alone with Sebastian is all he wanted. To let him know that there were no hard feelings. That he meant only to instruct, not to criticize. That Sebastian's opinions were as welcome as every other delegate's. Guilt or worry tugged at his abdominal muscles.

He drew the lapels of his black corduroy sport coat together and fastened two buttons against the morning chill. Late August and morning lows dropped into the fifties. An alarm clock, reminding him that the convention's business would soon be over. Whatever could be accomplished had to be done now. The red, white, and blue banners covering the buildings fluttered in strong winds. It added to his impatience as he paced the empty concrete sidewalk for two hours, looking for signs of movement in every direction.

Discussions continued in Sebastian's absence. Yesterday, they sent the last of the proposals, including the supremacy clause, to their respective committees. Today the process of voting on proposals that had already passed through their committees would kick off.

Those with thirty-four votes would be immediately adopted. Those with fewer than seventeen votes would be immediately rejected. Between seventeen and thirty-three votes, there would be another round of discussions before a final vote.

Assuming Sebastian to be a no, George calculated that his treason clause was five votes short of passing. Before his fight with Sebastian it was nine votes shy. Progress, but not the way he wanted it. Up all night anyway, he used the time to review, to practice his final plea. Though hopeful, he wasn't confident, even if Sebastian didn't show for the vote.

Was Sebastian's disappearance a ploy? he pondered, pacing up and down the sidewalk, alone, eyes darting toward anything that moved. As quickly as he dismissed the idea, it was replaced with a fear that he'd hurt Sebastian, perhaps beyond repair. The thought made him drop his head in shame. He felt like a bully.

Precisely at 11:00 a.m. the Centennial Bell halted his self-criticism, calling the delegates into the hall. Once the other delegates disappeared through the vestibule door, George took a last survey of the streets. Still no Sebastian, he sighed, as he entered Independence Hall.

A series of gasps cascaded from one corner of the Supreme Court chamber as George reached his pew, followed by a low round of applause. He turned his head, spotting Sebastian as he walked around the jury box, his head held low. Delegates patted Sebastian on the shoulders and back as he climbed the stairs. Sebastian didn't react; he moved like he was sleep walking.

The closer Sebastian came, the more alarmed George became. He appeared drawn, sullen, defeated. It was sad, George thought. He regretted having any part in Sebastian's physical decay. George moved to the side of the landing to give Sebastian room to enter their pew. Leaning down to place his lips near Sebastian's right ear as he entered the pew, George whispered, "I'm sorry. Please forgive me if I hurt you."

Without turning or looking, Sebastian replied in a barely audible broken breath, "No need," then took his seat. His head stayed slanted down and slightly away from George.

In the awkward silence, George felt the collective eyes upon them. The sound of Henri Ormond rapping the wooden cylinder to begin the proceedings brought some relief. It snapped eyes to the front as the day's business began.

One by one some of the issues came up for a vote. Dr. Alman's proposed clause declaring a woman's right to abortion didn't have enough votes for a discussion. Despite the fact that abortion had been protected by the Constitution for fifty-four years, only thirteen delegates voted to directly express it in the Second Constitution. No discussion, just a simple vote defeated the clause.

By an almost identical margin, a counter-proposal declaring that life begins at conception was defeated without further discussion. Introduced by Reverend Connors, it expressed the strong sentiment of the religious right. There would be no mention of abortion in the Second Constitution.

On the other hand, the proposal that would give states the right to replace the exclusionary rule, the rule created by the Supreme Court that threw out any evidence of a crime obtained by violation of a constitutional right, with civil penalties received forty-six votes. Law-abiding citizens never understood why evidence of a person's guilt should be thrown out because a suspect wasn't read their Miranda rights. The deterrent for constitutional violations would now come from monetary tort awards for violation of civil rights. It passed without further discussion.

Following next on the agenda was George's treason clause. Twenty-seven votes for, including President Adee's first vote. Fewer than he had expected, but enough for further discussion. Sebastian's return clearly hurt the odds.

He readied himself to give the opening remarks, expecting President Adee to give him the first and last opportunity to argue before any final vote. When she called for the debate on the treason clause, George raised his hand.

Several other delegates vied for recognition, but none more fervently than Sebastian. He sprang to life like a cat playing dead, waiting for his prey to get close enough. He hadn't raised his hand on any other provision. And George hadn't looked to see if he had raised his hand on the treason clause vote. It was payback, George surmised. The dagger Sebastian would thrust into his heart in return for having embarrassed him.

Before their blowup, George sensed a chance that Sebastian might support the clause, due to questions he'd asked that suggested he might be leaning in its favor. But clearly that was all lost. Whether out of spite or true conviction, Sebastian would do whatever he could to kill the clause if he got to speak first. George was certain of that and raised his hand higher and flagged more vigorously.

As the moments ticked by, George saw all hands withdraw, except his and Sebastian's. Apparently, no one wanted to interfere with what was shaping up to be an epic battle. It made him self-conscious. He repositioned his arm to half-mast, like he was taking an oath. Sebastian's elbow remained propped on the bench in front of him, his head periodically dipping down as if he was going to throw up.

President Adee's eyes fixed on George for a moment and then on Sebastian. Back and forth, back and forth, like she was watching a tennis match. It seemed like minutes passed to George. Her indecision, her hesitation gave birth to a sense of grief in his gut. Perhaps she wanted to defeat the treason clause? he worried, thinking back to her *Satan's wings* comment at the City Tavern. Maybe she just wanted to give Sebastian this opportunity for payback, the public forum where he could return his humiliation.

Perhaps she's right? he thought. Maybe he had been unfair and deserved Sebastian's retribution. As her gaze turned back to him, George slowly lowered his hand to his lap. He could not bring himself to force her to pick him based on friendship, loyalty, or shared values. The chamber stared at him with shocked faces, like a curtain had been opened to a bizarre but fascinating oddity that they all thirsted to see.

"Mr. Irving," President Adee called out. "You have twenty minutes," she directed with a rap of her gavel.

Sebastian sat back for a moment before pulling himself to his feet by tightly holding the bench in front of him. The wooden box groaned from the strain. When Sebastian sidestepped to the aisle, George noticed something very different in his demeanor.

He held the bench in front of him the entire time he shuffled along the pew. The crisp collar of his shirt hung around his neck like a loose yoke. There was room between the collar and his skin, something George never saw before. His skin was pale, almost green. To George it looked like he had lost fifty pounds in the few days since he last saw him. Like a man with an advanced disease. Is this what I did to him? George worried.

At the end of the pew, Sebastian released his grip on the bench and took an unsteady step onto the third landing. Instinctively, George grabbed his arm to steady him. Sebastian feebly pushed it aside and grabbed the railing on the right with both hands. George stepped backward, up one stair.

He watched with a lump in his heart as Sebastian carefully stepped down the three stairs, sideways, placing both feet on each step before taking on the next, tightly gripping the rail the entire time. The other delegates remained perfectly still, perfectly quiet. Only President Adee's direction to the sergeant at arms to "Get a chair" broke the silence.

Mr. Ormond quickly grabbed a chair and placed it in the center of the platform. The sound of the wooden legs contacting the hollow wooden platform resonated throughout the chamber, like tapping the body of an acoustic guitar. He then hurried to the edge of the stairs of the jury box to offer Sebastian his arm. This time, Sebastian took the assistance as Mr. Ormond practically pushed Sebastian up the small step to the platform.

Sebastian carefully squatted onto the wooden chair. He pulled a handkerchief from his right coat pocket and dabbed the beads of sweat on his face, catching his breath in preparation for what George knew would be a vicious personal attack.

"When you're ready," President Adee counseled, her tone clear that she did not mean to rush him. If he wanted sympathy, he achieved his purpose. If he wanted to focus all eyes on him so that the smallest whisper from his mouth would be heard as clearly as the ringing of the Centennial Bell, he had it. No one ventured a breath for fear of missing a syllable, an utterance.

"Madame President," Sebastian began in a failing voice. "Thank you for allowing me to be the first to speak on Mr. Comstock's proposed treason clause." George picked up the waver in his voice, as if Sebastian were having trouble speaking. It could be from anger, George thought. But it could just as easily be for effect, or the result of a startlingly sudden health issue that George could not explain without pinning a large portion of the blame on himself.

Rather than continuing, Sebastian looked deep into the eyes of the delegates and, at last, deep into George's eyes. It filled George with a sense of sadness, like he was looking at a dilapidated house that had once been filled with a lively family.

"It—" he started, and stopped several times before clearing his throat and forcing a grunt that brought blood back to his face. A very deep breath, and he tried once again.

"After my discussion with George the other day, I left this building angry. Perhaps more angry than I can remember being. I cursed you, George," he explained, looking at George, who saw trickles of moisture from the corner of Sebastian's left eye.

"I cursed you for the rest of that day and well into the afternoon of the next day. I cursed you until I realized that I didn't know why I was cursing you. You hurt me. You got under my skin, and no one has done that in sixty years." George didn't know where this argument was going. He suspected it was a setup. The precursor to some devastating insight that would make such common sense that everyone would have to vote against the treason clause.

"After all, I have the physical proof that I have a *thick* skin," he added, pointing to his belly. It drew a hearty laugh and vented the tension in the room. "So it was no small feat for you to get through it. But you did," he said, continuing to look at George.

"What I couldn't figure out, was how? What was it that bothered me so much? What exposed nerve did you hit? It was driving me crazy, and I couldn't return until I figured it out." He took a long pause as if he needed to gather his strength, his courage.

"When I realized what it was," he said, staring directly into George's eyes, "I didn't want to believe it." Sebastian seemed to be gaining strength. More peach than green filled his cheeks, his eyelids stayed up, his gestures were livelier. George sensed the final thrust.

"I was offended when you asked me what I believed. I tried to come up with an argument for the next time I saw you. I searched and searched for my beliefs. And I realized that the last thing I truly believed in was the thing that pushed me into this game, this racket, into politics."

The explanation of his father's demise at the hands of politicians showed a side of him that took George by total surprise, a human side. It was also a story that George heard time and time again. People drawn to public service for the right reasons, but succumbing to the seduction of the game.

"You asked me before—you apologized before, if you hurt me, my friend," he said to George with the softness of a mother singing her child to sleep. "You no more hurt me than a bottle of vodka hurts an alcoholic, a craps table hurts a gambler, an attractive woman hurts a cheating man. I hurt myself," he confessed, his body seeming to float up from the release of a great weight. "From the moment I strayed from what I believed in. Every day that I made the same excuses to myself as the politicians who screwed my father, I hurt myself."

George focused on the man, the purely human, flawed creature baring his soul in front of him. He forgot his treason clause, even the convention itself. Joy's sorrow bit at his throat, smothering him. He gasped for air through tiny gorges in his tightly clenched windpipe. Honesty was the most powerful persuader, he acknowledged, as he continued to listen.

"Once I realized that," Sebastian went on, "I spent the last three days reading it and re-reading it. *Naïve men with naïve intentions,*" he threw into the air, looking around with amazement. "Naïve men who knew something that I forgot, that I overlooked. That no matter how strong the protections, it is inevitable human nature that the strong, the powerful, the wealthy, and the greedy will constantly try to find ways to bend it to *their* will, for *their* gain, to line *their* pockets, and load *their* guns with ammunition. And then I realized," he said, barely able to get out the last words.

A long sigh that seemed to push the demons inside of him out across the oceans of the world followed. A release of tension, six decades of guilt and self-denial lifted off his shoulders. His face grew calm, placid, content. A rosy color returned to his cheeks, and in a moment he sprang to his feet. His eyes surveyed each pew in the jury boxes in front of him.

"I realized that *I* am the reason that we are here," the words, which came out softly, hit George with the force of a freight train, making the fine fibers inside the upper regions of his nostrils tingle and swell. Causing him to squeeze his nostrils together, to stop them from running. "I am the reason that we must pass the treason clause!" he exclaimed.

George could hardly believe what he heard. He listened with a sadness born of love as Sebastian outlined in detail how politicians sold out the people with as little concern as slave owners once had for the people they claimed to own.

"I came here with two things on my agenda. To stop the Second Constitution, if possible, and, at the least, to stop George's treason clause. To stop any chance that power could be taken away from my clients. The politicians who got large campaign contributions under *Citizens United,* local politicians who retired from politics to get high-paying jobs with the companies for whom they doled out sweetheart deals, even Supreme Court justices, grateful for their lifetime appointments and picked by politicians and special-interest groups based on how they would vote," he apologetically added, looking back at President Adee, who nodded in agreement. "The mental patients were running the asylum, the criminals were running the justice system, with no one to stop them, and we wanted that to continue."

On his feet, he paced around the platform, shifting his eyes from George to delegates throughout the chamber.

"If you truly want to stop the party, stop the game, and return this country to its citizens — to the ninety-nine percent, then I can with absolute certainty guarantee you that the only way to do that is to make politics as usual the highest crime against the people of the United States of America."

Amid the applause, George pulled out a handkerchief from the front pocket of his sport coat to catch the fluids dripping from his nose and eyes, blowing, and wiping, and applauding. Delegates left their pews and cradled Sebastian on the platform.

■ ■ ■

Over the three and a half weeks leading up to September 17, 2037, the date for the signing of the Second Constitution, the discussions took on a new quality. There were no private caucuses. Everyone met as a group, as a family, in Independence Hall and in the Bourse. Arthur Hanley no longer spewed anger. There were no opposing sides, only fifty women and men trying to do what was best for the United States' most precious commodity, its people.

The ceremony on September 17, 2037, seemed more like a graduation than a political ceremony. Fifty minds, fifty voices, fifty hands moved together like one. George pointed out in speeches and articles in the years to follow, that it took three years of bitter arguments for the First Constitution to be ratified. First by eleven states, then by all thirteen a year later, when it was clear that it would be ratified. He and Sebastian attended every legislative session in each of the fifty states to explain and argue for ratification. Many of the other delegates joined them, even those who would grow feeble with age and pass, such as President Adee.

It took just over two years for the ratification process to finish in 2039, unanimously ratified on the first vote in every state. Sebastian often reminded George that it was quickly and unanimously ratified simply because the people would have ripped politicians from office had they ignored their will.

The Second Constitution took effect on January 1, 2040. Under its terms there would be a Third Constitutional Convention in 2287 and every 250 years thereafter. On January 14, 2040, Sebastian Irving died. His husband asked George to deliver the eulogy at his funeral.

Temple Emanu-El on the upper east side of Manhattan could seat twenty-five hundred people. At least another five hundred stood to hear George's speech. The highest politicians in the land, all of the living re-framers, even George's law students who had helped him prepare for the convention came. Remembering back to President Adee's admonition not to be like Dante's Satan, he chose another portion from the *Inferno* to capture Sebastian's essence.

"Past the gate but before the river Acheron, it held those who could neither enter purgatory nor heaven. They were the *Trimmers* in life. Those people who were neither hot nor cold, who took no positions, who never tried to help anyone other than themselves, who spent their lives shielding themselves from perceived dangers. They were not good enough for heaven or purgatory. They were not even good enough for deep hell. Their epitaph, to paraphrase Dante, would for always be, *The world will never record their having been there.*" He had to pause for a full thirty seconds to keep his throat from closing and his posture from falling into a slumping, sobbing mess.

"Sebastian Irving's courage as a reframer, willing to admit and face his own shortcomings, to profess them to the world for the greater good, is by far the most difficult and bravest thing that I have ever witnessed. We as a people, as a nation, and as a beacon for the world, will be forever in his debt. I can assure you, I can assure you my old friend," he said, placing his hand on Sebastian's casket, "the world will forever record your having been here. And will forever benefit from your life."

Looking out over the mass of people crammed into the cavernous temple, he saw countless mourners wiping their eyes. After the ceremony, Sebastian's husband presented him with two bound journals that Sebastian kept daily during the Second Constitutional Convention. George was honored by the task of safeguarding Sebastian's inner thoughts for future generations. He would decide how and when to make them available to the public.

George mulled around, chatting for several hours. All complimented him on how well his speech captured the spirit, the heroism of what Sebastian had done. One of his favorite old law students, Bill Waverly, came to talk with him. Bill seemed so excited to tell George that he had just landed a job with a prominent firm in Chicago, handling matters for some of the biggest companies in the world. George listened intently, a little surprised that Bill didn't mention Sebastian's passing. As if the funeral were a networking opportunity, a high school class reunion where successful geeks could brag about their success to the car mechanic jocks.

"You did a great job at the ACLU," George praised. But Bill's reaction dismayed him. He stepped back and crossed his arms like he was being attacked. He wouldn't look George in the eye.

"Well, everyone has to grow up sometime," Bill responded apologetically. George let the comment drop. He preferred to let his students grow up on their own and in their own time.

CHAPTER 19

Washington, DC, November 12, 2059

Time reversed in Bill's mind as he sat alone in the witness room, guarded by the court officer. Lunch ended at 2:00 p.m. — the trial should have resumed, he calculated. Now it was 3:00 p.m., and still no one in the hallway. It felt like he had fallen down a hole to the center of the earth and was now climbing to the surface on the other side. Instead of hoping that someone would come for him quickly, he now hoped that no one would come before the end of the court day at 5:00 p.m.

Clearly, Beth had waived the privilege and was most likely blaming him, or setting up a story that she would insist he parrot. *How stupid!* The internal words bounced off the walls of his mind.

If he could just make it until 5:00 p.m. He'd have the night to discuss it with her and Paul. He couldn't testify, he knew that. But he knew that she would make him. Maybe Paul could come up with some way to avoid his testimony? To make the best out of silence. Nothing would hurt her case more than if he testified.

He again took to pacing to look through the square window; the green walls and soft lighting weren't helping a bit. He checked the clock on his celltop every few minutes. He'd never seen molasses run, but it couldn't be as tedious as waiting for the minute display to change just one digit.

In his head he started repeating the Gettysburg Address as slowly as possible, trying to time it to five minutes. Repeating the words extra slowly in the hope that more than five minutes would elapse by the time he next looked at the clock. Four minutes, dammit! he cried after his first recitation of the speech. The game took away stress, emotions, thoughts that didn't suit him. It shifted his focus from crazy imaginings of what was happening in court to the speech he had memorized as a kid.

Halfway through his third recitation, he heard the officer outside the room speaking in a low voice. No one had come down the hallway. He must be talking on a celltop or earpiece, he guessed. He gasped as the door opened, hoping to hear the officer say that they were adjourned until tomorrow. It was a different officer. Maybe they switched at lunchtime and he just didn't see it.

"Mr. Gordon will be here in a moment to speak with you, sir. I thought you would like to know," the officer said.

An instinctive "thank you" was the best Bill could muster. He drew several long, deep breaths through his nostrils and exhaled fully through his mouth, trying to sync his blood with the calm green décor. With a wad of tissues, he dabbed the perspiration forming on his forehead and around his nose while his heart pounded against his eardrums, like it wanted to get out.

The door opened and Paul took a step in, still holding the door. "I don't want to be disturbed by anyone, even the president," he instructed the officer.

Bill tried to stand but his legs didn't cooperate. Instead, he gestured for Paul to sit on the couch. Paul remained standing.

"What's going on? What did she say?" Bill managed to ask, his voice a little louder than appropriate for the small room. The volume scared him. He pushed back against the couch cushion and started another round of deep inhales and exhales.

"You know I can't discuss her testimony," Paul cautioned. "And you must know that anything you and I talk about here is not covered by attorney-client privilege. You understand that, don't you?"

"Of course, I know how this works," he answered, his inflection undulating in pitch while slowing in delivery—like a secret code between two members of an exclusive club, two co-conspirators. He looked for Paul's reaction and saw only stern eyes, the same eyes he remembered when his father would berate him because of a B+ or an A–. He sensed disappointment, not in his words but in his character. It made him panic. If Paul couldn't tell him what she said, how would he know what to say? He was blindfolded.

"The truth," Paul rattled, as if he could read Bill's mind. "You'll have to stick to the truth."

The truth? Bill pondered as if he had seen an apparition. A ghost that was feared and whispered about in dark places, but never seen. At least not by him.

Bill struggled to compose his thoughts. To come up with a plan. His assumption that he and Paul were thinking of the same strategy was showing stress fractures. Why wouldn't Paul tell him what she said? How could Paul's silence benefit Beth?

"Well then, can't you at least tell me what *you expect* me to say on the stand?"

"I can't tell you how to testify. I'm not going to put words in your mouth," he said, then paused. "We only have a few minutes. I need you to tell me straight up. If I put you on the stand, will the truth hurt the case?" No shade of gray in the question or in Paul's eyes, Bill thought, as he looked up at him from the couch.

"Truth is often a matter of interpretation," Bill responded, more to himself than to Paul.

"No it's not," Paul shot back. "Cut the bullshit. If you tell the jury about what you discussed with the president, will it help or will it hurt her? Clear and simple."

Clear and simple, clear and simple, the words tumbled around in Bill's mind, searching for a familiar experience to latch on to. Was anything clear and simple? Had anything been clear and simple in his mind since law school? Since he gave up the good fight at the ACLU? Since he stopped being a lawyer and started being a political broker? Paul's look of impatience went unsatisfied as he considered an answer.

A sudden, unexplained calmness overcame him. His shoulders relaxed, his breathing became easy. *Clear and simple, clear and simple.* How long had it been since he had a clear and simple thought, a clear and simple answer? An effortless smile formed on his bloated face. He looked up at Paul as if he were looking at an old friend, then paused, and finally answered.

"If I testify truthfully — she will get the death penalty."

Paul took a step back. Maybe it was a little too *clear and simple* for him, Bill thought. "She's not gonna like that," said Paul, and Bill laughed, knowing how true that was. "But it's clear we can't put you on the stand. You might as well come back with me while — while I explain it to her. Then we'll rest."

He walked with Paul to the courtroom, where the president sat waiting. A court officer and the reporting technician remained in the room, but Keri and the judge were absent.

"Can we have a minute?" Paul requested, looking at the officer. "We should be good to go in about ten minutes."

"I'll notify the judge and Ms. Marshall. But Mr. Waverly will have to wait outside. No contact with the defendant," the officer responded. Bill left the courtroom but loitered just outside, looking through the long vertical window in the door. He watched as both the officer and reporter exited the door to the left of the judge's bench.

Bill studied Beth's reaction. Just what he thought. Her face turned that American Beauty rose-red he was used to seeing anytime she didn't get her way. Paul was holding her back from running into the hall to attack him. It was the first time anyone had stood between him and Beth's wrath. He allowed himself to enjoy it for a moment, even though he knew that if he didn't back up her lies, her fate might be sealed and his along with it. She would never understand. He simply could not testify.

The court officer returned to the courtroom, forcing Paul and Beth to end their discussion. Paul leaned over her and whispered something. It had its effect. She seemed to calm down. To switch back to Dr. Jekyll as Paul signaled Bill to come in.

Judge Kneuaya flipped on the jury screens and turned toward Paul. "Mr. Gordon, please call your next witness."

Paul rose from his seat and turned to the camera. His head perked up as he looked to Keri and then back to the camera. "At this time, Your Honor, the defense is quite willing, ready, and desirous to rest so that the jury may do its duty and let the president get back to work." There was a slight air of indignation in Paul's tone superimposed on his thicker pretense of confidence, a tonal way of conveying to the jury, *I think their case sucks.*

Bill marveled at the gesture. But he wasn't sure that the jury held it in such high esteem. Their faces uniformly showed signs of surprise. Double takes, looking around as if the next witness might be in their jury booth.

It was still worth it, Bill considered, as he watched Keri stumble for a response. She tapped aimlessly on her celltop without looking at it. Her eyes squinted and she peered over at him — then Paul, then Beth. Like a card player reading the other players' faces. Bill sat erect, trying to portray an image of confidence and certainty. Puffing himself up like a tom turkey ruffling his feathers to appear larger. Like this had been their plan all along. Could the great Keri Marshall not know what to do? The thought made his head rise higher and his chest puff further.

"Any rebuttal, Ms. Marshall?" Judge Kneuaya asked. Bill didn't expect any. Keri had done a thorough job during cross-examination. She already called enough witnesses on direct to show that Beth kept her change of position solely to herself.

Keri stood, but hesitated. She looked at the judge, again at the president, at Bill, then at the twenty-three faces on-screen. But she didn't speak.

"You don't need to call witnesses today, Ms. Marshall, but I need to know if you plan on calling rebuttal witnesses," the judge offered. Keri continued to tap her celltop, even while standing. A brief look down, three definitive taps of the celltop, and she spoke.

"At this time —" Keri paused. "The prosecution calls William Waverly."

For a moment Bill thought he would wet himself. His groin went cold. All of the muscles in his extremities, his arms, his legs, seemed to lose strength. His head felt bloodless and his breath stopped. The only organ working seemed to be his heart, which pumped so fast and hard that it drowned out his thoughts. He couldn't decide whether to stand, to object, to run. He sat. Waiting, hoping for blood to make its way back to his brain along with his wits.

"Objection," Paul calmly uttered, taking his time to rise. Bill welcomed the seconds to allow more blood to circulate.

"Since Ms. Marshall has never been privy to conversations between Mr. Waverly and the president, she would have no basis to call him as a rebuttal witness. She has no knowledge as to whether his testimony would contradict the president's testimony. She wants to conduct a fishing expedition.

A witch hunt. To try to smear the president's testimony through clever cross-examination."

He was right, Bill thought. *Brilliant!* He never would've thought of that argument and here Paul pulled it out of his bag of tricks, so obvious that a child would have thought the same. The pounding of his heart reduced to a hum. Warmth flowed back into his groin, strength resurrected in his extremities.

Bill saw the jurors switching focus to Keri, but she didn't have a chance to speak.

"You can't have it both ways, counselor," Judge Kneuaya answered. "You can't wait until your client testifies to privileged conversations and then not expect to have her attorney testify to the same conversations. Overruled." The jurors' faces switched to the left and Bill knew they were staring right at him.

It all looked so different sitting in the witness box, Bill thought, trying to relax each muscle from his feet up. Trying not to look nervous. But everything took on a new meaning. The judge was no longer someone to convince. Keri was like a tennis player who would lob questions and he would try to lob back. He didn't even see Paul or Beth. His eyes were so focused on Keri and the jurors' faces, which seemed so much larger, that the rest of the room faded into a Gaussian blur. The twenty-three faces staring down at him from the screens were unbearable.

"Good afternoon, Mr. Waverly," Keri offered in a surprisingly friendly voice as soon as Bill was sworn in.

"Good afternoon, Ms. Marshall," he responded.

She started slow, taking him through his educational background, with emphasis on his connection to George Comstock. His research into the death penalty and his time at the ACLU. As he described each stage of his life to the jury, vivid images filled his mind. As if the witness stand was a portal transporting him back in time. A top student, constitutional scholar, champion of the weak and adviser to the powerful. Within fifteen minutes he felt like a new man, his old self.

"Did there come a time prior to the 2056 election that Senator Suarez told you that she had changed her stance on SAFTA?" Such a simple question, he thought. No terms or words or even inferences that added anything other than the main point. How could he answer no? Beth told them she did. He searched his mind for ways around it. Not to be argumentative, not to pretend that the question was confusing. That wouldn't work. He just wanted something other than *yes* or *no* that might make Keri worry that this wasn't going to go the way she wanted. He drew a blank.

"Yes."

"Do you remember the conversation?"

"Somewhat. Portions of it certainly."

"Do you remember your advice to her?"

"Generally," he hedged, even though it made him look cagey.

"And you told her *'absolutely it would not'* be treason?" she asked, reading Beth's exact words from her celltop.

He paused, hoping for an objection that didn't come. "Ethically, I don't believe I can divulge advice I may have given to a client." It sounded indignant, even to him. Most jurors pulled back one side of their mouth and dropped an eyebrow. The uniform expression for *bullshit,* he thought.

"The defendant has waived any privilege, Mr. Waverly. You are directed to answer the question. Do you need it read back?" Judge Kneuaya asked.

"No, Your Honor," he responded, but continued to pause, thinking of the least dangerous answer. "I told her that it *may not* be treason." He was cautiously pleased with his answer.

"*May not be* treason," Keri repeated without a question. She strolled around the small area in front of her counsel table, deep in thought. Bill envisioned the tough questions in his immediate future.

"By *may not,* do you mean it *could not* be treason, or do you mean it *could or could not* be treason?"

"I meant it *may not* be treason."

"So you said. But I think this jury has a right, a need, to know what you meant by that," she stated, pointing to the screens. It drew Bill's eyes to the screens, the larger-than-life images of the jurors looking at him for answers.

"Objection, counsel is making a statement for the jury, not a question for the witness," Paul interjected.

"Sustained."

"Okay. Then perhaps there is something you can tell this jury. Did you advise her that it *could be* treason?"

He answered quickly. "Certainly under specific circumstances it *could be* treason. Any lawyer would have told her that."

"Did you tell her that it *could be* treason if she spoke in support of SAFTA after she secretly changed her position?"

"Yes, of course."

"That it *would be* treason if she spoke in support of it after she changed her position?"

He didn't like the question. Changing *could* to *would* made it sound like he thought she was guilty.

"I don't remember using the word *would* in our conversations."

"Fair enough, Mr. Waverly," Keri conceded. "Did you tell her that it *could be* treason to not let anyone know that she changed her position? To not tell the voters, the media? To not put out a public statement that she was withdrawing her support?"

Damn, Bill thought. Too precise. "I'm sure you would agree, Ms. Marshall, that a jury *could do* anything. Anything is possible."

"I see," exhaled Keri; it sounded more like resignation than desperation. She stepped back behind the prosecution table, arranged her celltop in front of her, pressed her outstretched fingertips against the top of the table, and squared her shoulders toward Bill. Her posture made him feel uncomfortable.

"Let's do it this way," she resumed. "You were Senator Suarez's attorney when she decided to run for president, correct?"

"Yes."

"As her attorney, it was your job to advise her on the legality of her actions, decisions, and statements, isn't that true?"

"As a rule, yes."

"It was your job to keep her out of trouble, right?"

"I'm not sure I would put it that way," Bill answered. Her questions were coming too fast. He had to try something to slow her down.

"If you thought she might commit treason, it would be your job to tell her."

"Of course."

"And you told her, did you not, that there was a possibility that she could be found guilty of treason if she did not tell anyone that she no longer supported SAFTA? Yes or no?"

"I don't recall using those words."

"Whether or not you used those *exact words,* it's what you told her. Yes or no?"

"Yes. A possibility. There's always a possibility," he answered, trying to keep it within the bounds of possibility, not probability.

"And you told her that it *would be* treason if she ever said she supported it after she changed her mind?"

"Of course," he responded, without thinking. Suddenly, as if out of nowhere, Beth's contorted face, beside Paul, emerged from the background blur: her flared nostrils, gritted teeth, tight-lipped, squinted eyes Mr. Hyde face staring at him. Like he was a bull's-eye and she was a missile. It looked comical next to Keri's no-nonsense, matter-of-fact, I got you face. He knew which one to fear.

"And of course you asked her why she changed her position?" Keri slipped in as innocently as a baby's smile.

He was paralyzed. How could he answer? What could he say? Nothing he said so far was a lie. Maybe not the whole truth, but no lies. This would require either a lie or the death penalty. He rolled it around in his head. *A lie or the death penalty.* The jury, the people, could never forgive her if he spoke the truth. They would demand death.

"Mr. Waverly?" Keri nudged.

"Just tell them the truth!" Beth shouted. "Tell them how we discussed that it would hurt the people," she commanded, small white globs of foam forming on her lip. It wasn't the truth she wanted him to tell. She wanted him to tell them the truth according to Beth, the truth that she had invented.

Lying under oath meant nothing to her. She thought of herself as above a simple oath. Bill always knew that about her. What she didn't know about him, he realized with horror, was that it did mean something to him. It was a tenet that allowed him to keep his parallel worlds intact. That allowed him to stay in his ACLU–Comstock world, the world that made him feel significant.

The courtroom was bustling. Paul was standing, his mouth was moving, but Bill couldn't make out the words. They were muffled, as if his ears were filled with water. He saw Keri speak, then the judge speak. The sounds grew louder, but he couldn't make out the words. It scared him. He felt like he was dying, waiting for a bright light, waiting for it to be over.

"Mr. Waverly?" Keri's voice came into focus. They were waiting for his answer. He was waiting to die. Could he say that? Could he say that she told him how it would hurt the people? He saw his kids' faces as he said it to them in his mind. They looked at him with disgust. He wanted to hide his face, to throw up as if that would make the feeling go away. His kids' faces turned into his father's face. A stern, overbearing face whose lips formed the words *I told you so.* A lump pushed up his throat, making him gag. He had to fight to keep from vomiting.

"Mr. Waverly, we need your answer!" his father barked. He realized the voice belonged to Judge Kneuaya.

"Yes, I asked her why she changed her position," he said in tight, small words, anticipating the next question.

"And what did she say?"

Keri's calmness made the lump in this throat travel up toward his mouth. He tasted it. An oily, putrid taste. Why couldn't he be like her, or Paul, or Judge Kneuaya? Why did he have to be like Beth, that small rodent sitting next to Paul? If he lied for a rodent, he would become a rodent. He would wake up a cockroach. He would be a cockroach for the rest of his life. His children and grandchildren would have cockroach genes, rodent traits. He wanted to cry for them.

"With all due respect, Your Honor, I cannot betray a client's confidence. I'm sorry." His head hung down on the last word, Bill praying for it to be over. A small stroke or heart attack would be fine.

"If you do not answer the question," Judge Kneuaya countered, his anger barely under his breath, "the witness room you waited in today will seem like the Taj Mahal compared to where you'll spend the rest of your life. This court, these jurors, have devoted months to this trial. This nation has been made to wait on the outcome of this case. I'm not about to let you put your self-proclaimed sense of duty above them. Your client has waived the privilege — answer the question."

"Tell them!" Beth shouted.

"Remove her," the judge ordered.

She stood as the court officer came behind her, Mr. Hyde eyes glaring at him the entire time. Bill couldn't answer. He hesitated, weighing a lifetime in jail against an answer that would destroy her, destroy his worlds, expose him. Beth shot him a one-eyed stare as the officer turned her to leave the courtroom, a boxer's unbroken stare of intimidation. It made him angry, protective of his worlds, his children, and he spoke.

"She told me that it would be a disaster for Global Mundo. For her husband's company."

Everyone froze. Time froze.

"You liar!" Beth screeched as the court officer pushed her the final steps outside of the courtroom.

Bill went limp. Every ounce of his strength was exhausted. He felt neither hot nor cold, neither happy nor sad, neither safe nor scared. Just numb. It felt like an hour before Keri continued.

"One last question." She spoke slowly, softly.

"When Ms. Suarez said she vetoed SAFTA because she believed it was in the best interests of the country — at the veto ceremony where you were present — that wasn't true, was it?"

"No," he answered softly, dropping his gaze into his lap.

"And she knew it was false when she said that, isn't that true?"

"Yes," he exhaled, as if the weight of a thousand chains had just been lifted from him.

There were no further questions from Keri. The judge released Bill from the witness stand, but he couldn't move. He sat there as court was adjourned until tomorrow for summations. He sat in the witness chair as Paul, and Keri, and the spectators scrambled out of the courtroom, feeling that his mind was as empty as his soul.

CHAPTER 20

Washington, DC, November 15, 2059

Bill stuffed his scarf deeper into the opening of his collar as he walked two long blocks from the 7th Street Convention Center Metro Station to Mount Vernon Square in Northwest Washington, DC. It rained unmercifully over the three days since his testimony. A depressing rain. A cleansing rain, but not for him. Nothing could wash away the guilt he carried, a feeling of betrayal pummeled home by Beth's conviction yesterday.

An early polar vortex moved in overnight, freezing the rain-soaked sidewalks. Ice crushed under his boots as he walked on the 9th Street side of the small park next to the Carnegie Library. The sound amazed him. He had grown so used to walking on well-shoveled paths, being driven from door to door, his feet never touching the types of ground that ordinary people had to walk. The crumbling ice sounded silly, laughable. Why was there ice on the sidewalk, where people had to walk? Ice was for glasses, to keep his drink cold, he laughed, recognizing how removed his thinking had become.

But the joke didn't ease his dread over the early Saturday-morning meeting. George had asked to meet at 6:00 a.m. An odd location, an obscure park—very secretive, Bill thought. Not like George. Bill considered himself cold-blooded. The judgments of others couldn't pierce him, at least not since his father passed away twenty years ago. Only with his father did he prepare for a fight. To argue against expressions of unyielding disappointment. With anyone else, he could quarantine emotions, but not with his father — and not with George. Nor did he want to. Whatever criticism, whatever judgment George had for him, he felt it was deserved.

The emptiness of the park brought some relief. Since his testimony he'd become a celebrity. People came up to him everywhere he went, as if they were a relative or colleague. Most called him a hero, even Democrats. But he didn't feel like a hero. He felt like a serial killer who had breached every standard of society. At least his own standards.

His celltop vibrated so often that he had to charge it every day since his testimony, instead of every month. Most were faces he didn't know, or famous people whom he had never spoken with. Politicians, celebrities, and especially news personalities. He threw them all to his message center, even ones that could further his career or find him a new one now that he had testified himself out of a job.

The two calls that he had instantly accepted were from his sons.

"Wow, Dad, I didn't think you had it in you," he remembered Justin, his oldest, saying, as if there had been no silence between them. "You single-handedly brought that bitch down. Good going."

Justin's approving voice warmed like a strong poultice on an open infection. Bill told each of them about his urge to call them when he was sequestered. How he wanted them to know that his thoughts were of them before he faced the end of his career.

"The end of what?" Justin shrieked. "You're a hero. You could run for president. That's what everybody's saying. I'm so proud of you. I'm proud to be your son."

Bill had to choke back a lump that prevented words from leaving his throat. How could he explain? How could he take the only time his son expressed pride, a desire to be known as his son, and explain that he had betrayed everything that was important to him? His obligation to protect his client, to keep her secrets, his hatred of the death penalty? Visions of him loading syringes and handing them to Beth's executioner plagued him. All of his passion to fight the death penalty returned, met by the horror that he could be responsible for its application.

Bill watched George walk towards him on the ice-crusted path uncertain of whether to expect praise or condemnation. When he stood

George wrapped his arms around him and patted his back like he was burping a baby.

"I know how tough that was," George offered, squatting to sit on the bench. Bill now understood George's reluctance to take credit for the treason clause. Credit which he always passed to Sebastian Irving. It gave them a strange bond. A pain, a guilt that united them in a desire to fulfill a duty, to honor the sacrifices of others, to finish what they started.

"I spoke with Paul, and eventually Beth. I'm going to do the sentencing summation on Tuesday and I want you to help me," George explained.

The chill seemed to leave the air with the idea that he might have the slightest possibility to make this right. To turn his wrong into a right, by at least helping to save Beth's life. "What" — he paused to allow the back of his tongue to collect moisture — "did they say?"

"They agreed. They think it would be a huge help. Especially if you sit next to me at the counsel table. Between me and Beth." An image of Beth attacking him in front of the jury, trying to grab his throat, cut his jugular, seemed so real that his hand instinctively rose to protect the right side of his neck. He laughed, and George laughed along, their cloudy breaths projecting in front of them like two smokers.

"I don't deserve the chance," Bill answered, pulling his overcoat tighter. "What do you think her chances are?"

"Of not dying?" George replied with surprise. "Better than yours, I'm afraid."

Bill's body grew as cold as the bitter frost around him. As if there were no difference between the core of his body and the cold world he sat in, the way the horizon can fuse with the ocean on a misty twilight. No separation, no identity. He looked at George but couldn't speak.

"The blue folio?" George answered the blank stare. "I told you we'd talk about it at some point." Visions of unknown handlers stalking him ran through Bill's mind.

"I'm sorry about that," Bill answered, dipping his head.

"About what?"

"About having them pressure you to argue the motion to dismiss." George looked at him with a blank stare that Bill didn't understand.

"The only one who pressured me to argue that motion was you," George added with squinted eyes.

"*He* said they would find a way to make you do it," muttered Bill absently. His facial muscles relaxed, bringing a calmness to his face—relief that none of the horrors he imagined had taken place.

"Nope. No one contacted me, nothing," George declared, adding, "but that makes sense."

The logic escaped Bill. "Why is that?"

"Beth's execution would be their best chance of getting rid of the Second Constitution," George explained, his voice so determined that the pumps of his breath reached almost across the path in front of their bench. "Why do you think I agreed to help her? The Second Constitution will always be at risk from their kind."

Bill had never thought of that possibility. Aurelius was there for him. To help him use her. To give him whatever he needed to control her for their benefit, and his gain. His pulse quickened as he grasped how he had been played all along.

"Who exactly are they?" George asked. "This blue folio group?"

"*Syndicated America?* I thought you knew," Bill answered. "You seemed to know about the blue folio."

"No big secret there," George replied. "During the convention, Sebastian handed me his counter-proposal for the treason clause in a blue folder. Not a typical blue, a cobalt, metallic blue. I had never seen a folder of that color before. Clearly it was custom-made. When we were making the ratification rounds, he told me a little bit about it, and the journals he kept during the Convention explained most of it."

"This goes back to the convention?" Bill interjected.

"Of course! It was Sebastian's idea. He sketched out the framework for it before coming to the convention, in case he couldn't stop us. Powerful industry heads setting up a rump government, a secret government, out of official power, but who would control the economy directly. No more buying out politicians. They were too unpredictable, Sebastian told his clients."

Bill's teeth ached from the cold before he realized that his mouth hung wide open. He snapped it shut, with an audible pop. "Then why would they want to go back to the old way?" he asked.

"Probably didn't work out as well as they hoped," speculated George. "Every time they tried to manipulate a market, the attorney general shut them down. Keri started it with the auto industry. Without politicians relying on their money, there was no one to stop the AG from keeping them honest. Just look at the lower cost of road projects ever since the Second Constitution. Without friendly politicians, they can't jack up the prices and compete for government contracts."

"And if they take away the treason clause, they could roll back the clock?" Bill whispered, connecting a few dots in his head.

"That, the independent Justice Branch, and a few other reforms," George added. "I'm sure they drooled over your testimony, but not over you using the blue folio to intimidate Mr. Carroll. And not over hiring me."

Wheels turned quickly in Bill's head, but they didn't seem to match up. Slowly he saw how they'd manipulated him. At first, he got angry. Then the anger turned inward. *How could I be so stupid?* he admonished himself.

"You're a risk to them now. You've exposed them, even if just a little. They won't hesitate to get rid of you," George explained, patting Bill's leg for comfort.

Without his Secret Service protection and Aurelius to protect him, Bill felt exposed, naked, returned to a primal state of survival. The thought of Aurelius putting a bullet in the back of his head brought a strange comfort. A release from the guilt, the shame he couldn't quarantine.

"The only thing protecting you right now is your popularity," said George. "Enhance it! Stay in the spotlight. Make it dangerous for them to do anything to you."

It's the last thing that Bill wanted to do. He wanted to crawl in a hole and hope everyone forgot about him. But now that seemed impossible. If they couldn't get to him, they might go after his family. The thought ignited a wave of panic.

"See that young woman over there?" George asked, pointing his head twenty degrees to the right. "The tall one, dressed a little too fancy for an early Saturday morning in this weather."

Bill casually moved his head to the right by wrapping his right arm around the back of the bench. "She does look out of place," Bill agreed, his mind still occupied with his sons. He looked more intently; her facial features pinged a bell. Dark hair tied back, framing a flawless face, perfect complexion, serious eyes, ruby lips, too red for this time of morning.

"Oh my God," he blurted. "I know her."

Ignoring Bill's excitement, George casually asked, "I'm pretty sure she's been following me since Halloween. Not sure who she's with. Any ideas?"

"Yeah. She's a handler. She's with Syndicated America," Bill responded, ice filling his veins. "Her name is Clodia. I worked with her for a while."

"Hmm," George ruminated. "I thought she might be from Julius Stevens' office, spying to see if you guys hired me."

Clodia's presence made Bill paranoid. If they were following George, they could be following him as well. He hadn't heard from Aurelius since he asked him to pressure George. He worried that perhaps his exposing *them* by using the blue folio with Aiden Carroll wasn't forgotten. Perhaps it was more serious than Aurelius let on.

"Why would she be following you?" Bill asked.

"Probably a little intimidation. To make me think twice about getting involved," said George. "It's not the first time. They show up whenever I'm involved in anything that would cut into their industries. I never knew exactly who they were with, before now."

"They can be dangerous," Bill cautioned.

George didn't seem alarmed. "Not when they show themselves. If they wanted to kill me, I'd never see them."

Instinctively, Bill's eyes darted to every window, doorway, and alley across the street. He hadn't *seen* Aurelius in three weeks. That didn't mean he wasn't around, just that he wasn't showing himself to Bill. He could be stalking his prey, waiting for a perfect shot, Bill envisioned, his heart pounding.

George shot to his feet and started waving to Clodia as Bill watched in horror. "What are you doing?" Bill pleaded, trying to get George to sit.

"Just trying to be friendly," George joked. His side-to-side wave switched to an exaggerated beckoning motion, inviting Clodia to join them. "Look, now I've intimidated her," George laughed, as Bill watched her duck into an angled shadow in a small alleyway. Bill didn't find it funny.

Without warning, George walked across the frost-tipped grass in the direction of the alleyway. "What the hell are you doing?" Bill shouted, his voice cracking with fear.

"Come on," George urged as he walked faster. "We can't put up with this! Let's confront her."

Paralyzed, Bill stayed seated, frozen in fear. His voice disappeared, and standing — let alone walking — was impossible. He watched George make a beeline across the street and, without hesitation, jut into the same shadow that had swallowed Clodia. Certain that he would never emerge, Bill struggled against his paralysis. He wanted to run to George's aid, but could not. He wanted to run away, but could not. It left him suspended, helpless, frozen on the bench.

They're killers, Bill argued with himself, remembering how coldly Aurelius had offered to make the Aiden Carroll problem disappear. George must be dead, he deduced, his head jerking in all directions, looking for danger.

"Quadruple *U*." A strange voice snapped his head to the left. A tall man, his light complexion turned red from the cold or alcoholism and his face shrouded in stubble, walked toward him on the path. No stagger, Bill noted, closely watching the man's hands, which held a blanket wrapped around him.

"William Waverly, *WW*," the man added, getting closer to Bill. "*Double U* and *double U* equals *quadruple U*," he calculated out loud, stopping less than a meter from the bench. Bill's eyes stayed glued to the man's hands as he struggled to assess the threat. It could be some homeless man or a clever disguise for an assassin. He couldn't tell which and he couldn't take the chance of guessing wrong.

The paralysis gripping his legs released, as if shackles had been broken. He shot to his feet and began to move. The steps felt slow, labored, as he walked on the path, past the blanketed man and back toward the train station. Away from the man, away from the alley, away from George. He had no control of the direction, as if he were being pulled by an unseen force.

His steps quickened beyond a crawl, his head in constant motion glancing side to side, and his body occasionally turning 360 degrees to look for danger. He slipped behind the library, blocking his view of the horrors he was sure he would see if he looked into the alley where George had disappeared.

Breath seemed as dear as platinum as he panted from the strain of walking against fear. Hoarse breaths of cold air rasped in his ears to a background of blood pounding against his eardrums. By the end of the first full block he thought he could hear footsteps, someone running behind him. Pictures of Lee Harvey Oswald and Arnold Talbot being shot flooded his imagination.

One block from the train station and he broke into a jog. He had no energy to turn around. He couldn't divert his attention. Every ounce of focus was needed to make it just one more block so that he could slip into the subway station. I'm just being paranoid, he thought, as he continued to jog away from the sensation of someone running behind him, anticipating something horrible and grotesque to jump out and devour him at any moment.

"Wait up," a voice called from behind. He jogged faster, expecting to feel a sting that would drop him to the ground. Let it be quick, he prayed, striving against a lifetime of inactivity, refusing to give up the instinct to survive, no matter how futile.

The tap was lighter than he expected. On his shoulder, not on the back of his head. "Hold up," the voice repeated, and his legs gave in, coming to a wobbly stop. Running was useless. Time to pay the price, he thought, turning.

George was panting as loudly as Bill as the two stood in the middle of the sidewalk, barely able to move. He must have run full on from the alleyway, Bill surmised.

"You're out of your mind!" Bill squealed, trying to catch his breath. "I told you, they're killers. Dead stone-cold killers. Do you have a death wish?"

George's breath wasn't getting calmer, Bill noticed, worried that it might be a heart attack or worse. "Where did she get you?" he shouted, tearing off his gloves and frisking George's neck, searching for a barb or needle. "Did she stick you?"

"Stop that," George ordered, pushing Bill's hand away. Still gasping air, George stumbled toward a convex glass shelter. He sat on the empty bench, arched his back, and drew several long, steady breaths. Bill stood over him, looking down, silent and scared.

"They're not gonna kill me," George pushed out through calmer, more shallow breaths. "Not if they ever want to undo the Constitution. It would make me a martyr."

"It's not worth the risk," Bill pleaded, momentarily forgetting about his own fears. George turned and studied Bill's face for a moment before speaking. His face wore an expression of disappointment, a face Bill was used to seeing on his father. "Of course it's worth the risk," George responded in a low, downward tone, his head shaking. "What could be more worth the risk? There was a time you understood that, Bill."

The accusation hit Bill where it hurt. A recognition that his worlds had collided, his secret revealed. He knew he was a coward, and now George knew it.

"Isn't there anything you would take the risk for?" asked George, his breathing returning to normal.

Bill searched for an answer. "My kids. I would take any risk for my kids!" he yelled, looking away.

"What about their freedom? Would you take the risk to preserve their freedoms? Would you take the risk to guarantee your grandkids' freedoms?" George pushed in the same manner as Bill remembered from law school. Always another question, always another point.

"Of course!" Bill yelled, angry at the implication.

"It's not enough to just say it, Bill," George prodded. "You have to do it."

Do what? Bill asked himself, looking down the empty street, away from George. Dawn peaked and the sun was crawling over the horizon. Ice melted along the line of sun as it reached the sidewalk. It didn't warm him, though. He had no answer for George. Only a desire to change the subject, make small talk, then disappear back into his apartment. He looked at George, whose eyes were fixed, staring at Bill.

"You have to tell me everything about Syndicated America," George commanded.

"I have to go," Bill answered in a low voice, standing and ambling toward the Metro. There was no answer he could give. At least not a good one.

"You'll be there on Tuesday?" George asked.

"Yes," Bill answered without slowing or looking back.

CHAPTER 21

Washington, DC, November 18, 2059

Bill sat in the courtroom between George and Beth, not trying to hide his emotions. Deep furrowed lines across his forehead, eyebrows crunched where they met the outline of his upper nose. If the outward signs of fear and sadness could help the jury understand the gravity of their decision, he had no desire to hide them, even if he feared his own fate more than Beth's.

"Mr. Comstock," Judge Kneuaya called. The room stood silent as George rose from his seat and walked to the podium. The jurors were shocked on Friday, after they found Beth guilty of high treason, when Paul Gordon announced that George would take over the defense. Right after that, Keri announced that Julius Stevens, the attorney general, would take over the prosecution.

When tendering the prosecution, Keri had made it clear that she refused to argue for the death penalty—a sentiment buttressed by her presence in the gallery, sitting next to Paul Gordon, directly behind Beth, where the jurors' camera could see them, friend and foe aligned. It gave Bill hope as George reached the podium and paused.

"It has been a very long time since I have had the pleasure, the privilege of addressing a jury. So please forgive me if I stumble a little, and remember that I am perhaps too old to be doing this in the first place," he began. It drew a universal smile and instantly introduced the jury to an icon they had only read about in history books, with the same reverence as a George Washington.

"First, let me tell you that I am not here to argue with your finding that Mrs. Roche-Suarez is guilty of high treason. She *is* guilty of high treason. Each of you has done what I'm sure was a difficult, soul-searching task. You are all patriots, and this entire nation owes you a debt of gratitude for protecting their freedoms."

The comments went beyond what was allowed for a summation, Bill calculated, watching Julius holding the side rails of his chair, debating whether to object. For any other lawyer, it would have been pandering, trying to gain the jurors' trust by paying personal compliments, appealing to their sense of ego. But not for George. No one would ever think that was his motivation. And Julius couldn't very well interrupt the reincarnation of George Washington.

George's words were simple and understandable. Bill found himself transported back to the lecture halls of William & Mary, to discussion groups with George leading up to the convention. He tried to forget about himself, about the precipice he stood on, and focus on the words.

"Nor will I try to convince you that the defendant is a nice person. How could anybody who steals the freedoms, the rights, of an entire people to line her own pockets, be likable. Even if it was only one time. One instance, in a lifetime of good public service where she fought to raise people above their plight, to improve the quality of life, education, and to provide greater opportunities for people whom society too often ignored. A hundred lifetimes of good deeds never excuses one instance of betraying the trust of the American people."

Reverse psychology, Bill thought. At least that's what he would think if it was a trial attorney tactic. Point out her good deeds through the back door. But it didn't come off as a tactic, it came off as the sincere truth. She was guilty of high treason and deserved punishment, no matter how much good she had done.

"I'm going to ask you to do something for a little while, just for a few minutes. I want you to assume that after I finish speaking, that you assume, that you believe wholeheartedly, that you will find that Beth Suarez must be given the death penalty."

Bill hadn't expected this, nor did anyone else, from the reactions he observed. It jolted Beth out of her thousand-meter stare and threw open the eyelids of the jurors, like forty-six shades recoiling so quickly that they kept flapping uncontrollably before coming to a rest. But instead of seeing her death, he saw his own. A penalty handed down by a detached board of directors of Syndicated America, to be carried out by his own handler, he pictured.

"Now that you have decided in your mind, and in your heart, that she must die, I want you to visualize it, to see it happening. Picture her waiting for the day of execution, knowing the date, the time, the minute, the second that she will draw her last breath on this earth."

Bill pictured himself looking over his shoulder at every turn, for the rest of his life. Checking for Aurelius, or someone he sent. Worrying if that was going to be the day, the moment of his execution. A death sentence seemed easier. Only one day of misery.

"Picture her being strapped onto a gurney, intravenous lines plugged into her veins, connected to vials of sedatives making her drift off into unconsciousness, not sleep, not rest, but unconsciousness. Picture other vials of paralytics bringing her heart, her lungs, all of her vital organs to a grinding halt as her body convulses. An unconscious, involuntary fight for the most primal prize — life. A fight that she will lose."

George stood still, silently looking at the jurors. In the silence Bill foresaw himself lying on the ground, blood pouring out of his head, his last seconds of consciousness spent in regret. The days he would never have with his sons. The grandchildren he would never know. Sacrificed to maintain a balance in a world of wealth where he didn't belong. The pawn never wins — he got it now.

"We all will die someday," George added slowly, then paused to let the reality sink in. "For most of us, those last moments will be painful, filled with fear and sorrow, whether it's because we grow old or because we betrayed the nation.

"What I want you to see, to feel, is that your decision is real. Your decision to impose a sentence of death will have real, physical consequences. It will end a life," he added, "and it can never be undone."

Bill knew the strategy from his ACLU days. Jurors had to understand what a death penalty meant. Not some abstract principle, but a killing. Taking a life. Maybe not an innocent life, maybe not a murder, but taking a life all the same. For those who believed in God, they were taking over his position. For those who believed that life is precious and sacred, it was taking away the most precious, the most sacred. For Bill, it was never more real than at this moment. He could feel his own physical death and it was making him angry.

"Now that you have resolved that she must die, and in full knowledge of what that means, I would challenge you to ask yourself one question — only one question." He paused. Bill was uncertain if it was for effect or to gather his emotions before continuing. George slowly looked at Beth and then looked to each and every one of the twenty-three pairs of eyes on-screen, before asking, "Why? Why must she die?"

He stood silent for almost a minute, still looking at the jurors. Bill watched as the jurors' eyes dropped in unison, each popping up again after differing pauses — the time it took for each to answer the question in their minds, Bill figured.

"Is it because you want to set an example so that no one else will betray our trust? If so — does that require death? Why would it be necessary for our society to end a life in order to send that message? Wouldn't an entire lifetime behind bars, isolated from the world, isolated from family, without the possibility of taking a single breath of freedom before death, be message enough?"

Some eyes dropped again in contemplation. Others stayed raised, centered between subsiding eyebrows and gentle crow's-feet. Shoulders collectively relaxed, Bill sensed, along with attitudes among the jurors. Those still willing to consider death were easier to spot, and they were decreasing as George continued.

"Or is it because you're angry at what she did? How could you not be angry? She betrayed your trust. She betrayed all of us. You must be angry. I'm angry. We have every right to be angry." George's hammer pushed the nail into the jurors' minds as deeply and effortlessly as every lesson Bill received from his professor. A few might still thirst for blood, but they would know that it would only scratch an angry itch and not dispense justice.

"But if we are to kill her, if we are to put her to death because of anger, then I submit to you ladies and gentlemen that it would only be the action of an angry mob. Even if that mob consisted of the entire population of this great nation, it would never be more than an act of anger. Justice and vengeance are not the same. Justice makes things right. Vengeance makes wrong linger, like an unwelcome guest that never goes away. It harms each of us. It is a seed that once planted grows into a noxious weed, choking the crops that feed us, choking all that is good." George dropped his eyes, as if he was crying. Not a single juror's eyes diverted. Bill studied them as they edged toward their individual cameras, like they were trying to touch George.

"Your courage to find her guilty has saved the freedoms of every citizen of this nation," George continued, his head remaining down and still. Bill tried not to look at him, to keep his eyes forward, but the urge grew too powerful as the pause lingered. Finally he turned toward George and saw him lift his head, take a single step closer to the camera and fix his eyes solidly. Still he didn't speak, he just stared at the camera, his eyes moving imperceptibly, as if he was counting the eyes on the other end. A breath, a sigh, a signal that he had only one last thing to say, and George whispered:

"Your decision to spare her life will save our souls." His voice choked. "The soul of this great nation and the souls of every citizen. And I thank you."

Bill was filled with a sense of patriotism he had long forgotten. A feeling of warmth breathed back into his existence after a lifetime of hypothermia. It brought exhilaration and it brought grief. How much of his life had he wasted? What part of Beth's fate was his responsibility? George returned to his seat, and out of impulse, Bill grabbed both George's and Beth's hands.

Julius' summation on the death penalty was a pale copy of Keri's summation on the treason charge. Her brilliant explanation of why Beth's veto was treason overshadowed Paul's mantra of "just don't vote for her in the next election." After her summation, no one doubted that it had to be high treason. But that didn't mean that it had to be death, and Julius didn't understand that. His use of Keri's arguments fell flat as did his hope of running for president.

Bill barely listened to Judge Kneuaya's instructions; the possibility that the jury's decision could mean Beth's death transformed Bill's exhilaration into a spiraling panic. Anything can happen in a trial, he repeated to himself. It's not over until it's over.

The instructions were short. Judge Kneuaya read them with the gravity of a man burying his only child. Anger can be a powerful motivator, Bill thought. But he was certain that after George's argument, not a single juror could ignore what their decision would mean.

Looking at their faces, he saw twenty-three professional poker players. Not a twinge or a twitch. Eyes looking straight ahead. No telltale signs of their inner thoughts to give him comfort as they retired to deliberate. He knew the wait would be unbearable.

The officer had Beth stand while he placed handcuffs behind her back. Bill asked if she could wait in an attorney room on the same floor, with him. They could wait in there while the officer stood guard outside. They started to walk past Keri and Paul, who both wished her good luck. Bill could see that Beth was puzzled.

"Bill," George called from the front of the courtroom, where he was talking with the judge's clerk and Julius. Bill begged the officer to hold Beth in the courtroom for a moment while he went to the counsel table. As he reached George's side, George turned and whispered, "We have a note."

They couldn't have been deliberating for more than five minutes. There was no evidence for them to ask for in a note, Bill thought. The note could only mean they were asking for an explanation of the instructions, or they could have made their decision, nothing else. It seemed too short for either.

Everyone stood as Judge Kneuaya entered. Bill walked up to the bench with George and Julius at the judge's wave of his hand. The judge laid the note flat on his bench and turned it around for them to read.

"We have our verdict," Bill read the note to himself.

"Five minutes?" Bill blurted unintentionally, garnering a belittling gape from Judge Kneuaya. It's not over until it's over, he kept repeating in his mind, trying to convince himself that such a short decision could mean anything. He didn't want to push the cork out of the champagne bottle until he was certain, even though every instinct told him the jury could not have agreed on death so quickly. It would be over in minutes, and Beth would be spared. He was certain, at least hopeful.

As the judge and jury performed the tightly choreographed ritual of reading the verdict, Bill felt relaxed and miserable. "Life in prison," he heard the foreperson say. Beth wouldn't die. He didn't cause her death, he rejoiced.

Above the applause, Beth leaned over to Bill's ear. "Don't forget me," she pleaded. "Please don't forget me." Her wretched cry bled every stitch of power from his body, as if his aorta had dissected, leaving no strength. He couldn't stand with George and Beth for her sentencing. He couldn't be by her side as the correction officer led her out of the courtroom in handcuffs. George's congratulations were nothing more than muffled sounds without meaning.

He sat, motionless, stoic, as the courtroom emptied. It felt like he was alone for the first time in his life. Like an orphaned eighteen-year-old with no relatives to take him in. Too old to be taken care of by society. The judge's bench, the juror screens, counsel tables, the witness box were familiar, but devoid of meaning. He searched them, trying to paint them with some importance in his life, but he could not.

From the hallway he heard busy sounds, but he figured that the media had moved to the lobby or the street. The court officers wouldn't let the halls turn into media centers. Besides, he was yesterday's news. Last Wednesday's news to be exact. George and Paul and Keri and Julius were today's news. Paul and Julius would be the main players, he thought. Even though Julius lost his argument for the death penalty, he wouldn't give up the stage.

At some point court officers would kick him out of the room. But he would wait until the last minute, until there were no more voices outside. He didn't want to see anyone, he didn't want to talk to anyone, ever. He didn't want to think about anything. He just wanted to stay until there was quiet, and slip outside to obscurity.

Voices from the hall grew a little louder and the words became more distinct. He heard two people talking as they walked to the courtroom door. A male and a female voice. In the long rectangular window he caught a glimpse of them walking closer, just their torsos. A tall man in a black suit and a smaller, slender woman in a simple blue dress. Keri and George, he recognized as they opened the door and peered in at him.

Of course they would be the ones to come back and try to console him, he thought. They were good people, but he would rather be alone. George nodded. Keri spoke. "Are you okay, Mr. Waverly?"

He laughed at the formality. "After what we've been through, I think you can call me Bill," he offered with an air of defeat in his voice. "I can't imagine that I'll ever be all right again," he confessed, unafraid to show his true emotions, his shame.

Keri and George stood outside the railing separating the spectator seats from the counsel table where Bill remained seated. George gingerly placed his fingertips on the railing, as if he was going to play the piano. Keri leaned over, resting her forearms on the rail, and folded her hands as if praying. They both looked directly at Bill as if they all knew a secret that no one wanted to speak of.

"I told Keri about Syndicated America," said George, piercing the silence. Bill wanted to vomit. He shouldn't have told George and now two people knew about it. Twice the danger. He shook his head and looked down, away from them.

"You must know how much danger you're in?" Keri asked. "We can help you; I think we can help protect you."

"And what will it cost me?" Bill shot back through clenched teeth. "My life? My sons?" Tears silently streamed down the sides of his face.

"Hopefully not," Keri replied softly. "They wouldn't be in more danger than they're in now anyway." It made sense to him. "We've never had anyone who would discuss this before," she continued. "We knew they were out there. They had to be out there. They weren't going to just disappear after the Second Constitution. We didn't even know what they called themselves."

"Probably because they've killed anybody who could talk," Bill struck back.

"Honestly, we have no idea what they're capable of," George interjected. "But Keri can get your Secret Service protection back, or put you into a witness protection program. She can have you watched around the clock."

Bill didn't like the idea of being watched around the clock. But looking ahead, he didn't see any life for him. He would spend the rest of his life looking at shadowy alleys, waiting for the tap that would end his misery. After the friendly media attention shifted to accusations, as it always did, no one would hire him. There would be no protection then. SA could kill him and the nation would be grateful. Either way it would be a death sentence.

George stepped from behind the rail and sat next to Bill. Bill looked away, afraid that eye contact would seal his fate. He felt George's hand cup his shoulder and softly rub.

"Come on, Bill," George urged. "You're one of us." There were no words Bill would rather hear. An affirmation that he was still part of this world, his ACLU world. "Life just got in the way for a while and you forgot that," George added.

Bill played out the scenarios in his mind. A lifetime of hiding from an organization with unlimited capabilities — a protected witness, squirreled away from his family. Or being out front, an exposed target, with the world watching as he exposed a cancer that virtually no one knew existed. Fear seemed so endless, so tiring. At least fighting would be interesting, he decided, remembering what it felt like to pour his heart and soul into defending death-row inmates.

"Fuck it," he uttered out loud. Looking first at George and then at Keri, he asked, "What do you want to know?"

Printed in Great Britain
by Amazon.co.uk, Ltd.,
Marston Gate.